Mindanao

S U L U

Basilan

S E A

JOLO   GROUP

Jolo

SAMALES GROUP

A R C H I P E L A G O

Siasi

TAPUL GROUP

atata

C E L E B E S   S E A

0 ——————— 20 miles
20 kilometers

The Songs of Salanda

H. ARLO NIMMO

THE SONGS
OF SALANDA

and Other Stories of Sulu

UNIVERSITY OF WASHINGTON PRESS

SEATTLE & LONDON

Library of Congress Cataloging in Publication Data

Nimmo, Harry Arlo.
The songs of Salanda : and other stories of Sulu / H. Arlo Nimmo.
p.   cm.
ISBN 0-295-97334-X (alk. paper). — ISBN 0-295-97335-8 (pbk. :
alk. paper)
1. Anthropologists—Philippines—Sulu Archipelago—Fiction.
2. Bajau (Southeast Asian people)—Fiction.   I. Title.
PS3564.I47S6   1994
813'.54—dc20   93-42674   CIP

The paper used in this publication meets the minimum requirements
of American National Standard for Information Sciences—Permanence
of Paper for Printed Library Materials, ANSI Z39.48–1984.

To Marc Scruggs

Contents

Preface

Probably every anthropologist who has ever conducted field research thinks that he or she has a novel, or at least a short story, among the experiences encountered in the field. We swap these stories with one another at professional meetings, include them in our cocktail party repertoire, or share them with our students. But ironically, most of them never reach the articles and monographs we publish—ironic because they are often among the most significant experiences of our lives. Thus many of us are left with a sense of frustration when we review our publications, since so few of these personally meaningful events ever appear on those pages. That, at least, was the case with me.

During the 1960s, I spent over two years in one of the most beautiful parts of the world, the Sulu Islands of the southern Philippines, among a unique people, the nomadic boat-dwelling Bajau. The moment I entered Sulu I knew I was entering a land rich in material for the storyteller. And probably I began my first story upon my arrival. But I never wrote it down. I was too busy learning a new language, conducting interviews, attending ceremonies, taking censuses, observing fishing techniques, unraveling genealogies, and generally learning the culture of the Bajau. After an appropriate time in the field (perhaps a little longer than most), I returned to my university and wrote my doctoral dissertation. It was eventually published as a small book. Over the years I wrote another book and some twenty articles about the Bajau. But with the publication of each book and article, I always felt a slight letdown. Something was missing. There was much more to the Bajau and my experiences among them than I conveyed in my anthropological accounts of their sociocultural system. But the tradition of anthropological writing did not allow the expression of those other things, even though I was convinced that they were critical to understanding what the Bajau and Sulu were really all about. My sense of frustration led me to write for popular publications, where I could describe my field experiences more personally. But still something was lacking. I still felt bound to the mere recitation of facts. The individual people and the important events of their lives were missing. When at last I tried my hand at fiction, I was finally able to speak from my reservoir of experiences and to delve into the missing dimensions of my years in the field.

The following stories are composites of people, places, and events I encountered or heard about in Sulu. All the names are fictitious. I experienced most of the events and knew most of the people described in this book, but not necessarily in the sequence or context described here. I have used the real place-names of Sulu, but the events I describe did not always occur at those places. This is not a great departure from anthropological description. The articles and monographs that result from our field work are also composites of individual observations, arranged in such a way as to provide understanding of the cultures we study. We frequently use pseudonyms for people and places we do not wish to identify. We have traditionally striven to make our research and the resulting publications 'scientific,' but most of us would admit that anthropological interpretation is, ultimately, more art than science. Certainly we seek to pursue our data within an agreed-upon framework of investigation, but in the final analysis we are individuals perceiving reality through the personal lenses of our own cultures. Our interpretations are uniquely our own. These stories of mine perhaps differ from that tradition only in that they make no effort to be scientific; they are very personal explorations of my experiences, moods and emotions during the two years I lived in Sulu.

The Songs of Salanda

I arrive where an unknown earth is under my feet.
I arrive where a new sky is above me.
I arrive at this land, a resting place for me.
O Spirit of the Earth! The stranger humbly offers
his heart as food for thee.

Traditional Maori chant

I

Sulu

I lay on the top deck. Beneath me, the cargo ship pulsed through the night, leaving an iridescent trail in the disturbed waters. Above me, familiar constellations seemed nearer and somehow distorted. On a darkened island shore, silhouetted by the moonlight, the sea tossed muffled breakers. In a few hours the dawn would break and the day would bring me to Bongao.

Home was an ocean away. Between here and there were all the familiar reasons people seek frontiers. And a few new ones, too. On the surface, my quest was prosaic enough. I was a doctoral candidate in anthropology en route to an isolated people to collect data for a dissertation. But the academic degree was simply a vehicle for a far more personal quest. I was seeking answers to questions I had not yet formulated, following moods and emotions rather than rationality and intellect. I sensed something was not quite right about the culture that had spawned me, and I felt a need to leave before it consumed me as it had consumed my brother and countless others who still lived.

A trail of strewn aches lay behind me, a young lifetime of little hurts from trying to fit into spaces not intended for people like me. And so I left. I wanted to learn if this were what the world is all about, or if some place existed where

I could live more easily. And that is why, on this particular night, I lay on the top deck of a converted mine sweeper in the Sulu Islands of the southern Philippines.

I awakened to a spectacular dawn. The world was red. I watched the sun climb above the horizon to reveal the blues and greens that color the sea world of Sulu. Like the scattered stones of a brilliant emerald chain, the Sulu Islands stretch across the azure sea between Mindanao and the great island of Borneo to comprise the southernmost provinces in the Republic of the Philippines. Small volcanic islands and even smaller coral islands and a myriad of reefs provide homes for the people of Sulu.

Most of Sulu's people are Muslims, but those whom I was seeking are not. Outcasts in the eyes of the Muslims, they are the Bajau, a small group of nomadic boat-dwellers who ply the Sulu waters in single-family houseboats. Their movements are limited to some 250 square miles of sea, southwest of the large island of Tawi-Tawi in southern Sulu. Within this area are located five main moorages or villages, and two tiny cemetery islands where the Bajau bury their dead. These tropical seas are fished by the Bajau, but the many small islands are farmed by Muslims upon whom most Bajau are dependent for the vegetable portion of their diet. I had come to spend two years with the Bajau, to live a life on the sea.

I first heard of the Bajau while I was a graduate student. One day, as an uninspiring lecture drew to a close, the professor reviewed the dominant subsistence patterns in Southeast Asia and mentioned that a little-known fishing people of the southern Philippines spend their entire lives upon the sea, wandering from island to island in small houseboats. They stirred my then-romantic interest in things anthropological, so I decided to write a term paper on the sea nomads of Southeast Asia. A brief trip to the library, however, convinced me data was not available for such a project; what little material

I could find was superficial and impressionistic, so I chose a different topic.

That seemed eons ago. The sun was high in the midday sky when the ship blasted its horn through the noisy strains of a scratchy recording of Sousa marches and clumsily nudged the wharf at Bongao, the small port town of southern Sulu that would be my home base. From the top deck, I watched the crew toss heavy mooring ropes to the barefoot, bare-chested stevedores on shore. Herds of half-naked children appeared, seemingly from nowhere, to watch the mooring and then scramble onto the ship. A few men in sarongs and turbans stopped to see what the vessel had brought from the outside world. The warehouse at the wharf was bright red, but the other buildings, most built on piles over the reef, were of unpainted wood. They appeared to grow from the sea and the green slopes of Mt. Bongao that climbed lazily behind the small port town and then fell abruptly to the sea. A single dirt road led from the wharf through Bongao town and stopped at the forested interior of the island.

With a population of about five thousand, Bongao was the main port and administrative center for the Tawi-Tawi Islands. Like most of Sulu, it was more Indonesian than Filipino. Manila was Catholic and lay hundreds of miles to the north, while Sulawesi and Borneo were Muslim and only a few sea miles south and west. Manila's western veneer hid its Asianness—the Hilton, Coca Cola, rock music, the English language. I sensed in Manila that I hadn't yet gone far enough. But in Bongao, as I watched the people come to meet the ship, I knew I was in Asia.

I picked up my typewriter and duffle bag, bade the captain farewell, and climbed off the ship. My appearance on the wharf caused a minor stir, with many curious stares and comments in a language I could not yet understand. I returned the stares with a forced smile I hoped would appear friendly, and set off down the road to find the *convento* of the American Catholic priest stationed in Bongao. A tired, mangy dog crawled from under a house to give a few ritual barks as I passed. A cow raised big brown eyes and chewed a leisurely cud. A puzzled old woman with bare, gnarled feet and betel-blackened teeth stopped in the middle of the road to stare at me. A young man, clad only in briefs, interrupted his bath from a five-gallon tin of water to shout something about an American to his friend down the road. Two small boys scurried away from me, stumbled, and almost fell under the weight of the heavy fish they carried on the pole stretched between them. All along the road, comments were exchanged by passers-by. The only word I could understand was the recurring "American."

I finally reached the *convento*, having collected a small entourage of curious children and undernourished dogs. I met Father Raquet, who had been forewarned of my arrival. He offered to put me up until I could find space at the Bajau moorage I planned to study. I accepted his offer but hoped it would be a short stay, since I was eager to start living with the Bajau.

That evening, after a dinner of fresh tuna, Father Raquet opened a bottle of sherry, a gift from an English globetrotter who had spent a few days with him. We sipped the mellow drink during what turned out to be the first of many pleasant evenings I was to spend with the kind priest. We talked of Sulu and of ourselves. Father Raquet, a short, wiry man with a quick wit undulled by thirty-some years in the boondocks of Sulu, reminisced about his years in the Philippines. I listened, and watched a huge moon emerge from the sea and sail through wisps of clouds.

Early the next morning, Father Raquet and I sped over the still waters in his small speedboat. As we approached the Bajau moorage in the channel between Bongao and Sanga-Sanga Island, dozens of houseboats became visible, moored haphazardly to poles placed at lopsided angles throughout the shallow reef upon which the settlement floated.

In one of those little houseboats, I planned to spend my next two years.

2

Masa's Wife

I sat on a rock at the beach and looked out at the Bajau houseboats. It was my second day on the island and I was wondering if I were cut out to be an anthropologist. Father Raquet had left me, somewhat uneasily, with my duffle bag of basics. I had set up quarters of sorts in one of the crumbling army barracks abandoned since World War II, when the Japanese occupied them. I knew the Bajau were reserved and would be reluctant to welcome an outsider, but I wasn't prepared for the reception they gave me. Whenever I approached a group on the beach, they hurried to their boats. Thinking that children would be a good entry to the community, I tried to befriend them. But they were even more terrified than the adults and ran away screaming as I approached. Such a group had just taken off across the reef. I sat on the rock and seriously doubted whether I could last the two years I planned to be in Sulu.

After a few minutes of self-pity, I waded through the low tidewaters toward the moorage. About three dozen houseboats comprised the moorage. A finger of exposed reef jutted out from the land and created a little bay. Within this, the moorage was located. On the reef, a man was cutting planks from a large log for the boat he was building nearby. I approached him and sat on a log to watch him work. He glanced at me without acknowledging my presence and continued his work. After about ten minutes he stopped, leaned on his axe, and looked me over. He was probably about my age, in his middle twenties. He wore only shorts. Like most Bajau men, he had a lean, muscular body, the sort that most Americans achieve only through diets and gymnasiums. His thick, black hair was bleached to shades of red by the sun, which had darkened his body to deep brown tones. I smiled what I hoped was a friendly smile, and he returned a broad grin that revealed strong, white teeth.

He dropped his axe to the ground, walked to the log, and sat next to me. He fumbled in his shorts and pulled out a crumpled pack of Filipino cigarettes. He offered me one, put one in his mouth, and lit us both up. I'm not a smoker, but I realized the need for the social act, so I stifled a cough at the strong cigarette. He continued to smile at me as he smoked. Finally he asked, "Melikan?"

In the few words I knew of his language, I told him I didn't understand.

He repeated, but still I didn't understand. He pointed to himself and said, "Pilipino." He then pointed to me and asked again, "Melikan?"

Finally, I realized that "Melikan" meant "American." I responded vigorously in the affirmative. From then on, Melikan was my name among the Bajau. We both laughed and he said something else which I didn't understand.

A small group of children who had been playing at the far end of the reef approached us, attracted by our conversation. In the presence of the Bajau man, their earlier fear of me disappeared and they crowded around to look me over. They ranged in ages from five to ten, boys and girls, and were naked save for an occasional necklace, earring, or bracelet. Their hair was sun-bleached to shades of red and blond. The man returned to his work at the log as the children clustered around me. I took advantage of their curiosity to expand my knowledge of their language. At that time, the Bajau language, called Sama, was unrecorded, so there was no way I could learn it before my arrival in Sulu. I had studied linguistics and languages related to Sama, but I was still essentially ignorant of the Bajau language. I picked up things from the reef and pointed at objects to learn words. I jotted the children's responses in my small notebook, and they were fascinated by the strange marks I made on paper. I learned their names and told them my name. I pointed at the man working on the log, and they responded "Masa." The man turned and smiled, and returned to his work. This was my introduction to Masa, who was to remain my closest friend for the next two years.

The children's voices attracted others to our group, and eventually a few men and women from the boats wandered over. The children lingered, but the adults stayed only a short time. Some smiled shyly; others offered no smiles. Eventually my curiosity-appeal wore off, and the children resumed their play at the far end of the reef. Masa waded out to his houseboat, and I was again left alone. The tide was coming in, so rather than find myself stranded on the small reef, I waded back to the beach in the rapidly rising water. I returned to my barren barracks and recorded my initial interaction with the Bajau in my journal. A lonely afternoon passed into a lonelier night until I fell asleep, occasionally wakened by the still strange sounds of the jungle that surrounded the rotting barracks.

My morning visits to the moorage became routine. Each morning I saw Masa and we struck up a friendship in my very limited language. Through pantomime I asked him if I could stay in his boat, and through pantomime he let me know quite clearly that he was not interested in a houseguest. I learned that he lived with his wife and two young sons, both under five. I met his wife the third day as I watched Masa build his boat. She came to the reef with the two children to bring Masa a drink of water, but mostly to see me up close. She was a lovely young woman, and very pregnant. Masa patted her stomach, smiled at me, and said, "Denda," a word within my small Sama vocabulary which meant "girl." They wanted this child to be a girl. His wife smiled widely, held her stomach, and also said, "Denda." I nodded in agreement. She returned to the boat, leaving the boys to play on the reef within the watch of their father.

The days passed into weeks as I made more and more friends at the moorage. The children were no longer afraid of me, and several patient adults conversed with me in my limited, but growing Sama. Masa continued to be my important contact. Through a great many gestures and a good deal of imagination, we were able to communicate about most matters; when insurmountable hurdles presented themselves, we simply changed the subject.

One day while I was sitting on the reef surrounded by a group of children, Masa approached to ask if I would like to go fishing with him. It was the first time I had been invited to go anywhere with a Bajau and I eagerly accepted. Masa's brother-in-law joined us, and we fished the deep waters beyond the moorage until we had a sizeable catch.

When we returned to the moorage, Masa suggested I eat with him and his family. I was delighted, realizing I was making an important entry into their life. After a rather unappetizing meal of boiled fish and cassava, we sat at the end of the boat smoking Masa's strong Filipino cigarettes. He then said it was too late for me to return to my barracks and suggested I sleep in his houseboat. I found a space on the hard deck and lay down, happy with the realization that I finally had been accepted into the Bajau community.

It was a terrible night. The deck of the boat was incredibly hard. In addition, I was unaccustomed to the rocking of the boat, not to mention the various sounds of the family's nocturnal activities. But I made it through the night and awakened with the family. They invited me to join them in a breakfast of cold fish and cassava.

About halfway through the meal, Masa's wife retired to the back of the boat and began to groan softly, groans which I'd heard through a portion of the night. The onset of her labor had begun. Masa cleaned up the breakfast remains and called to the neighboring boat. Shortly, two women arrived—one about Masa's age and the other an ancient woman who looked a few years beyond death. I later learned they were Masa's sister and mother-in-law. They ignored me and went directly to Masa's wife, speaking to her in low tones. The old woman changed to a green blouse and yellow sarong, the traditional attire of female shamans, as I learned later. Masa remained at the back of the boat and invited me to smoke with him. I did so. I felt somewhat uncomfortable in the presence of the imminent birth, although no one else seemed disturbed by my presence. Men wandered by the boat, some stopping to talk to Masa, and two more women came to assist Masa's wife. The children left the boat to join playmates on the reef.

Judging by the sounds coming from the other end of the boat, the birth was drawing near. I couldn't see what was happening, but the women were clustered around the expectant mother. The old woman was chanting as she massaged Masa's wife. Before long I heard the cry of a baby. One of the women called out to Masa, "Denda!" Masa smiled at me and I congratulated him on his new daughter. He nodded and then picked up his axe and indicated he was going to the reef to continue work on his boat. I felt awkward in the boat, so I decided to return to my barracks and record the events of the preceding twenty-four hours. I wrote for about an hour and then succumbed to sleep. When I awakened it was midafternoon, and I returned to the moorage.

Masa's houseboat was covered with citrus branches, which I later learned were protection against evil spirits believed to prey upon newborns. I waded to the boat and discovered Masa sitting at the bow with his two sons. Inside, the same women were still attending his wife, and the old shaman was still chanting as incense burned in a coconut half shell.

Mouthing his words slowly so I could understand, Masa said, "My wife is very sick. Do you have medicine for her?"

"I have no medicine," I said. I had only aspirin and penicillin ointment, neither of which seemed appropriate.

Masa asked me to enter the boat to see his wife. I crawled in behind him as the women made way for us. Masa's wife lay on a mat, her head resting on a pillow. The new baby slept at her breast. She smiled at me wanly. I touched her forehead. I knew nothing about childbirth, but I realized that the woman had a high fever and was obviously suffering from more than the usual problems of delivery.

"Do you have medicine?" Masa asked me again. I remembered that a public health doctor was stationed in nearby Bongao. He would know what to do. But on the other hand, I thought, maybe I was over-reacting. Bajau women had been delivering babies for centuries before I came upon the scene. They knew better than I how to deal with the crises of childbirth. So again I told Masa I had no medicine.

The midwives obviously planned to spend the night with the young mother. It was hardly a night for an additional houseguest, so after a few more words with Masa, I said goodbye and returned to my empty barracks for another night of jungle sounds.

At about noon the following day, I returned to the moorage and went to Masa's houseboat. He greeted me at the entrance and I learned that his wife was still very ill. Three shamans were inside the boat, conducting a ceremony over burning incense as the midwives watched. Masa told me she had worsened and asked me to look at her.

When I saw her, I knew she was critically ill. Her lips were parted and dried; her eyes were half-closed and glazed.

"Do you think the doctor in Bongao could help her?" Masa asked me.

"Possibly he could," I responded.

Masa's mother-in-law, named Laka, looked up and said, "His medicine is not for our people. He does not know how to deal with the *saitan* that cause our illness." *Saitan* are spirits the Bajau believe cause illness and other misfortune.

"But you haven't helped my wife," said Masa. "She's getting worse."

"These are very powerful *saitan*," said Laka. "It takes time to get rid of them."

"Let us at least try the doctor's medicine. It can do no harm," reasoned Masa.

"I do not trust those doctors. They stick needles in you and cut you open. Our ways are better."

Masa asked me if this were true. In my limited vocabulary, I told him sometimes doctors do that; but only to help, not to hurt. "But," I continued, "they also have medicines that can help."

"See," said Masa to Laka. "Maybe the doctor has medicine that will help my wife."

She ignored Masa, glared at me, and continued the ceremony as if the discussion were closed.

Masa asked me, "Do you know this doctor?"

"I don't know him well, but I've met him."

"Would you go with me to get some medicine for her?"

Old Laka turned and shouted angrily, "You are a fool. Those doctors know nothing about us. Only we know how to deal with these *saitan* that are making your wife sick. Don't you trust us anymore?"

"I trust you," said Masa patiently, "but maybe some new *saitan* have come to make her ill. Maybe the doctor knows how to get rid of these new *saitan*."

"Maybe Masa's right," said one of the midwives. "It cannot

hurt to try. We won't let the doctor stick needles in her or cut her open."

"You're fools," said Laka. "Those doctors know nothing about us."

"I will try the doctor's medicine," said Masa. "After all, she's my wife."

"But she's my daughter," said Laka. "I gave birth to her."

"The husband has rights in such matters," said one of the midwives. Others in the boat agreed, but the shamans alone formed a knot of opposition.

"Will you come with me to get the medicine?" asked Masa.

"I don't think he will give her medicine until he has seen her. I can write a letter asking him to come if you can find someone to take it to him. If he's available, he might be able to come this afternoon."

Masa agreed to the suggestion. I found paper and pen in my shoulder bag and wrote a note to the doctor. I told him what I knew about the case, which wasn't much, and stressed the critical nature of the woman's illness. The note was given to two nephews of Masa, who set out in a small dugout for Bongao, about three miles over the sea. I was certain the doctor would come if he could get away. I had met him briefly and was impressed with the young man's dedication. He was the only doctor in all of southern Sulu, and he was trying to make inroads into the communities of the area. He had been totally unsuccessful in reaching the Bajau, and he might see this as an entry into the community.

Meanwhile, the shamans returned to their ceremony. Masa and I went to the reef where he continued to work on his boat. I stayed with Masa for a while, adding some new words to my vocabulary, but I sensed he would rather be alone, so I walked to a group of children playing at the far end of the reef and was soon surrounded by them. They gave me more words for my growing vocabulary, and as they went back to their play, I studied my language notes. My proficiency in Sama improved daily, but it was a frustrating business. I shall ever be sympathetic to anyone trying to learn a second language.

As the hours passed, I wondered if the public health doctor would be able to make it to the moorage. Finally, however, I saw a motor boat approaching. As it became more visible, I recognized the doctor. He turned the motor off and poled the boat through the shallow waters. He greeted me and I waded out toward him.

"I'm glad you came," I said, "although I'm not sure there's much you can do."

"We shall see," he said as he shook my hand.

We went to Masa's houseboat where a small crowd gathered. We crawled inside the boat, and with Masa at his side, the doctor briefly examined the ill woman. Her condition looked the same as when I last saw her. The doctor spoke Sama and asked questions of Masa and the midwives regarding the illness. He then turned to me and spoke in English. "She apparently has hemorrhaged a great deal. There must be some further complication also, because she has a very high fever, a sign of infection somewhere. She probably should have a blood transfusion, but that is impossible here. She also should have an injection to fight the infection, but if they are like most people here they will oppose it. Let me try."

He spoke to Masa in Sama, and told him of the seriousness of his wife's illness. He suggested that the best way to treat it would be with an injection. Immediately cries of opposition arose from the shamans and the midwives.

The doctor explained to Masa, "Your wife is very weak because she has had no food for several days. If she is to live, she must have food in her body. The only way I can give her food is through a needle from a tube. Will you consent to this?"

After some thought, Masa announced, "We will use the doctor's medicine. He can use the needle."

Immediately the shamans opposed the suggestion. The

midwives and others in the boat were quiet, however, apparently having come to share Masa's feelings. The shamans told Masa of the folly in letting the doctor give more pain to his wife and how ignorant he was of their spirits.

Masa finally lost his patience and shouted angrily, "For three days I have watched you treat my wife, and for three days she has grown sicker. What you are doing does not work. Do you want me to wait more days until my wife is dead? We have tried our way. It does not work this time. Now we must try another way."

The shamans were obviously angered and offended. "You will be responsible if she dies," Laka hissed. "Do not come to us for help when she is dead."

They angrily left the boat and Masa told the doctor to do what he had to do. The doctor immediately opened his bag and prepared a shot, which he injected into the young woman's arm. Next, he took out a bag of dextrose and fastened it to the low ceiling. He unraveled the plastic tube, attached a needle to it, inserted the needle into her arm, and secured it with a strip of adhesive.

"That is all I can do now," he told Masa. He then turned to me. "I will leave another bag of dextrose. When this one is empty, replace it with the other one." He instructed me in the simple method of changing bags. "I will also leave some pills. If she gains consciousness, give her two of these every three hours."

He turned to Masa. "I am very busy in my office, and it is difficult for me to come here. I suggest that tomorrow you bring your boat to Bongao and moor there so I can come and see your wife more easily. Your wife is very ill. It may be too late for my medicine to help her, but I shall do the best I can."

Masa and I walked with him to his boat and watched him speed across the reef toward Bongao. I stayed with the patient until both bottles of dextrose were administered. I then removed the needle from her arm, and covered the puncture with a bandage. She was still unconscious. I needed a break from the tensions of the moorage, so decided to go back to the barracks to spend the night. I left two pills with Masa and told him to give them to his wife if she regained consciousness.

I waded through the shallow waters toward the beach, looking forward for the first time to the lonely privacy of my empty barracks.

I awakened early the next morning and walked to the moorage to see how Masa's wife was responding to the medication. When I arrived at the houseboat, Masa was in good spirits.

"The doctor's medicine is good," he said. "My wife awakened this morning and I gave her the pills. She's sleeping now."

The midwives and Laka were still in the boat. Laka did not look happy and mumbled something about the spirits. At Masa's encouragement, I went into the boat and examined his wife. Her fever was still high, but she appeared to be asleep now rather than comatose.

"Do you think we should take her to Bongao?" asked Masa. "Maybe it's not necessary since she is better."

"We should not take her to Bongao," said Laka. "There are different saitan over there which might bother her now that she is already weakened."

"What do you think?" Masa asked me.

I strongly felt she should be taken to Bongao so the doctor could continue his treatment. On the other hand, I was not interested in getting further involved in the schism that had developed. Nonetheless, I told Masa, "Yes, I think she should be taken to Bongao. She looks better now, but if she is not given more medicine, she will weaken."

Masa shared my feelings and told the small group they should prepare to go to Bongao.

Although unhappy with the decision, old Laka remained

with her daughter, as did the other midwives. Also in the boat were Masa's two sons and an old man who I later learned was his father-in-law. Masa invited me to accompany them. Three other boats containing various relatives came with us.

It was still quite early as we poled the heavy boats out of the moorage. The sun was up but its rays were not yet hot. Awakening sounds from the island were muffled by the expanse of water. Masa poled the boat through the shoals as I sat at the stern with a steering paddle. When we reached the edge of the reef, we caught a favorable current which moved us swiftly along.

We were no more than ten minutes away from the moorage when suddenly I heard a shriek from within the house, "She is dead! She is dead!" Other screams followed. I looked in the house and saw the family clustered around Masa's wife. Her old father reared up, dismantling the frail thatch roof. Masa rushed to the group. All were screaming, and several of the women lay on the deck, flailing arms and legs as they howled their grief. The old man seized pans, pots, dishes, and fishing equipment and smashed them on the deck as he screamed at the top of his lungs. The other boats quickly came to us and joined the violent mourning. Some jumped aboard to see the body, only to fall on the deck in spasms of grief. Masa sobbed quietly as he bent over his wife, while Laka huddled against the side of the boat, crying loudly and cursing the spirits.

I was totally unprepared for all of this. I had no idea that Masa's wife was so near death, nor did I know the Bajau reacted so violently to death. I remained at the back of the boat, grieved at her dying and shocked by the violent behavior around me. Several persons had to be controlled by others to prevent injury to themselves and destruction to the boat. Two men from the other boats took charge of ours and decided to return to the moorage.

As we approached the moorage, word was shouted that Masa's wife was dead. Everyone came out to meet us. The women wailed as they waded fully clothed into the deep waters to meet the boat. They tried to get aboard and would have capsized the boat had the men who had taken charge not kept them off. They followed us, wailing loudly. The men shouted, flailing themselves and breaking everything within reach. When we finally reached shallow water and the boat was moored, it was swarmed with screaming, crying mourners. Virtually everyone in the moorage, men, women, and children —well over two hundred people—were at the boat, shrieking and crying in their grief over the death of the young woman.

I slipped from the boat and waded to the exposed reef to sit on a pile of rocks away from the activities. I had never been so close to death before. I only knew death at funerals after the corpse was properly prepared for inoffensive viewing. Masa's wife had died almost before my eyes. Although I did not know her well, I had felt an intimate part of her struggle to live. I was also disturbed that I had let myself become involved. I was the one who had suggested that Masa call the doctor and submit to his medication. I began to wonder what I was doing here. I had no business coming into these people's lives. They didn't invite me. They couldn't care less whether their culture was documented in the dusty pages of academe. I had really botched my first entry into the field. What kind of an anthropologist was I? As I continued to grieve the woman's death and to feel sorry for myself, I looked up to see Masa and Laka approaching.

Laka had won, I thought. Now the moorage would never again try modern medicine. Maybe it was just as well. They had lived several millennia without it and probably could live several more. And they certainly could live without an anthropologist.

Masa's eyes were red from weeping and tears came to

mine as I sensed his deep sorrow. Old Laka said, "Your medicine is strong, but some *saitan* are stronger than all our medicine. Come. Help us prepare for the funeral."

Masa and the old shaman put their arms around me, and we waded through the rising tide toward the funeral boat.

3

The Saitan

It was early morning and several months into my field research. I sat at the stern of the little houseboat where I was now living, bored out of my mind with the research I was supposed to be doing. It was one of those days. I didn't want to be in the Philippines, but I could do nothing about it since I was stuck among some of the most remote islands of the archipelago.

As I watched the family next to me prepare their nets for a day of fishing, Laka came splashing through the low tidewaters.

"Where are you going?" she asked me. The Bajau greeting is usually totally removed from any real interest in the answer.

"Nowhere," I replied. "Where are you going?"

"Over there," she responded, indicating no particular direction.

"You look very tired," I said out of genuine concern. Old Laka and I had become good friends after our stormy introduction. She was one of the most powerful Bajau shamans, and through her I had learned a great deal about the Bajau spirit world.

"I'm tired," she said, as she stopped at my boat to rest. "The saitan keep me busy."

"What have they been up to?" I asked.

"The usual," she said. "They tricked my grandson into going to Borneo."

"Tricked him?" I asked.

"Yes," said the old woman, shifting her cud of betel. "He's been away for almost a month, and we didn't know where he went. I asked the *saitan* where he was, and they said they tricked him into sailing to Borneo. But I didn't believe them." She went into a long harangue about the lying trickery of the *saitan* and the danger of ever believing the things they say. "So I had to go to Borneo last night to see for myself."

"You went to Borneo last night and are back now?" I asked cautiously. The round trip to Borneo normally took at least a week by Bajau boat.

"Yes," she said matter-of-factly. "That's why I'm so tired this morning."

"I see. How did you go to Borneo?" I ventured.

"I flew," she said sharply, as if any fool would know.

"You flew? By yourself?"

"Of course. Flying always makes me tired, and it was even worse last night because I was flying into the wind."

"And how is your grandson?" I asked.

"Who knows," she said disgustedly, spitting a red blob of betel juice into the water. "After I got there, I couldn't find out a thing. And now this morning my daughter Maini is sick. I have a feeling it's the same *saitan* that tricked my grandson, so I've got to go over and see what I can find out."

Laka's adventures with the *saitan* were beginning to stir me from my lethargy.

"What will you do?" I asked.

"This is a stubborn *saitan*," she said reflectively. "I'll have to use a *ta'u-ta'u* and take the *saitan* to Lapid-Lapid."

I became enthusiastic and forgot I was bored. Ta'u-ta'u were wooden anthropomorphic images made by some of the Bajau shamans to house spirits they exorcise from patients. Once a *saitan* is in the *ta'u-ta'u*, it is taken to the little island of

Lapid-Lapid and left with others there. I had seen the ceremony only once, and I was not allowed to accompany the shamans to Lapid-Lapid for fear I would be harmed by the many evil *saitan* who dwell there.

"May I come and watch the ceremony?" I asked.

"If you want to," she yawned. "I don't know how successful it will be. I'm so tired today. Sometimes I wish people didn't need my help so often. It's tiresome being the best shaman in Tawi-Tawi."

She turned and waded toward her daughter's houseboat. I grabbed a notebook and pencil and followed her. We greeted people along the way and soon arrived at the ill woman's houseboat. As we crawled into the low craft, I saw Masa and other members of the family sitting around Maini, who was lying to one side looking rather feverish.

"How is she?" asked Laka, as she felt her daughter's head.

"About the same," said Biti, the patient's husband.

"It's the *saitan*," announced Laka. "Did you make the *ta'u-ta'u*?"

"Yes," replied Biti. He rummaged through some bundles at the side of the boat and pulled out a wooden figure, crudely anthropomorphic, about two feet tall.

Laka looked at the figure. "It's not very good," she said critically, "but I suppose it will do. Hand me the incense."

She lit the incense and placed it in a coconut half shell between her and the patient. She then chanted in a language understood only by herself and the *saitan* to whom she was speaking. As she continued to chant, she held the crude wooden image over the patient, moving it in circles. I knew from other ceremonies I'd seen that she was inviting the *saitan* to leave the patient and enter the image. She continued chanting for about five minutes while the rest of us sat quietly watching the ceremony.

Just as the ritual was beginning to bore me, old Laka clutched the image to her breast. Her eyes rolled back and she fell to the deck in a trance, babbling frantically. Her arms and legs flailed at some invisible force as she shouted through clenched teeth. Suddenly she stopped and her body curled around the image. When she gained consciousness a few moments later, she announced, "I have the *saitan*. Maini will feel better soon. Get the boat ready so we can go to Lapid-Lapid."

Masa and Biti left to ready the boat. Laka leaned over to spit a mouthful of betel juice through a small crack in the wall.

"May I go with you to Lapid-Lapid?" I asked.

"Of course not," she said sharply. "There are too many *saitan* there, and I don't want to be responsible if you get harmed by one of them."

"But you won't be responsible," I said, even though I knew my argument was futile. I had already tried several times to go to Lapid-Lapid with Laka. But I continued anyway. "I'll write a letter to Father Raquet absolving you of responsibility if anything happens to me."

"What good would that do? I would still be the one to blame. It's too dangerous. You can't go."

I knew the matter was settled, so I said no more. I felt that I must visit the little island since it appeared to be important to the religious life of the Bajau, but obviously this was not going to be the time. I sat back and watched the remainder of the ceremony as Laka offered food and cigarettes to the wooden image before taking it to the boat made ready for the trip. She climbed on board with Biti and Masa and they paddled away. I went back to my houseboat, resentful of Laka's stubbornness and prepared to be bored for the rest of the day.

Several weeks later, I was again sitting at the prow of my houseboat, watching the early morning activities of the moorage. This time I was not bored, but I was trying to think of a profitable, not too strenuous way to spend the day. It was high tide and my boat bobbed pleasantly as the morning sun warmed my bare legs. Masa's boat was moored some thirty feet from mine. He stepped onto the back deck, stretched to a noisy yawn, and shouted a greeting. I responded as he climbed into the small dugout tied to his houseboat and paddled in my direction. Masa had remarried about four months after his wife's death. His new wife was the younger cousin of his first wife, and the marriage was deemed an appropriate one by the moorage.

"What are you going to do today?" he asked, as he maneuvered his little boat next to mine.

"I haven't decided yet," I replied. "How about you?"

"I talked to Laka and Biti this morning," he said. He paused, and I waited for him to continue.

"We've decided to take you to see the ta'u-ta'u on Lapid-Lapid."

I almost fell overboard from surprise. For weeks I had tried to talk Masa into taking me to see the ta'u-ta'u. Always there were excuses—It was too far away; the seas were too rough; he was too busy; but most important, the saitan were so evil that I would most certainly become ill within their presence. But today, for no apparent reason, Masa made the proposal himself.

"I don't know why you want to see the ta'u-ta'u," he continued, without waiting for my reply. "You'll probably be disappointed. But you've asked us so many times, it must be important to you. Since you've been good to us and shared your medicine and food with us, we'll take you—if you still want to go."

I assured him that I definitely wanted to go and was ready to leave immediately.

"I've told you before that it's dangerous for you to go to the island," Masa said. "You're not accustomed to the saitan and don't know how to treat them." For five minutes he lectured me on the great dangers, illnesses, and possible death that might await me if I pursued my hazardous request. Again

I said that I understood the dangers, and again I offered to write a letter absolving him of any responsibility.

"We must first go to Laka's boat."

I grabbed my camera and notebook and joined Masa in his small boat. Within minutes, we were in Laka's houseboat where Biti was waiting.

Laka grunted a greeting to me and said that a ritual must be conducted to ask the *saitan* to refrain from mischievous interference during our trip to the island. Incense was lighted and the three of us held our hands on our crossed legs with palms upward as Laka flattered the *saitan* and asked them to allow our safe passage to Lapid-Lapid. We then sprinkled a sweet-scented tonic, a favorite of the *saitan*, over our hands and faces while Laka told me that en route to the island I should not laugh, shout, urinate, defecate, spit, nor look over my shoulder. Once on the island, I should touch nothing.

"Are you sure you want to go?" she asked in conclusion, and then added matter-of-factly, "You might die, you know."

"I want to go," I said adamantly.

She shrugged her shoulders, spat, and said, "Let's go."

We crawled onto the deck, climbed into a smaller boat, and paddled away from the moorage. As we moved across the glasslike surface of the early morning waters, Laka spoke further of the *saitan*.

"The *saitan* on Lapid-Lapid are not spirits of our people. That is why they are so evil. Our spirits once lived among us. They know what difficult lives we lead and they don't harm us unless we anger them. But the *saitan* on Lapid-Lapid are different. They are like the land people. They dislike our people and make us ill—they even kill us."

She continued to explain the harassment of the Bajau by the spirits. The *saitan* are present everywhere—land, sea, sky— but they are known to congregate on certain islands, which the Bajau avoid. Such was the island we were now approaching, and it bore additional infamy as the home of the *ta'u-ta'u*.

As we neared the beach, Laka announced we should refrain from speaking until we had visited the island and were back in the boat. It was a small island, no more than a quarter of a city block in size. Scrub vegetation covered all but the center, where a small rise was topped by a large tree. As we beached our boat, Laka gave me a shiny black stone to carry for additional protection from the *saitan*. We followed a path into the dense tropical foliage of the island's interior. I was sandwiched between Laka and Masa to ensure my safety. Periodically, Laka silently stopped to leave small offerings of food and betel to the temperamental *saitan*. Soon we arrived on the small rise, in the center of which stood a tree some twenty-five-feet tall. The tree housed about thirty *ta'u-ta'u*, whose blank faces and grotesque features seemed to grow from the tree. Some had obviously been there many years and were almost completely devoured by the growth of the tree. Others were recent. Dozens of small green and white flags, traditional Bajau offerings to spirits, were scattered throughout the tree. This macabre scene was punctuated by occasional bursts of sound and movement from a species of bright green lizard, about a foot long, which also inhabited the tree. Their sinister heads darted long, thin tongues at us. The only other sound was the murmur of the sea, which the dense foliage blocked from our sight.

I took my camera from the case slung over my shoulder. I didn't have to look to see my companions' disapproving glares. I took about a dozen shots, jotted down some notes, and about thirty minutes after our arrival, indicated I was ready to leave. They had been ready for some time. We kept our pledge of silence until we paddled away from the island.

"You see," I said, "the *saitan* didn't mind my visit."

"It's too early to tell," said Laka, obviously unconvinced. The others said nothing.

We returned to the moorage and I spent the rest of the day working on my field notes. That evening, shortly after dinner, I began to feel the warning stomach cramps of dysentery. It turned out to be one of the most severe attacks I experienced in the field. Four days later I was still on my back but beginning to recover. Masa and Biti, having just returned from fishing, stopped by to check on my health—or lack of it.

"You're lucky you're recovering," said Masa.

I uttered agreement and added that the medicine I used was effective for dysentery.

"The medicine is useless before the *saitan*," said Biti.

"*Saitan?*" I asked.

"Of course, *saitan*. It was they who made you sick. We told you it was dangerous for you to visit the *ta'u-ta'u*, but you insisted."

"But the *saitan* didn't make me ill. It was some food I ate."

"Perhaps so, but it was the *saitan* who made the food bad," insisted Biti.

I tried to convince the men that the *saitan* had nothing to do with my illness. Again I explained the germ theory of disease. The men listened politely and said that I might call them germs, but to the Bajau they were *saitan*. I changed the subject.

I was worried about their diagnosis. I had yet to witness all the Bajau religious ceremonies, and if the Bajau thought their *saitan* didn't like me, they would probably bar me from their ceremonies out of concern for my well-being. I would never be able to understand their religious life, one of the main areas of my research. Somehow I had to convince them that my illness was a coincidence, that I was immune to the behavior of the *saitan*. I had to visit the *ta'u-ta'u* island again and return unscathed.

It took me three months to talk Masa and Biti into taking me back to Lapid-Lapid. Laka would not even listen to me. Unashamedly, I reminded the two men over and over of the many favors I had done for them, and that they had once told me I was like a brother to them. Finally they agreed to take me back, weary of my repeated requests. Again I heard the long lecture about proper behavior before the spirits, and this time they did ask me to write a letter, to be deposited with Father Raquet in Bongao, absolving them of any responsibility for misfortunes which might befall me as a result of the visit. With dour predictions of impending disaster from almost everyone in the moorage, we set out for the island.

My argument was that I was immune to their spirits since I was not a Bajau. I told them of the spirits of my people in the United States. They had never heard of them, of course, so I told them this proved that spirits are only concerned with the people who believe in them. They answered that spirits are geographical—if Bajau went to the United States they could be harmed by American spirits, just as Americans who came to Sulu could be harmed by Sulu spirits. They used me as an illustration. I told them about the god who Christians believe created all the world. But the Bajau had never heard of the god. Are the Christians wrong or are the Bajau wrong? This gave them pause. Finally they agreed to take me—from sheer exasperation, I think, rather than from the convincing nature of my arguments.

Our trip to the island was without mishap, and we observed the tabu on speech when we beached the boat. As we walked the path to the *ta'u-ta'u* tree, we followed the other tabus of the island. We left offerings and we took great caution to avoid offending the *saitan*. When we reached the tree, however, I took photographs and, to the unspoken horror of my companions, I bumped a *ta'u-ta'u* when I stumbled over a root. Masa and Biti glared at me as I smiled an apologetic smile. When we were safely back at sea, a flood of reprimands rushed from Masa and Biti. Bumping the *ta'u-ta'u* was the most foolish of all the foolish things they had seen me do since I arrived. If I became sick and died, it was no one's fault but my own. The men were angry and concerned. I had no idea my mishap would upset them so much and I was genuinely sorry.

They sensed my feelings and softened their words, but then told me I was in grave danger and must promise to be more careful in the future—if, as Biti added pessimistically, there were to be a future for me. We returned to the moorage and word of my transgression soon spread. The entire moorage was concerned.

I went to my boat to be alone with my wounded sensitivities, escaping into an Agatha Christie novel for the remainder of the afternoon and eating some cassava and dried fish in solitude at sunset. I went to sleep early avoiding my usual nightly visits to the houseboats since I didn't feel like facing any more reprimands and questions. At about nine o'clock, I awakened with severe stomach cramps. I tried to ignore the symptoms, but fight as I did, they continued. I gulped down an overdose of Kaopectate, but the cramps persisted. I was determined to ride it out alone and not let the Bajau know of my illness, but, there is no way in the world for an attack of dysentery to follow a quiet course. Try as I did to stifle my illness, it resounded throughout the moorage.

Masa was the first to reach my boat. "You are sick again," he said, frightened.

I nodded greenly, and again hung my head over the side of the boat. Within minutes the entire neighborhood moved their boats over to mine to discuss my punishment by the saitan. Laka came to the boat and questioned me about my behavior and the symptoms of my illness. She looked at the bottle of medicine I was taking and dismissed it as useless against the evil saitan. She instructed Masa to light incense, the prerequisite for all Bajau ceremonies. She kneaded my entire body with her strong, gnarled hands as she spoke to the saitan responsible for my illness. I was in no state to remember her exact words, but her monologue was a request that the saitan remove my illness since I was a stupid American who had unintentionally and without malice offended them. She flattered the saitan and continued to tell them of my ineptness in dealing with the Bajau spirit world. Next she mixed an herbal concoction and rubbed it over my forehead and stomach. After more flattery to the spirits, she bent over my face and blew into my mouth and nose. Fortunately, the blowing was a brief part of the treatment since Laka's addiction to betel gave her a breath that would sink a battleship. After some more kneading and more chanting, she announced that I might be all right by morning, but only if the *saitan* allowed it. She left, as did the rest of the party except for Masa and Biti, who stayed with me the entire night. I awakened only once during the night to vomit, and by morning I felt quite well—albeit somewhat hollow.

For the next few days, my illness and recovery were the talk of the moorage. My experience greatly reinforced the Bajau belief in their spirit world as well as Laka's renown as a curer. When Biti insisted my illness was caused by the visit to the island, I no longer challenged him. A week later when I dropped my camera into the sea and Masa told me the spirits were still punishing me, I said nothing. Two months later the pictures I had taken of the *ta'u-ta'u* were returned blank. I didn't tell anyone.

4

Child Bangsa

Probably the loneliness was the most difficult part of my field work. And a strange sort of loneliness it was, too, since I was almost always surrounded by people when I was at the moorages. When I first arrived among the Bajau, I attributed my loneliness to the fact that we didn't speak one another's language. But after I knew the language well enough to converse, I became more aware of the cultural chasm that separated us: a different set of values, a different sense of aesthetics, a totally different view of the world and everything within it. As an anthropologist, I came to understand the Bajau world view; but as a man, I couldn't always appreciate it.

It was the children who eventually saved me from my loneliness. I don't know what I would have done without them. Whatever I did or wherever I went, I usually had an entourage of curious, smiling children in tow. Their antics and companionship brightened me out of many bleak days. They marveled at my odd gadgets. Some would watch for hours as I typed my field notes. After discovering what my camera was all about, they struck poses whenever they spotted it. But their favorite gadget was the tape recorder; they would listen for hours to the songs I had recorded, sung by people they knew in the moorages.

Bangsa was my favorite child. He was a boy of about eight with wide-set, oval eyes, and his large, white teeth were always displayed in a broad grin. By Bajau norms, he was somewhat neglected. His mother was dead and he lived in a houseboat with his father and an older, unmarried brother. While his father fished and worked with his brother, Bangsa wandered the moorage, usually in my company. Our relationship was cemented when he asked me to cut his shoulder-length, lice-infested hair which caused him ceaseless irritation. I insisted he get his father's permission, which readily came. I then shaved his head and uncovered the liveliest array of vermin I've ever seen. Within minutes, word traveled among the children that the anthropologist was giving free haircuts, and I was soon beleaguered with requests from young boys admiring Bangsa's shorn, pale scalp. Before the day ended, I gave haircuts to about a dozen children, not to mention several adults.

After I acquired my outboard motor, the children became even more attached to me in hopes they would be chosen to take the rides I parceled out each day. I tried to be democratic in choosing who went, but since Bangsa was always by my side, he received more than the others. The other children came to understand that Bangsa was my shadow, so they did not resent the preferential treatment he received. After I got my own houseboat, he sometimes slept with me and shared my fish and cassava. He frequently accompanied me on visits to other Bajau moorages and on my occasional trips to Bongao to pick up supplies and mail. And throughout it all, he taught me his culture, sang into my tape recorder, and hammed it up for my camera.

In the early days of field work, Bangsa helped me learn his language. In general, the children were much more helpful in teaching me than were adults. They were not hesitant to point out my errors, whereas the adults were often too polite or embarrassed to do so.

One day I acquired a bunch of coconuts from a land-dwelling family, and I arrived at the moorage in my boat to distribute them among my friends.

"Do you want a coconut?" I asked the wife of one of the men who had taken me fishing the previous day.

She looked at me suspiciously and then spied the coco-nuts in my boat.

"Have one," I said, handing it to her. She took it smilingly while her children giggled.

"Have a coconut," I said to old Laka, as I handed her one. She laughed uproariously and disappeared with the coco-nut inside her boat. Nearby, two teenaged girls laughed as I paddled by.

As I was beginning to wonder what was so funny, Bangsa paddled up in his small dugout.

"Have a coconut," I said, placing it in his boat.

He laughed loudly, splashing the water with his paddle. "This is what you're calling a coconut," he said, grabbing his penis. He held up a coconut. "This is a coconut." He carefully pronounced the word, accenting the vowel I had slurred.

I looked back to see old Laka listening to Bangsa's expla-nation with a big smile on her face. "Hey, Melikan! I'm still waiting for that penis!" She laughed and crawled back into her boat.

One of my favorite pastimes in Sulu was watching the sun-sets. Most Bajau were indifferent to the spectacular displays of color which splashed across their watery world each eve-ning, but Bangsa was an exception. He came to appreciate the colors of the sunset as I did, and he often joined me for my evening pause to see what the setting sun had to offer. And each day we'd see a different display as we quietly sat side by side watching the kaleidoscopic movements of the sky. Sometimes the west was ablaze with pinks of every conceivable shade, and on other evenings, subtle blues, greys, and lavenders left us wondering how so much loveliness could fill so few moments. Occasionally the entire earth was dipped in flowing reds, and I better understood why the Bajau called the sunset "the blood of the sun." Once when we were at sea, yellows turned us into bronze men sailing our amber boat over a sea of molten gold into an orange sun. Never before nor since have I felt so completely a part of the world around me. And Bangsa was an integral part of that world.

Bangsa's bright smile and cheerful presence helped me through more than one grey day. I remember a particular day when everything seemed to go wrong. Bangsa and I were returning from a visit to another moorage. About halfway home, my small motor died, and while I was trying to revive it, it fell into the sea. Fortunately, I always secured it to the boat with ropes in case the clamps loosened, so with Bangsa's assistance, I pulled it from the sea. We then erected a makeshift sail which took us on our way until a sudden wind came up and snapped the frail pole we were using as a mast. Heaving seas and a downpour followed the wind, soaking us to the skin and nearly capsizing the boat. When we finally reached the moorage, shivering like half-drowned rats, we paddled gloomily to the houseboat of a friend. As I stood at the prow to jump to the houseboat, I lost my balance to an unexpected swell and fell into the shallow moorage waters. Bangsa tried to grab me but only succeeded in falling in himself. It seemed the last straw as I dragged myself into the houseboat. Bangsa, ahead of me as usual, fell onto the deck and broke into peals of laughter. I started laughing, too, as the hilarity of the series of preposterous incidents struck home. I grabbed Bangsa and we rolled on the deck, laughing until tears rolled down our cheeks. Our hosts stared at us nervously as if they thought the crazy American and his boy companion were possessed. Then they, too, caught our mood, and all of us—adults, children, and an aged grandmother—laughed uproariously as the rain pounded the world outside.

I came to love Bangsa very much. And in his own way, I think he loved me, too. When I sat cross-legged in houseboats of friends to talk away long evenings, he would crawl into my lap, listen to the adult conversation, occasionally correct my speech, and eventually fall to sleep. I'd then take him home, tuck him into his end of the boat, and write the notes that usually occupied the last hours of my day. I would put out the little lamp and be thankful for his presence, which filled an otherwise empty night.

Early one sunny morning I drydocked my boat to clean the accumulated parasites from its hull. The low tide had exposed a glistening bar of sand and a bed of brilliant green kelp at the edge of the moorage. As usual, about a dozen children surrounded me to see what I was up to. They watched disinterestedly for several minutes, some chewing on the remnants of their breakfasts, when Bangsa discovered the bed of kelp. He jumped into the shallow waters to detach some of the long strands and draped them over his little brown body that glowed nakedly in the morning sun. He then began dancing on the white sand. The other children, attracted to his dance, decked themselves in kelp and joined his movements. I stopped work to watch them. They danced for about half an hour. Their little brown bodies, draped with the brilliant green kelp against the white sands and the blues of the sky, blended with the gentle movements of the aqua sea. They looked like a group of sea elves, recently emerged from the warm waters to dance a rite to a happy deity who spread benevolence over a sparkling world.

Bangsa saw me watching and decided I should participate.

He signaled his companions and they danced toward me with long strands of the sea weed. Tugging and pulling me to the sand bar, they draped me with kelp and, using me as a maypole, danced around me until I was entwined in green, like some sea creature from the primordial deep. Then, attracted to the breakers at the edge of the reef, they ran off to splash in the frothy water, leaving me in my bonds. I sat on the sand in my green garb, watching their antics until they finally dispersed to individual pursuits. Bangsa came to me, undraped my kelp, and returned with me to my boat to finish the job his dance had interrupted.

Everyone in the moorage assumed I would take Bangsa with me when it came time for me to leave. His father was equally enthusiastic, thinking his son would have a much better life with me than in Sulu—and probably also thinking that he might share in his son's good fortune. Bangsa and I never talked about it, but I knew I would never take Bangsa to America. Bangsa belonged in Sulu to his people, to the sea, and to the islands. But I knew it would hurt very much when I had to leave him. That happened sooner than I expected.

One morning he told me he was going with his father to visit relatives at a moorage some twenty miles away. They planned to be gone for about five days. The five days extended into two weeks and then three. I missed Bangsa tremendously and was becoming anxious about his return. I asked various people in the moorage when he and his father were coming back. No one seemed to know anything of their whereabouts. Several days later, I noticed his father's houseboat at the edge of the moorage. I approached the boat and saw his father repairing fish nets at the prow.

"When did you get back?" I asked.

"Last night," he said, looking up from his work.

"Where's Bangsa?" I asked.

"He's dead," he said, sadly.

I was stunned. "Dead?" I asked. "How? What happened?"

"The *saitan*," he said, continuing work on his nets. "The *saitan* got in his stomach and made him sick. He died in two days."

A great hurt welled within me. I stumbled back to my boat and sat alone. Several children stopped by to see me, but I was in no mood for their usually pleasant visits. I poled my boat to the edge of the moorage, engaged the motor, and sped away to an uninhabited islet some two miles away. There, I moored the boat in the shallows and walked up the beach to fall into the shade of a cluster of coconut palms. I don't know how long I sat there, quietly harboring the pain of Bangsa's death as I stared, unseeing, across the water.

Suddenly, I jumped to my feet and yelled as loud as I could, shouted until my throat hurt, screamed at the senselessness of Bangsa's death. I picked up coconuts and smashed them on the beach, broke fallen limbs against tree trunks until my strength was spent. I fell to the beach, exhausted, and quietly wept into the soft sand. I don't know how long I cried, but when I looked up, the sun was setting. I went to my boat and headed toward the moorage, alone in a grey sunset flowing into a black night.

5

Lam

I shouldn't have liked Lam, and I didn't. He was gross, self-centered, loud, insensitive, and downright unpleasant. Had it not been for the special circumstances of that period of my life, I would never have tolerated the man beyond our first meeting.

Lam was Chinese, married to a Bajau woman, and he made his living as a fish-buyer. I met him during my first week in Sitangkai, a village of house-dwelling Bajau. I had just finished my morning coffee and was sitting on the deck of the house where I was staying, watching the men of the household load their boats for a day of fishing. I planned to wander around the community that day to make myself visible to the Bajau before inflicting my questionnaires upon them. As I downed the last of the coffee, a Bajau youth paddled up to the deck in a small dugout boat.

"Mr. Lam wants you to come and bring medicine," he said in Sama without introduction.

"Who's Mr. Lam?" I asked.

"Mr. Lam. Over there." He pointed over his shoulder to the houses beyond.

Realizing I wasn't going to get much information from the boy, I asked my host, who was tossing fishing nets into his boat, the same question.

"A Chinese. A fish-buyer. He lives in the big blue house." He pointed in the same general direction the youth had indicated.

"Why does he want medicine?" I asked.

"I don't know," responded my host. He untied the boat and poled it through the shallow water.

"His wife is sick," said the boy.

Apparently word had already spread that I had medicine—only aspirin and penicillin ointment, but valuable commodities, I had discovered, in communities with no physicians.

Out of curiosity, and realizing it would be a way to introduce myself to some of the community, I decided to accompany the youth. I got my bag that contained my small store of medicine and stepped into the young man's boat. Within minutes we alighted on the deck of Lam's house. We were met by several other Bajau youths, and they led me into the main room of the house. The house was much larger and better constructed than most in Sitangkai, and the room we were in had amenities—such as two easy chairs, a table, and curtains at the windows—not found in most homes.

Attention was centered on a young, very attractive Bajau woman seated on mats in the center of the room and surrounded by a number of other women, probably relatives. She was in obvious discomfort, and wore only a dark blue sarong, which she pulled over her shoulders and held at her throat. As I entered, Lam, a wiry Chinese man in his forties, entered the room from another door.

"Give her medicine." He said to me in fractured English.

I was immediately put off by his abrasiveness, but thinking his coarseness perhaps was due to his inadequate command of English, I held my tongue. I asked, "What's wrong with her?"

"Show him," he ordered the young woman in Sama as rude as his English.

The young woman turned her back to me and pulled

down her sarong to reveal a swollen, infected area on her lower left shoulder. I knelt to examine it closer. Lam knelt beside me. He was a short man, thin on the verge of skinniness. His thick, straight hair was not subdued by the heavy oil it seemed to ooze. His thin-lipped mouth was small, but heavily and greenishly toothed. He avoided my eyes when he spoke to me.

"Give her medicine," he demanded again in English.

I ignored him and looked more closely at the infection. It looked like a large boil. I discovered that the young woman had suffered from the painful swelling for four days and had been unable to sleep the previous night. As I was gleaning this information, I was interrupted by Lam in his rude English.

"Give her medicine. Don't worry. I pay."

With a good deal of self-control, I told him I didn't know if my medicine was appropriate for her infection, I was not a physician, and I did not expect any payment. It should have been obvious to Lam that I did not like him, and I think it was. He retired sullenly to the side of the room and didn't speak again.

I dressed the wound with some penicillin ointment. While I didn't think it would help much, I also thought it would do no harm. I gave the young woman two aspirin tablets, hoping they would ease her pain, and announced that I would leave. She smiled at me in appreciation.

Lam barked in Sama at the young man who had brought me, "Take him back."

I walked out with the young man, got into the boat, and was paddled home. Lam did not accompany us, nor did he offer a word of gratitude. I hoped I would be able to avoid him for the remainder of my stay.

During the next few days, my time was occupied in making my presence known to the people of the community I had come to study. I wandered through the village, trying to make sense of the maze of rickety walkways that connected the pile dwellings built above the shallow reef waters and chatting with persons who looked friendly, explaining to them why I was there.

On the evening of the third day after my encounter with Lam, I was sitting on the deck with members of my host's family, awaiting the evening meal, when the same young man who had taken me to Lam's house again approached in his dugout.

"Mr. Lam wants you to come to dinner," he said, as his boat rubbed against the pilings of the house.

"Now?" I asked.

"Yes."

My initial feelings toward Lam had not changed. During the last few days I had learned he was reputedly very rich, did not associate with the few other Chinese in Sitangkai, and was generally disliked. I was prepared to turn down the invitation but began to wonder whether my interpretations of his behavior were biased by my own cultural expectations. The man had obviously been uncomfortable in my presence, and maybe his speech was offensive only because of his minimal command of English. At any rate, I wasn't looking forward to the inevitable dinner of fish and cassava; perhaps Lam's fare would be better. I accepted the invitation, passed the word on to my host, and got into the boat with the young man.

We arrived at Lam's house, where he was awaiting us on the deck. He flashed a nervous chartreuse smile and ordered me to follow him inside. We went through the main room and on through a door leading into a large room that seemed to serve as his office. A huge desk sat in one corner. In the center, a long table extended almost the entire length of the room. A chair was at either end. Lam indicated I should take one chair while he took the other. We sat looking at one another over a table top about twelve feet long while a pressurized kerosene lamp hissed illumination from the ceiling.

Lam shouted in Sama, "Bring beer!" At first I thought he was talking to me until I looked toward the door and saw a strapping young Bajau man standing like a sergeant-at-arms, wearing only a sarong of deep green and a *bolo*, the blade that is part of the dress of most men in Sulu. The man slipped out the door and shouted, "Beer!"

Within minutes, Lam's wife—her name, I learned, was Najima—came in with two bottles of beer and two glasses filled with ice. She smiled at me and looked much better. I asked if her condition had improved, and she smiled affirmatively.

"Go now!" Lam shouted to her with his usual tact. She stopped smiling and left immediately. The sergeant-at-arms closed the door behind her, locked it, and planted himself in front of it with his muscular arms folded over his bare, powerful chest, staring straight ahead at the blank wall across the room.

"Drink your beer," Lam commanded me, having filled his own glass and sporting a foamy moustache to reveal he had sampled it.

I did as ordered and was reminded that beer over ice really is not bad in the tropics, especially when the alternative is beer at room temperature. We drank in silence as I gazed at the only adornment on the walls of hand-hewn boards—a calendar advertising a Chinese medicinal ointment.

I was startled out of my observations by Lam's shout, "Jaffir! Four beers!" Jaffir, apparently the sergeant-at-arms, opened the door and repeated the command. Again Najima brought in the beer. After placing two bottles before each of us, she was peremptorily told to "get out" and bring dinner. She left and Jaffir again assumed his position.

I didn't like the silence but could think of nothing to say. Before I finished my first bottle of beer, Lam had started on his third and ordered Jaffir to get more. This time Jaffir brought in the beer himself—an entire case, which he placed in the middle of the table. This seemed no breach of household etiquette. At any rate, Lam said nothing.

"You don't like beer?" he asked, looking at my still unfinished bottle.

"I do," I said. "I'm a slow drinker."

"You saved my wife's life," he said suddenly, looking out the window behind my back.

"I doubt that," I said.

"Your medicine caused the sore to break. Now it is getting better. You saved her life. I owe you much."

"It would have broken and healed without my medicine. Maybe the medicine speeded up the process. Maybe it did nothing at all."

"You saved her life," he said adamantly. "I owe you much."

Somehow I knew Lam didn't believe what he was saying. And I knew that he knew I knew he was lying. We made eye contact for the first time since I met the man. He looked quickly away and took an enormous swallow of beer. Deep guttural sounds came from his end of the table, and he spat the resulting phlegm onto the floor between us. I looked away and tried to think of other things.

Jaffir opened the door to a knock. Najima entered with steaming bowls of food which she placed before us.

"Whiskey now," he said to me. He shouted the same order to Najima as she went out the door.

"Eat," commanded Lam. He began eating his food, slurping noisily and rapidly, so immersed in it that he soon seemed unaware of my presence.

I sampled a spoonful and was surprised at the succulent flavor. It was delicious, and I was soon eating with a relish, which, if it did not surpass, certainly challenged Lam's.

"This is delicious," I said.

"Of course," said Lam, speaking for the first time in Sama, apparently drunk enough to give up the effort of speaking English. "I taught her how to cook it. You've been around them long enough to know their food is suitable only for a bunch of savages. Chinese food is the best in the world."

I've long felt that Chinese cuisine is one of the best in the world, but I resented hearing it from Lam. My feeling was intensified by the fact that he spat food across the table as he said it.

"What is this?" I asked him.

"Soup—shark's fin."

I have since eaten shark's fin soup many times in Chinese restaurants around the world, but never have I found any as delicious as it was that night.

Lam finished, shoved his plate away, and yelled at Jaffir for more. Almost immediately, Najima and some female assistants began bringing dishes until a dozen steaming bowls covered the table. I ate with a gusto that, in retrospect, almost embarrasses me. I had eaten nothing but fish and cassava for almost a year, and I gave free rein to my appetite in a gastronomic orgy. Although I probably ate as much as Lam, I could not compete with his style. His table manners were absolutely swinish. He spilled food on the table and floor, ate with his hands when it was more expedient to do so, belched, and spat out bones. Particles of food stuck to his face and juices ran down his arms. We talked little during our attack on the food, commenting only on the merits of the dishes, all of which were delicious. If Lam had taught his wife to cook Chinese food, he was a marvelous teacher and she an honor student. He washed down his enormous mouthfuls of food with beer and Johnny Walker scotch which he sloppily mixed. By the end of the meal, he was very drunk.

Jaffir didn't leave his post. He seemed totally oblivious to us unless Lam barked a command at him.

Finally, Lam stopped eating. He shoved the plates away and lit a cigarette.

"You and I are alike," he said.

Beyond a common taste for the food we had just eaten, I hoped I shared nothing with Lam, but I asked "How is that?"

"We're both civilized men stuck living with a bunch of savages. These people. . . ." He waved his hand toward Jaffir, who surely must have heard him but didn't flinch a muscle.

"They're not savages," I said. "And many of them happen to be my friends."

"They live like animals. You've seen how they live . . . like pigs," he continued.

Involuntarily, my eyes swept the litter surrounding Lam and saw again the rice stuck to his chin. Jaffir opened the door to a knock, and Najima entered with another young woman and began clearing away the dishes.

"Why do you live with them if you don't like them?" I asked.

"Business," he said. "I have a good head for business. They're stupid, like babies. They don't know how to use money. I give them credit, and they have to sell their fish to me. All my wife's family works for me because they owe me money. You saw my wife. She's beautiful. It's good to take a beautiful young girl to bed."

The thought of Lam in bed with anyone repulsed me.

"She was lucky to marry someone rich. She knows it. If she wasn't married to me she'd be out fishing all day like the rest of them. Isn't that right, Najima?"

She didn't look up from the pile of dishes she was stacking, but said, "Yes." The two women then left the room.

We sat in silence—Lam in a drunken stupor and me wondering how I could ease out of the evening. The problem solved itself when I looked down the table and saw Lam snoring loudly, his head resting in a puddle of beer on the table top. I looked at Jaffir, still at the door, and told him I was ready to leave. He nodded, opened the door, and accompanied me through the main room of the house and out onto the deck where my faithful boatman was waiting. I said goodbye to Jaffir, and the young man paddled me back to my house.

I didn't see Lam for several days. When I finally did see him being paddled past my house, he pretended not to see me, suddenly becoming very interested in something in the other direction. A day later I saw him on the main walkway of Sitang-kai, and since it was impossible for him not to acknowledge me, he simply grunted. I chalked his behavior up to his usual bad manners and, perhaps, embarrassment over his drunkenness.

About two weeks after our fabulous dinner, he again sent his messenger to invite me to his house—this time for drinks, not dinner. Again he caught me at a time when I was trying to think of a way to pass the evening, so I accepted his invitation. When I arrived, he was already drunk. We went into the same room where we'd had dinner, taking our seats at either end of the long table. Again, Jaffir stood in stoic attention at the door. Lam stumbled his way through our initial conversation in his smattering of English and then gave it up for Sama, muttering in disgust, "It's terrible that two civilized men have to speak in this barbaric language to be understood. You should learn Chinese."

I said something noncommittal to the effect that I'd like to someday. As usual, Lam didn't listen to my response and shouted to Jaffir that we needed whiskey. Jaffir relayed the command and Najima appeared with a bottle of Johnny Walker scotch. I nodded and smiled at her. She returned my smile as she poured a glass half full of the liquor. As she was filling a second glass, the bottle slipped from her hand and fell onto the table, spilling about half its contents before she could set it upright. Lam leaped from his chair, ran to her and struck her violently in the face, knocking her to the floor. I jumped up and went to her side as he returned to his chair, shouting,

"You stupid, clumsy bitch! I'll make you pay for that whiskey you wasted. Get out of here!"

Najima rose to her feet, holding her hand to her face. Jaffir opened the door for her with the first emotion on his face I had ever seen—a combination of anxiety, fear, and hatred. Najima left. Jaffir closed the door and resumed his position.

I returned to my seat and said to Lam, "Was that necessary? It was an accident, you know."

"Clumsy bitch. She's always breaking and wasting things. She should be out in the boats crawling around with the rest of those animals."

I don't know why I didn't leave. It seemed the more I was around the man, the more I disliked him. I've met only a few people who have no redeeming qualities. Lam is one of them.

He began mumbling about how hard he had to work to support all his wife's family, and how he had to watch them so they wouldn't steal him blind. He then began talking about his own life. He was born in Sandakan, a small city on the northeast coast of Borneo, some fifty miles across the sea from Sitangkai. His family had come to Sitangkai as fish-buyers when he was a small child. At that time almost all the Bajau still lived in boats, and his family's house was one of a dozen strung along the coast of tiny Sitangkai Island. He was about twelve when World War II began, and the Japanese arrived to make Sitangkai their headquarters for military operations in that part of the Philippines. One day when he was out fishing with a Bajau family, the Japanese rounded up all the Chinese inhabitants of Sitangkai and executed them. His father, mother and all his siblings were killed. He had nowhere to go. He had relatives in Borneo but there was no way for him to get there. Frightened by the execution of the Chinese, the Bajau left Sitangkai in their houseboats to live in the outer reefs and islands.

Lam went with them, living for the duration of the war with several families who befriended him. After the war he left the Bajau to work on a smuggler's boat that made runs from Borneo to Manila. He became increasingly involved in smuggling and eventually acquired his own boat and crew. He intimated that he'd made a fortune in smuggling but had given up the business about five years earlier because it was becoming increasingly dangerous. Then he returned to Sitangkai, and established his fish-buying business. He had married Najima two years ago.

He ranted about the other Chinese families in Sitangkai. He hated them because of their superior attitudes. They looked down at him because he'd married a Bajau. But he didn't care, he said. He had more money than they. That's why they didn't like him, because he was so wealthy. He could buy them all out if he wanted to. Or, better yet, he could indebt their fishermen, and thereby take away all their workers, forcing them out of business. But he had better things to do than waste his time on the Chinese in Sitangkai. He had the best house in Sitangkai, and they were jealous.

He then began a similar tirade about the Bajau: the awful food he'd had to eat when he lived with them during the war, how dirty they were, their simple-mindedness and downright stupidity, how ignorant they were at business and how easy it was to cheat them. He was like a *datu* in his household, and they were all his servants—if not his slaves. He could sleep with any Bajau woman he wanted, and he usually did. It didn't bother them. They were like animals who have sex with anyone who comes along.

I knew it was useless to argue with him, so I said nothing. He was drunk, and besides he never listened to my responses, even when he was sober.

Within minutes, Lam began to nod off and I took my leave. Back in my room, lying on my mat, I thought of the terribly lonely life Lam must lead. And for the first time, I almost felt a tinge of pity for the man.

The weeks moved on as I became increasingly immersed in my research. I saw Lam periodically. Usually he pretended he didn't see me, but if he couldn't avoid an encounter, he would grunt a greeting and hurriedly move on about his business. I learned nothing new about the man, only verifications of what he had told me and what I gathered through my own impressions. He was unpopular with the small Chinese community of Sitangkai as well as with the large Bajau population. The Chinese considered him gauche and uncouth; the Bajau considered him miserly and mean. I concurred with both opinions.

It was about a month after my previous encounter with Lam. I was now living in a small house by myself, seeking the privacy I could not find in the extended household where I had spent my first few weeks in Sitangkai. Several times during this period, Lam sent his messenger to invite ("demand" is a more appropriate word) me to drink with him. I had made excuses, not being in the mood to deal with his various obscenities. I was sitting on my small deck watching the tide come in when Lam's young messenger paddled up. He told me Lam wanted me to come and drink beer with him. I was enjoying the mood of the rising tide and had no desire to leave it for Lam's company. In order to get rid of the young man, I told him to tell Lam I would come later after I finished a few chores. I had no intention of going to Lam's house, but did not want to have the messenger returning with a more adamant request when Lam heard of my refusal—a frequent occurrence in the past. The messenger left. Unfortunately, I am a basically honest person, so I soon began to feel pangs of guilt about having lied to Lam. After about fifteen minutes, I decided to go to Lam's house and have one beer with him.

When I arrived, he was already drunk. I joined him in the usual room, and Jaffir was stationed in his familiar place. Beer and scotch were brought in, and it all seemed a rerun of the other nights I had spent there.

"I thought you would not come," he said in Sama, not even attempting English.

"I thought about not coming," I said, honestly.

"You are the only friend I have in Sitangkai," he said. "I drink with no one else."

If I were Lam's only friend, I shuddered to think what his enemies must be like. I said nothing, unable to think of anything appropriate to say.

"When a man is as rich as I am, he has to choose his friends wisely."

"Why did you choose me?" I asked. "You don't know anything about me."

"Sometimes you don't have to know. Sometimes you can tell without knowing. I know we are alike."

Silently, I again began to refute Lam's claim of our affinity. Then I began to understand what he meant. We were both outsiders to the culture we were living in. The difference between us was that I was a visitor for a few months, whereas he was probably in Sitangkai for life. Perhaps I would behave like Lam if I knew I were in Sitangkai for life. As it was, I could hide my anxieties, frustrations, and hostilities because I knew I would be leaving in a few months. I had met Europeans caught in Asia in various ways who lived lives not much different from Lam's. Probably there is no greater frustration or loneliness than living in an alien culture.

"They would all like my money," he continued. "But they'll never get it. They'll never find it."

He looked at me expectantly, but I had nothing to say.

He turned to Jaffir and said: "Get out."

Without a word, Jaffir left the room.

After Jaffir left, he looked down the table and said in a stage whisper, "Gold is the only way to keep your money.

Pesos, rupiahs—even dollars—they're not reliable. But everyone always wants gold."

"I suppose that's true," I said.

"Have you ever seen gold ingots?"

"No," I replied.

"I'll show you some real gold. Stay here." He pushed his chair back, spilling the glass of scotch in front of him. He ignored it, and walked unsteadily through the door.

I sat alone, listening to the hissing kerosene lantern hanging from the ceiling and thinking how harshly it intruded into the softness of the tropical night. Within five minutes, Lam was back. He was carrying a parcel wrapped in what looked like a sarong. He carefully locked the door, came to my end of the table, and placed the parcel before me. He removed the cloth to reveal a wooden box about the size of a large cigar box. On the top was the figure of an elephant in what appeared to be ivory inlay. He lifted the lid. The box was filled with gold pieces, each about the diameter of a silver dollar, but many times thicker.

"This is gold?" I asked.

"Of course," he said. "Pure gold bullion."

I picked up a piece and was impressed by its weight. I had never seen such gold.

"Where did you get all of this?"

"I bought it. This is where I put my pesos and dollars. Gold is the only safe investment. I saw what happened to pesos and dollars when the Japanese were here. They were worth nothing. Who knows who will come next? But whoever comes, they will be interested in gold."

The box contained several hundred gold pieces—I'm sure Lam could have told me the precise number. Each seemed to weigh a pound but, in reality, weighed only a few ounces. But whatever the amount, I knew a sizeable fortune was on the table before me. It all seemed unreal: Here I was, sitting at this rough-hewn table in this crude house with this bizarre Chinese man in the remote Philippines . . . handling a fortune in gold.

"I'll put it away now," Lam said, interrupting my reflections. I put the piece back in the box. He closed the lid and rewrapped it in the sarong. "You're the only one who has seen this box. No one else knows anything about it." He picked up the box and left the room. He was back shortly, empty-handed, with Jaffir reinstated at the door.

The rest of the evening fell into the routine I'd come to expect. Food was brought in which Lam slopped all over himself and the table. He drank himself into a stupor, spilling the abominable mixture of beer and Johnny Walker all over himself, the table, and the floor. He cursed the Bajau, the Chinese, and anyone else who came to mind. The evening ended with him falling asleep, his forehead in the debris on the table.

I stared at him in silence. Jaffir stood at attention. The only sound in the room was the hiss of the kerosene lantern. I felt sorry for Lam, but it was difficult for any compassion to overcome my revulsion at the general obscenity of the man.

I told Jaffir I was ready to leave, and I went home with a vow that I would never again set foot in Lam's house.

I spent the next day working on a paper I planned to present at an anthropological association meeting in Manila the following month. There was no urgent need to finish the paper, but I didn't feel like talking to anyone, so I chose to talk to my typewriter instead. It was a hot day without a breeze, and my house with its galvanized roof heated up like an oven. When evening finally approached, I retired to the deck to catch some of the breeze I hoped would come up. As the sun was splashing its usual spectacular display across the western sky, Lam's messenger approached in his dugout. His message was the same. Lam wanted me to come and drink with him.

"Tell him I can't come tonight. I'm working on a paper."

It was true. I did plan to continue work on the paper, but regardless, I wouldn't have gone. I had no intentions of ever returning to Lam's house.

The boy left, and I hoped the matter was settled. I went into the house, lit a kerosene lamp to deal with the gathering darkness, and began reading the pages I had written that afternoon. About ten minutes later, I was distracted by someone calling my name. I went to the door and was surprised to see Lam climbing onto the deck from his boat.

"I came to talk with you," he said, in Sama, quite sober.

I wasn't happy to see him, but I invited him in. As he seated himself at the paper-cluttered table, I said, "I'm sorry, but I don't have anything to drink except coffee."

"Never mind. I don't want anything to drink." As usual, he looked everywhere but at my eyes when he spoke to me.

We sat almost a minute in silence. I waited for him to make a move. He'd never been in my house before, and I knew he must have come for a reason, especially since he was not drunk.

"I thought you might like to know about the fish-buying business here in Sitangkai. Since you're trying to learn about these people, you might like to know how they sell their fish."

Lam had never expressed the least interest in my research, so I was somewhat surprised by his announcement. Nor did I believe him for a minute. He had come for some other reason, I was sure. But until he got around to stating it, I thought I might as well take advantage of his sobriety and his knowledge of the fishing business. I had talked to a few of the Chinese fish-buyers and was just beginning to unravel the intricacies of the system that operated beyond the Bajau fishermen. So I decided to see what enlightenment Lam could offer.

I began plying him with questions. As I suspected, he turned out to be a bad informant. He gave mostly monosyllabic answers with little elaboration. His mind was obviously on something else. We had talked for about half an hour when

I realized I had learned as much as I was going to from Lam. It had not been wasted time, but neither did I gain any great insights.

"Would you like some coffee?" I asked. He said yes, so I made us each an instant cup with the hot water I kept in a thermos bottle.

About halfway through his cup, which he slurped and sloshed as loudly as he did his beer, he suddenly said while looking out the window, "I played a joke on you last night."

"Oh?" I said, trying to remember a joke from the night before.

"Remember the gold I showed you? That wasn't real gold. It was only brass. I wouldn't keep gold in my house."

I looked at him, inwardly puzzled. I know little about gold, but I was convinced that what he had shown me was indeed gold.

"I drank too much beer. That's why I fooled you. But since you're my friend, I had to tell you the truth."

"You certainly did fool me. I thought it was gold."

He laughed and said, "That would be an enormous amount of gold."

I agreed that it would be, and Lam changed the subject to some irrelevant aspect of fishing. It was obvious that Lam had decided he erred in showing me the gold and had come to tell me the lie I'd just heard. He probably awakened in terror, realizing he'd revealed his carefully guarded secret. I had no intention of telling anyone about the gold, but Lam, of course, did not know that. We talked for another half hour with no further mention of the gold. As I was beginning to grow tired of Lam, we heard someone shouting his name.

We went onto the deck. Struggling through the low tide waters some ten feet away was a young Bajau man I'd seen at Lam's house.

"Fire! Fire! Mr. Lam!" he shouted. "Your house is on fire!"

Lam gave a cry of anguish as he looked in the direction of his house. A discernible and growing glow intruded into the night above the intervening rooftops. Lam and I both jumped into the boat with the young man and helped him pole it through the rapidly lowering waters. The shallow waters allowed us to get no closer than a hundred feet from the house, so we left the boat and waded the remaining distance. A dozen people huddled on the far end of the large deck that stretched to the south of the house. Among them were Jaffir and Najima as well as other faces I recognized from Lam's household.

"What happened?" demanded Lam, accusingly.

"No one knows," said Najima. "The fire started upstairs."

"Throw water on it!" shrieked Lam. "Don't stand like idiots!"

"There is no water," said Jaffir, pointing to the bare reef, now almost totally drained by the low tide. Only a few cans of drinking water stood on the deck and they were useless against the flames that leapt from the back of the house.

Lam seemed to struggle with himself for a moment, and then, as if coming to a decision, gave a loud curse and ran toward the house. He made a slight hesitation at the door and then entered the smoke-filled interior.

"He will die!" said Najima, frantically. "Someone must get him!"

No one moved for a full minute, and then Jaffir broke from the group and ran to the house, also hesitating briefly before entering. I thought he had a good chance of reaching Lam since the flames appeared to be localized in the back of the house, some distance from Lam's quarters, where I assumed he had gone.

We all watched the house in silence for several moments. By now quite a crowd was gathered, but no one made any effort to save the house. There was, in fact, very little that could be done, since the only remaining water was confined to a few tidal pools scattered over the reef. Finally, Jaffir emerged from the house, coughing and rubbing his eyes. He stumbled over to our group and gasped, "I couldn't find him."

Suddenly, a small explosion rocked the deck, and an enormous burst of flame instantly devoured the interior of the house. The heat became so great we had to leave the deck and move out to the periphery, where most of the townspeople were now gathered to watch the fire. Lam's house was a roaring blaze and there was no way the man could ever escape. I sickened at the horrible death Lam was experiencing. Timbers began to fall through the floor, hissing on the damp reef and adding a new odor to the smells of the fire. I stood in fascination, not fully believing the man I knew as Lam was being burnt to death by that awesome fire.

Within an hour the fire burnt itself out. I waded toward my house, feeling a need to be by myself. When I entered, the kerosene lamp was still burning. I extinguished it and lay in the darkness, staring at the stars through the window before me, thinking of Lam. Finally, I fell asleep.

I awakened midmorning to brilliant sunshine, and I immediately thought of Lam. I made a cup of coffee and, as I drank it, I decided to visit Najima to offer my sympathy. Probably no one was sad that Lam was dead, but the proper rituals would have to be observed.

I paddled my boat through the high tidewaters and began asking passersby where I might find Najima. I was directed to a small house that belonged to some of her relatives. As I approached I saw Najima, Jaffir, and several of their relatives loading items into one of Lam's larger boats. I climbed onto the deck and expressed my sympathy to Najima. I looked over at the burnt piles sticking above the water, grim reminders of Lam's death. I learned that Lam's charred remains had been found and were now buried near the Bajau cemetery.

"Are you going somewhere?" I asked Najima, as she directed the placement of bundles into the boat.

"Yes," she said. "This place has only sad memories for me. Jaffir is taking me to Borneo. We have relatives there."

She picked up a small, obviously heavy wooden box about the size of a cigar box. On the lid was a figure of an elephant inlaid in ivory. She looked at it quietly and then handed it to Jaffir, who stood in the boat. He held it for a moment, thoughtful and intent. Then he carefully tucked it into a small compartment under the seat.

I went home and worked all day on my paper for the Manila conference. By evening, it was finished.

6

An Unexpected Source

They were the only Chinese family I knew in the Philippines, and even they were not exclusively Chinese. Somewhere in their past was a Filipino ancestor upon whom they called when the economic or political occasion demanded it.

The Wu family operated a small store and trading launch in the fishing village of Sitangkai. The mother was dead, but the father was very much alive and looked as if he would live for another century or so. He and his only daughter, unmarried and fortyish, operated the family business with the dubious assistance of a silly, effeminate son, probably in his early thirties. Two other sons, much younger, were away at college in Manila. The family's hopes were pinned on them. All of their energies went into making enough money for the sons to complete their education so they could find good jobs, and take over the economic chores of supporting the family. The sons knew this was expected of them and they accepted it as readily as they accepted the money that was sent to them each month.

I came to know the family because their store was the only one in town that had cold San Miguel beer. I discovered their cold beer shortly after I arrived in Sitangkai, and within a matter of days the family and I had established a warm, friendly relationship. As I drank their cold beer, they told me bits and pieces of their lives. They were unrelated to the other Chinese in town and, perhaps because of their Filipino ancestry, did not socially interact with them. Nor were they on intimate terms with any of the Filipinos in Sitangkai, probably because of their Chinese ancestry. They kept to themselves, although they were outwardly friendly to everyone and were generally well liked by the townspeople.

The daughter was very attractive, but her beauty was somewhat marred by the toughness of her character. Since her mother's death, when the younger brothers were infants, she had managed the family business. It was not easy, and the experience had left her as hard as the bright red polish that always adorned her nails. No one seemed surprised that she never married. She was the sort who would probably remain single unless a very sound economic reason for doing otherwise came along.

The older son must have been a great disappointment to his family. He was a rather absurd man who giggled like an infatuated schoolgirl. He dressed flamboyantly and spent most of his time striking dramatic poses in the store as he arranged his hair and talked incessantly in a high, whining voice to anyone who happened by.

The father was a wizened, shriveled-up old man with a face like a dried apple. But his mind was as sharp as a kris, and he had a humor and a tongue that were notorious in the little town.

The family was greatly respected by the townspeople, and admired for their honesty and hard work. Everyone knew the old man and enjoyed his wit. The daughter was a member of the town's governing council and had actually served as mayor when she filled in for a few months after the incumbent died. The older son had no special talents, but he was a kind soul and everyone tolerated his eccentricities. The two young sons were model Chinese sons, industriously improving themselves so they could take over the reins of family.

It was a hot, airless day when I learned of the family's financial disaster. I had just returned from a four-day fishing trip with some Bajau friends and stopped by the store to have a cold bottle of beer. Rather than the warm smiles and greetings that usually welcomed me, I was confronted with gloom. The old man served me with a weak smile and returned to the back of the store, where he conversed with his daughter in low tones.

"Is something wrong?" I finally asked the son, who was unhappily cleaning his long nails at the table next to me.

"You haven't heard?" he asked sadly.

"No. I've been out fishing the past few days."

"It's dreadful," he sighed, placing the nail file on the table and holding out his hands to admire his work. "Our launch was hijacked by pirates from Borneo. We'll never get it back. We're ruined."

The old man and his daughter came from the back and sat next to me.

"That's terrible," I said. "When did it happen?"

"We heard about it yesterday," said the daughter. "The launch was returning from Borneo with supplies. We invested all our money in the trip, and now it's all gone. We have nothing to send to the boys."

"Was anyone hurt?" I asked.

"No," continued the daughter. "The crew was left on a small island near Omapoi. They were picked up a few hours later. We'll never get the launch back." She was obviously much more concerned with the loss of the launch than with any hardships the crew might have suffered.

"We have no money to send the boys, and it is time to pay for their new term. They will have to come home," said the father.

"They will not come home. They must stay in school," said the daughter, with a determined clench of her fist. "We'll think of something."

"Can't you borrow some money until you get back on your feet?" I asked. "Some of the Chinese in town would probably loan you some money."

"Of course they would be happy to loan us money at their outrageous interest rates. I will not pay those rates."

I wished I could help them, but I could think of nothing. At that time I was struggling through the red tape of trying to transfer funds from the States to Manila. I had little cash to spare until the transaction was completed, whenever that might be. I finished my beer, again expressed my sympathy, and left them to their misery.

"Hey, Melikan! Did you hear about the shipwreck?"

It was the following morning, and I was having my first cup of coffee as I watched my neighbors prepare their boats for a day of fishing. The question came from a Bajau friend as he and his brother paddled to my deck, their boat laden with fish from the night's work.

"What shipwreck?" I asked, as their boat bumped against the piles of my deck.

"At Siculan. . . a big Chinese ship from Hong Kong went on the reef. The old people say the *saitan* did it again, but I think it was because the lighthouse was out."

Siculan was a small island with a seldom-functioning lighthouse that marked a very treacherous passage. Few outside ships ever navigated the area, since it was inadequately charted. Outsiders who tried it usually had problems. Only a year before, a cattleship went aground because of the delinquent lighthouse. The local people feasted on beef after the ship, awaiting help from Manila, ran out of feed and had to get rid of the cattle. The more superstitious residents blamed the shipwreck on the *saitan* believed to reside on the island.

"Any beef on board this time?" I asked.

"No. Mostly lumber and spices from Indonesia."

"Much damage to the ship?"

"I don't think so," said my friend as he tied together a string of fish. "The captain has gone to Bongao to wire for help from Manila. Have some fish." He tossed the string of brilliantly colored fish on my deck and shoved off to continue his way home.

"Thanks," I said. "Want to go out to the ship with me later?"

"Sure. Stop by this afternoon after I've had a chance to get some sleep."

I picked a handsome tuna from the string and prepared it for breakfast.

It was strange to see the big grey ship in waters usually populated by the small hand-made boats of the Bajau. It loomed sinisterly as we moved into the shadow of its disabled hull. Members of the crew watched our approach without interest, bored with their unexpected stopover in one of the backwaters of Southeast Asia.

"Hello," I shouted as we neared the grey hull. "Do you speak English?"

Some of the sailors looking over the ship's rail expressed surprise to see a foreigner on the Bajau boat. One of them shouted back: "I speak English. Can I help you?"

"Can we come aboard?"

"Wait." The man disappeared and returned shortly with another man who apparently had more authority.

"What can I do for you?" he asked.

"I'd like to visit your ship, if I may."

After a pause, he said, "Of course," and directed me to a ladder on the opposite side of the ship. My companion and I climbed the ladder. On deck, the man who invited me aboard was waiting. I told him my name, shook hands with him, and introduced my friend. He introduced himself as Mr. Chan, and said he was acting captain in the absence of his superior.

He offered to show us around the ship. During the course of our tour, I learned that the ship was en route to Hong Kong from Indonesia with a cargo of lumber. In spite of misgivings, they had decided to cut some days from their home trip by risking a passage through the southern Sulu Islands. In vain they had looked for the warning lighthouse the previous evening, until the distressing crunch of their ship confirmed that it was not operating. No serious damage was done, but they needed special assistance from other ships headquartered in Manila. Their concern was not with the cargo, which was nonperishable, but rather with the wasted time and the expense of dislodging the ship. At the conclusion of our tour, Mr. Chan invited us into his office, where he offered us cold drinks. We accepted.

"The crew is getting bored. We've been out five days, and now it'll probably be a couple of weeks before we get back to Hong Kong."

"Maybe they can visit some of the local sights," I suggested. "There are some beautiful spots around here."

"That's impossible. The local authorities won't let us off the ship. This is, of course, not an international port, and we don't have the proper papers to leave the ship. I'm sure they would bend the rules if we slipped them enough money, but I'm not that bored yet."

"Maybe the time will go faster than you think."

"Probably slower than I think," said Mr. Chan. He opened another bottle of beer. "Are there girls in this town?"

"Not the kind you want," I said.

"We'll pay them. What we really want are Chinese girls. They would help pass the time. I could make it worth your while if you could arrange for some girls to come here."

"I'm afraid there aren't any girls like that in Sitangkai," I said.

"How about boys?"

"Nothing in that department either."

"That's too bad," sighed Mr. Chan.

The conversation drifted to other topics, and within an hour we left the ship to return to Sitangkai.

It was a moonless night, a "night of the dead moon," as the Bajau called such nights. A Bajau friend and I were spearfishing with lanterns in the shallow waters between the grounded ship and Sitangkai. The ship was entering its fourth day on the reef. Apparently Mr. Chan had made his request to other visitors, because the word was out that the men would pay for Chinese women. One enterprising Sitangkai merchant was considering a trip to Borneo to get some Chinese prostitutes, but he cancelled the trip when he realized the ship might be off the reef by the time he returned.

I had just speared my first fish of the evening when we noticed another boat moving silently through the water some distance away. Beyond the light of our lantern the darkness was unfathomable, and I could not identify the boat nor its occupants.

"Who is it?" called my companion, a common greeting at such times on the sea.

No answer came from the boat as it moved quietly away from us.

He called again. Still no answer. Soon the boat was beyond calling distance.

"I think it was the Wu boat," said my friend.

"What are they doing out here?" I asked.

"Maybe fishing," he suggested as his interest returned to the illuminated reef floor.

"Strange they didn't answer us," I said.

"They're strange people."

Two days later I was sitting on my small veranda, drinking a cup of coffee. It was a refreshingly cool morning after a night of rain. The tide was high, and the little town seemed to float as it sparkled in the bright sunshine. Three children were diving from a boat into the channel that fronted my house. I watched them as I contemplated how I might pass the day. I didn't notice the boat moving down the channel until it was practically in front of my house.

"Good morning," called the Wu daughter. She and her brother were being paddled by two Bajau youth.

"Good morning. Where are you going?"

"We've been fishing," the daughter said. "We're on our way home." They both looked as if they'd been up all night.

"Did you have any luck?"

"Yes. Very good luck." The boat passed out of sight, and my attention returned to the antics of the children.

Toward evening, I walked over to the Wu store. As I entered, the old man spied me.

"One beer coming up!" he shouted, as he took a bottle from the refrigerator. "This is a cold one I've been saving especially for you." He laughed and placed it in front of me. He seemed in great spirits.

"How about some peanuts?" asked the daughter from the back of the store. She came forward with a small saucer of salted peanuts. She looked refreshed and rested. Her face was almost soft from the same high spirits that her father radiated.

I pulled money from my pocket to pay for the refreshments. "Oh no!" cried the son, running over from his perch behind the counter and giggling happily. "This is on us. We are celebrating."

He went to the refrigerator and took out three bottles of beer. "This is a happy day for us," he chattered as he handed bottles to his sister and father, and kept one for himself. It was the first time I had ever seen any member of the family drink beer. And it was certainly the first time they had given me a free bottle.

"What's the occasion for the celebration?" I asked.

"Money!" squealed the son. "We have money for a launch and for the boys."

"Where did you get it?" I asked, using the same frankness I knew they would use with me.

The daughter opened a bottle of nail polish, stretched her left hand before her, and began applying the bright red lacquer to her tapering nails. She smiled mysteriously and said, "From a very unexpected source."

7

Monsoon Night

I'd been on the launch for several hours waiting for the captain to accumulate enough passengers willing to brave the trip to Bongao. For a week I'd waited for the weather to clear so I could make the three-hour trip across the Sibutu passage, but the northeast monsoons had set in with a determination to stay for some time. Day after rainy day passed to the accompaniment of turbulent seas. Today, however, I was ready to risk the seas and rain for a few days in Bongao where I could speak English with Rob and Steve, Peace Corps volunteers who stayed there about six months before they could no longer stand the isolation. I had to leave Sitangkai or crack up. I chose the former. Field work was getting to me, and I needed a break to regain my perspective.

Our tiny round-bottomed launch chugged out of Sitangkai's main channel at about eight in the morning. Within an hour we were beyond the protective reef and riding the heaving swells of the open sea. Being a nonswimmer, I was always a bit nervous on the rough sea, but normally my fear subsided if my fellow passengers were unconcerned. My fears didn't subside this time, however. The other passengers were obviously worried about the angry black swells boiled by the rip tides of the passage.

A strong current caught our little launch and threw us off course as swells broke over the deck and drenched us. A wall of water roared over the launch, sweeping away the frail roof that was our only protection from the rain and threatening to swamp the boat. The captain ordered everyone to bail. The men found five-gallon tins and we bailed furiously. Children screamed while women chanted Arabic prayers for divine assistance. The breaking swells drenched us with sheets of water, making our efforts futile. Somehow we kept the boat from swamping until a disgruntled current tossed us out of the rip tides to again ride the giant, smooth swells.

We soon had the bilge cleared and, en masse, we collapsed on the deck. Every nerve, muscle, and bone seemed to leave me. Others lay around me. Family units huddled together with whimpering children. The rain was still falling in sheets when we docked at Bongao. I stopped at one of the shacks on the waterfront and asked for a San Miguel. The old woman in charge said nothing and quietly brought the beer. After a couple of beers, I was ready to brave the rain again for the half-mile walk to the Peace Corps house.

I didn't expect to find warmth and cheer at Rob and Steve's house, and I didn't. The week of rain was getting to them, too. The incessant drumming on the metal roof made normal conversation impossible and everything was said in semishouts. A table littered with beer bottles bore witness to the cruelty of the rain. Rob had read through their sizeable paperback library and, out of desperation, was halfheartedly paging through a Thackeray novel. Steve was at the typewriter in a desperate mood to communicate with a world beyond rainsoaked Sulu. They offered me dry clothes and warm beer. Both I accepted eagerly, and I then collapsed into a wicker chair which was still warm from the recent habitation of Sloopy, the resident dog. After discussing recent Bongao gossip, we talked about food, the topic that inevitably emerged when we met. For half an hour we tortured ourselves with reminiscences of great dinners we had known, the ingredients of which had never seen the shelves of Bongao shops.

Four beers later we were very drunk. We tried to out-obscene one another by thinking up epithets for the pounding rain. It took us half an hour of coin-flipping to decide who would face the rain to replenish the beer supply. Rob lost. He donned a raincoat to enter the howling night while Steve and I put together an unsavory dinner of dried fish and cassava. By the time the food was on the table, Rob was back with new curses for the rain and new reports about the weather. Locals were dourly predicting three or four days, maybe even another week, of rain. The planes were not coming because of the soggy landing strip. There seemed little to do but drink.

As we were having a before-dinner beer, Sloopy jumped up on the table and grabbed one of the few pieces of fish. Rob chased him, grabbed the fish from him, and gave him a swift kick. Sloopy howled as he retreated under the table to lick his wounds. We all agreed the dog was becoming too brazen and needed to be reminded of his proper lowly place. We ate the food—including the fish rescued from Sloopy—and then returned to the chairs in the living room. Sloopy had taken advantage of our absence to curl up in one of the more comfortable wicker chairs. It happened to be Rob's chair, and Rob was still smarting from Sloopy's theft before dinner. He ran to the dog, grabbed him by the scruff of his neck, and heaved him across the room, where he hit the wall with a howl. New curses were hurled at the dog as we settled down to another beer.

The rain, which seemed to be letting up during dinner, began falling with new fury on the metal roof. Conversation was impossible over the sound of the downpour, so we drank our beer in silence. The rain found hitherto unknown holes in the roof, and we had to rearrange our chairs periodically to escape the drips. Small puddles slowly widened until they joined to dampen the floor of the entire house. Occasional bursts of obscenities hurled at the leaking roof punctuated the din.

Sloopy unwisely sought protection under Steve's chair. Steve sniffed and suggested that maybe someone's outhouse had washed under the house. Further sniffing revealed that Sloopy's usual strong doggy smell was becoming even more doggy in the dampness of the house. So again the animal suffered the brunt of our frustration as he was chased out of the room and threatened with a night in the rain if he didn't learn to stay away from our sensitivities. He yelped into the darkness of the kitchen.

As we opened our last bottles of beer, the kerosene pressure-lantern sputtered to announce that it, too, was running out of fuel. We had to choose between going to bed or going out for more kerosene and, of course, beer. The thought of sleeping in damp beds appealed to none of us. Besides, it was only eight o'clock. Rob begged out of the coin-flipping since he had made the earlier plunge into the rain. Steve and I flipped. I lost. We pooled some pesos. I found a rain coat, and with an empty bottle for kerosene, I went into the windy, wet darkness as the lantern gave its last burst of light before yielding to the darkness.

I stumbled through the heavy rain and oozing walkway to the small store that normally stocked the commodities we needed. Flickers of light visible through the flimsy walls announced that someone was inside. I pounded on the door and, after announcing my identity, was allowed in. There was plenty of kerosene, but no beer. The old woman who owned the store said that the only thing she had to drink was some "hot stuff." The "hot stuff" was a particularly vile brand of rotgut called Black Knight, which advertised itself as "Scotch-like Whiskey." The "like" was printed in very small letters. No self-respecting scotch or whiskey would claim it as even a distant kinsman. I was faced with the choice of buying the evil concoction, with perhaps some Cokes to make it a bit less vile, or going farther down the slippery path to pound on other doors in the rain. I decided to switch to the Black Knight despite the old adage. With kerosene and Black Knight in hand, I returned to the house. I was glad the label of each bottle was distinct, since it would probably have been difficult to distinguish one from the other on taste alone.

When I approached the house, the door was open and Rob was furiously sweeping something out into the rain. With a string of obscenities directed at Sloopy, he told me the dog had answered a call of nature in the front room, which had been discovered by Rob when he slipped and fell in it. Sloopy was still howling in the kitchen corner.

Rob and Steve were none too happy with the Black Knight but agreed that it was no night for wandering about town in search of beer. The Black Knight was doubtless its usual unpotable self, but our taste buds were numbed by the many beers, so we drank it with only a few mumbles about real scotch. Steve went into the kitchen and found some pieces of dried fish which he stacked on a cracked plate and placed on the box that served as our table. While we gnawed in silence on our sad version of hors d'oeuvres, Sloopy slipped in from the kitchen and insanely snatched a piece of fish from the plate. He beat a hasty retreat to the dark kitchen, but we pursued him with a chorus of reproaches and violent threats. By the time we found him in the dark kitchen with the aid of the lantern, he had finished the fish and was looking very guilty but satiated.

We agreed that this was the last straw. The dog had to go. Rob and Steve recalled all sorts of offenses he had committed in recent days, but tonight was the end. We were about to toss him into the wet night when the idea emerged from one of our drunken heads that we should tie him up and throw him into the sea. For some grotesque reason, it seemed fitting.

After searching, we found a rope. Sloopy sensed something evil and eluded our pursuit behind chairs and tables. Finally we caught him, and two of us held him while the other bound his legs. Ignoring the angry rainy night, we left the house and carried Sloopy to the dock behind the house. The black night made it impossible to see the ocean, but we could sense the turbulent waters which occasionally added a salt spray to the rain that drenched us to the skin. Sloopy was yelping and trying to break from the ropes and our hold.

Something happened. I still don't know what it was, or even if it was an actual event, but the three of us simultaneously realized what we were about to do.

"Jesus Christ!" moaned Steve as he slumped to the dock and sat with his head in his hands.

"Goddam, fucking rain!" shouted Rob. "Son-of-a-bitching, motherfucking place! I hope the whole goddam, cocksucking island washes away! Rain, you son-of-a-bitch! See who cares! Fuck, fuck, fuck, fuck, fuck, fuck, fuck!" he screamed as he stumbled through the darkness to the house.

I bent down and untied the struggling dog. Sloopy yelped away into the night. I sat on the dock. Steve got up and lurched past me to the house. An occasional taste of salt sprayed my lips only to be washed away by the drenching rain. I don't know how long I sat there. Maybe only a few minutes. Maybe an hour.

When I finally went back to the house, the kerosene lamp was sputtering again. Rob was snoring loudly in a corner. Steve was hunched over the typewriter, asleep atop a half-written letter that would probably never be mailed. I left the door open in the event Sloopy should decide to come back, and I fell asleep on the wet floor.

The next morning we awakened with heads as big as beachballs and mouths filled with the taste of stockyards. For some reason, perhaps understandable to members of the canine world, Sloopy had returned. He wagged a forgiving greeting to our hungover remains. Never was a dog treated so kindly by three men. In lieu of a cold shower, Steve walked through the still-falling rain to the nearest store to buy something for breakfast. He came back with eggs, a loaf of bread, dried fish, and a can of corned beef. The corned beef went to a happy Sloopy while we devoured the rest with cups of coffee.

A month later, Steve and Rob left Sulu. We never talked about that night.

8

The Possessed

The night was very late and we had done all the fishing we were going to do. Masa sat at one end of the small dugout and I at the other, quietly thinking our private thoughts. Masa's two small sons lay curled together, sleeping on the flimsy deck. Beneath them in the hold, an occasional fish gave a desperate lunge in an attempt to rejoin the sea. It had been a long night, a successful one. Tired, we awaited the rising tide which would allow us to pass over the reef to our home moorage near the isolated islands of Lioboran.

Surrounding us were the lanterns of other boats, with men perched on the prows searching the illuminated shoals for the last few fish of the night. The sky was black, but the sea around us, studded with lanterns, looked like an inverted starry sky. Periodically the stillness was punctuated by the songs of tired fishermen, singing to pass the final hours of their labors.

My mind was elsewhere and I did not clearly hear the songs until several were sung. Slowly, I recognized them as a type called "wind songs," and recalling my role as anthropologist, I decided to learn more about them from Masa.

"Do you ever sing wind songs?" I asked.

"Sometimes," he replied, "when I'm fishing by myself and feel lonely."

"Old Laka told me the wind will come when they are sung," I said.

"You don't feel any wind coming up, do you?" laughed Masa. "They've been singing for about a half hour. We should have a real typhoon before long."

"Do some people sing them to call the winds?" Overhead, clouds opened to reveal three stars, the only ones in the night.

"Probably. There are lots of fools around—like some of the shamans."

"Don't you believe in the powers of the shamans?" I asked.

He didn't answer for a minute. Then, taking a final drag from his cigarette, he tossed the butt into the sea. It made a short, sharp hiss as it hit the water and disappeared.

"I don't believe most of them," he finally said. "A lot of them are charlatans." He thought for a moment. "Others are honest. I don't know what they do, but they seem to cure some people."

"Maybe they're actually able to communicate with the *saitan*," I suggested.

"I doubt it," he responded, somewhat cynically.

"Don't you believe in spirits?"

Again he thought a while before he spoke. "I was doubtful about them until about two years ago. One night I was out fishing. It was dark, like tonight, and I was fishing alone. It was late and I was tired, so I decided to take a nap. I moored the boat near Baliungan and went to sleep. When I woke up, I saw a bright light on the beach. When I looked closer, I could see that it was a strange creature—like a man, but it had only one leg and was shiny green. It had a horrible smell. I pulled in my anchor and paddled away as quickly as possible. I told my family about it when I got home, and Laka said it was a ghost."

"Do you think it was a ghost?"

"I don't know," he said, "but it wasn't human."

"How about *saitan*? Have you ever seen a *saitan*?"

"No," he said. "Laka says they're invisible. But I've seen a boy possessed by a *saitan*."

"Where?"

"At Baliungan—near the place where I saw the ghost."

"How old is he?"

"About eighteen. He's been possessed by the *saitan* since he was a small child. All the best shamans in Tawi-Tawi—even one from Zamboanga—have tried to drive out the *saitan*, but none have been successful."

"How do you know he's possessed by a *saitan*?"

"You can tell," he said as he reached over and covered his sleeping sons with a sarong. "Sometimes he falls over in a trance—just like the shamans. Then he begins screaming and breaking things. He even attacks people. Since he's become older the *saitan* possess him all the time and he has to be tied up so he won't hurt people. His family built a special house where they keep him tied up."

"That's horrible," I said.

"I know. His family feels terrible about it, too, but there's nothing they can do. He's too dangerous to be free."

"Do you know the family?" I asked.

"Yes, for many years. My father traded fish for their cassava when I was a child. Now I do the same. They're good people."

"Do you suppose I could see the boy?"

"Someday when we're fishing near the island, I'll take you to the house. Do you think some of your medicine might drive away the *saitan*?"

"I doubt it," I said. "But I'd like to see him anyway."

"The tide is coming in now," announced Masa. "We can start home."

The following morning I recorded the story of the possessed boy and filed it with other data on spirit beliefs. Several weeks passed before I thought of the boy again. I had been away from Tawi-Tawi visiting some house-dwelling Bajau communities farther south, a stone's throw from Borneo. When I returned, Masa told me he was going to Baliungan to trade fish for cassava. He invited me to accompany him and I accepted. I was interested in learning more about the barter transactions that the Bajau carry on with the land people, and I also remembered that the possessed boy lived on the island. I asked Masa if we could visit the household. He replied that we could.

My interest in the boy was threefold. First, I wondered if perhaps he could be helped. Second, I wanted to learn more about his possession in light of Bajau spirit beliefs. And third, I was downright curious to see a young man so uncontrollable that he had to be tied up in a specially built house.

We sailed early the following morning on the strong currents of a receding tide. A robust wind blew our boat across the rippled waters as swiftly as it blew the clouds across the sky above us. Even Masa was surprised at our speed, and evening found us moored off the village of Baliungan. Masa's wife cooked the fish we had caught en route as his two sons watched her hungrily. Masa and I resurrected the roof, which had been dismantled for sailing. When we finished, the food was ready, and we encircled the cooking pots to eat in the sunset. With the sun went the wind, and a still night brought out a silver slice of moon in a black sky studded with hundreds of stars. Tired from our long journey, we all drifted to sleep early. I didn't stir until I heard Masa building a cooking fire in the colors of dawn.

The early morning revealed the village of Baliungan. It was like dozens of villages in Sulu. Corrugated tin had not yet replaced the nipa-thatched roofs of the houses. Walls were of woven coconut fronds, and each house had a wide deck where morning activities signaled the awakening of households. Like most of the "land" villages of Sulu, it was built over the shallow waters of the beach. Residents farmed the inland fields and fished the surrounding waters to provide a self-sufficiency that dates back centuries in that part of the world. The awakening forest added its sounds to those of the arising village as we sat to the breakfast Masa prepared.

"Would you like to see the possessed boy this morning?" asked Masa as he dipped a dish overboard to wash it in the high tide. "I want to see if Makan has cassava to trade before I go fishing."

I agreed to his plan, and within minutes we were paddling the heavy boat to shore. We moored at the small wharf that served the village and walked to shore while Masa's wife and sons stayed behind in the houseboat. Our presence, especially mine, brought questions and comments as we walked through the village. Masa answered the curious residents. We reached our destination and walked across the walkway that led from the beach to a deck where a family awaited us.

The usual greetings were exchanged. Masa gave them a brief explanation of my presence and then asked Makan, a man about fifty years old and head of the household, if he had cassava to trade. He replied affirmatively, and Masa told him that he would return in three days with fish.

"Do the saitan still possess the boy?" asked Masa after the trade negotiations were settled.

"Yes," said Makan. "It is getting worse."

"May the American see him?" asked Makan. "He might have some medicine to help him."

"I don't think I have medicine to help him," I said hastily, not wanting to raise false hopes.

"Yes, you can see him," said Makan. "My wife is about to feed him. I don't know why Allah has cursed us this way."

We followed him and his wife, who carried a tin pan of fish and rice. We walked to the far end of the deck to a small house, about ten by ten feet. Makan opened the door and invited me to look in.

In the center of the single-room dwelling lay a young man

sleeping. His hair was long and matted. He wore no clothing and he had no cover for sleeping. He was secured by ropes stretched from each corner of the house. One was tied to each of his wrists and ankles so that his movements were limited to only a few feet in any direction. There was nothing else in the house.

"We must tie him," explained the father. "Otherwise he would hurt himself. He tears up all the clothes we put on him, so we have given up trying to cover his nakedness. We are so ashamed we have to treat him this way. But he attacks others if he is free."

I sensed Makan's great sadness. Mentally disturbed people in Sulu are generally tolerated and move freely about the communities where everyone looks out for them. It must have been terribly painful for Makan's family to have to tie up their son.

Makan's voice awakened the young man. He lay motionlessly and blinked at the light from the opened door. As he noticed us, he stood up, and with a piercing screech he lunged at us. Involuntarily, I stepped back, forgetting about the ropes, which jerked him to a halt. He continued to scream and to fight with the ropes as they tore into his already raw wrists and ankles.

"Food! Food!" shouted his mother as she held the dish out for him to see. He immediately stopped screaming and knelt in a docile position. The old woman stepped into the small house and placed the plate of food in front of him. He grabbed the food with both hands and stuffed it into his mouth. Within minutes, he devoured the food, licked the plate clean, and picked up the droppings from the floor. He then hurled the plate at us as he screamed. I turned as the plate bounced off my shoulder.

"We had better leave him alone," said Makan, as he stepped back and closed the door. We walked to the main house as the screaming continued.

"Do you think you have medicine to help him?" asked the mother, not hopefully.

"I'm afraid I don't," I said.

I was very disturbed by the young man. He seemed more like a mad animal than a teenage boy. In spite of Masa's description, I was unprepared for him.

The family offered us coffee and we sat on the deck and sipped the hot, syrupy beverage.

"How long has the boy been this way?" I asked the father.

"Since he was a small child. He was not so bad then. Occasionally he had temper fits and we could not control him."

"How long have you had to tie him up?"

Makan thought for a moment. "Probably about two years. We didn't want to, but we had to do something. He wasn't violent all the time, but we never knew when he might be possessed. He burnt down the house once. And then he almost killed his younger sister—the girl over there." He pointed to a pretty teenager sitting in the doorway. "He's become worse since we tied him up. Sometimes he's not violent. Sometimes he sits and cries for hours."

"That's worse than his screaming," said the mother sadly.

"Did something happen when he was a baby that might have started the attacks?" I asked.

"I can think of nothing," said Makan.

"It was the *saitan*," said the mother. "They are evil. And these are very powerful *saitan* who possess him. We have tried the best shamans in Sulu and none have been able to help him."

"Does your country have medicine that might help him?" Makan asked. A scream from the little house interrupted him. "Sometimes I think it would be better if he died. Then the *saitan* could not torture him."

"I have a friend in Bongao who is a doctor," I said. "She might have medicine for your son. It won't cure him, but maybe it will calm him. If you wish, I'll ask her about it."

"We would be greatly indebted to you if you did," said Makan. "We've tried everything."

Masa suggested we leave in order to reach the reefs we planned to fish before the tide lowered. We said goodbye to the family and returned to the houseboat.

Several days later I was back in Bongao. I picked up a packet of mail from the post office and wandered down to the wharf, where I planned to read it as I watched the early evening activities of that always changing place. As I approached the wharf, I saw Sister Evangelista sitting at the end with a fishing pole. She was a Filipina M.D. who, with two other Filipina nuns, had arrived in Bongao about eight months after I did to establish a small hospital. Sister and I had become close friends. She was engaged in a lively conversation with a Muslim man who was fishing next to her. I didn't know Sister Evangelista was a fishing enthusiast, but I long ago had ceased to be amazed at the remarkable woman's many talents and interests. I walked over and sat beside her.

"So, you're a fisherman too," I said, settling into a comfortable position.

"Aha!" she cried. "My handsome young anthropologist is back in town and hasn't been to see me. Are my charms failing?"

"I just arrived," I said. "I planned to stop by to see you after reading my mail. Even you take a back seat to my mail."

"Do you know Mr. Hussain?" she asked, nodding to the man. "He works for the Bureau of Fisheries." We nodded greetings to one another. "And this is our resident anthropologist. If I weren't already married, I would have captured him long ago," she laughed.

"My fate," I said. "The most beautiful women are always married. How's the fishing?"

"Not bad," she said, showing me a half dozen sizeable fish in her bucket. "I've been here less than an hour."

"And I've been here two hours. See what I have," said Mr. Hussain. He held up a small, undernourished fish. "I can't compete with her."

"I gave up long ago," I said.

"You flatter me," said Sister Evangelista, standing up. "I must go. My little break is over and duty calls."

"May I stop by the clinic tonight?" I asked. "There's something I'd like to discuss with you."

"Of course," she said. "Better yet, come to dinner—if you don't mind eating late. These fish should be ready about eight o'clock. Can you wait that long?"

"Your dinners are worth waiting for. I'll be there."

She made a parting remark to Mr. Hussain, and then left with her pail of fish.

"I don't think my luck is going to improve," he said as he wound up his line and left with his little fish.

I was left alone and began reading my letters. When I had finished, the sun was almost gone. I watched the last dark splashes in the sky, and then walked to the seaside bar for a beer to kill time until eight o'clock and dinner with Sister Evangelista.

When I arrived at the clinic, the waiting room was empty except for a lay worker who was writing in an account book at the desk. She greeted me pleasantly and told me Sister Evangelista was waiting for me upstairs, where she and the other sisters had living quarters. I went to the stairs and announced myself.

"Good timing," Sister said. "Dinner is almost ready."

A small table was set for two in the living room. "The other sisters ate early," she explained. "They have work in the clinic." She came from the kitchen with a bottle of wine. "Just as well. We'll have the wine to ourselves. They don't like it anyway. Down deep I think they disapprove of my taste for wine."

"You're entitled to one small sin," I said.

"I have a bundle of them," she laughed. "But none of them is terribly serious—at least I don't think so. Let's have a glass of wine before dinner."

She filled two glasses and led me to the couch, where we sat as she handed me a glass. She sipped hers "It has suffered a bit during the ride from France, but all in all it's not bad."

"I haven't had wine in so long that anything would taste good." I took a sip from the glass. "It's actually quite nice."

She told me of events at the clinic and in Bongao during my absence as we drank the wine. We then moved to the table, where she served a delicious dinner of fish curry, saffron rice, and sauteed green papaya.

"The fish didn't look too promising by itself, so I decided to curry it." She added after tasting it, "It's not bad."

I took a bite, and concurred, "It's delicious. You should publish your recipes."

"I have no recipes. I simply go to the kitchen and start tossing things together. It usually works out, but not always. I've had my share of disasters."

We returned to the sofa with final glasses of wine.

"On my last fishing trip I discovered a real challenge for you," I said.

"What kind of a challenge?"

"A young man, about eighteen, who's very emotionally disturbed, probably beyond help."

"Tell me about him."

I told her of my visit to Baliungan and all I could of the possessed young man. She asked me many questions about him, most of which I couldn't answer.

"Did he seem to have any physiological abnormalities?" she asked.

"I couldn't see any, but it was hard to tell."

"We've discovered that many of the so-called mental problems of the past actually have a physiological basis which can be treated medically. I would have to examine him, of course, to see."

"That won't be easy," I said. "He's violent, although his mother said he has quiet moods when he sits and weeps."

"It breaks my heart," Sister Evangelista said sadly. "If only I could have reached him when he began having these problems. The greatest frustration of my work here is that so many of the patients have gone too long without medical help and there is little I can do when they come to me. My only consolation is that I am able to reach some in time, and as our clinic and reputation become established, we will reach more. Sometimes it seems our steps are so small."

"Your steps are much bigger than you realize," I said.

She smiled at me. "I suppose you're right. I'm not sure there's a lot I can do for the young man. Even if I could find a physiological basis for his problem and treat it, he doubtless has severe psychological scars, which only a person much better qualified than I could handle. The least I can do is prescribe medication which might control his violence. Such a tragedy. How the poor child has suffered. And how his parents have suffered."

"Do you think he might be possessed?" I asked. "The Catholic church believes in possession, doesn't it?"

"Some of the Catholic church believes in possession. Not this representative. I've read a great deal of the literature on possession, and the documentation leaves a lot to be desired. I don't rule it out—I rule out few things—but I'm not convinced. When can we go see the young man?"

"My schedule is totally flexible for the next week. Whenever it's convenient for you."

She thought a moment and suggested, "How about Wednesday morning? We should be able to get back by early afternoon, shouldn't we? If we leave early?"

"That should be no problem," I said.

We worked out our plans, and after discussing recent books we'd read, I departed.

Sister Evangelista and I left Bongao early Wednesday morning. A very grey dawn had become a slightly less grey morning as we sped across the steel-colored sea in the little speedboat we borrowed from Father Raquet. The sound of the motor precluded any conversation, so we both enjoyed the privacy afforded by the purr of the engine and the expanses of the sea. Within an hour we were within sight of Baliungan, and minutes later we had moored our boat at the little wharf that served the community. Sister Evangelista's white habit, my red beard, and the jaunty speedboat brought a crowd of curious villagers to watch our arrival. Helping Sister from the boat, I explained to the spectators that we had come to visit the household of Makan. They gave us directions, which I didn't need, and we walked to the edge of the village with a small entourage of curious children. Sister Evangelista chatted with them in her limited Sama and, as usual, managed to form instant friendships with most of them.

When we reached Makan's house, he was standing on the deck, having seen our approach.

"Hello," I shouted to him. "We've come to visit you."

"Please come in," he smiled. Other members of the household joined him on the deck.

We crossed the walkway that led to his deck. A few of the children followed us, but most stayed behind.

"Have you eaten?" asked Makan.

"Yes," I replied. "This is my friend I told you about. She is a doctor and may have some medicine to help your son."

Makan looked down, and his wife, standing beside him, began weeping.

"Our son is dead," said Makan, looking at me sadly.

"Dead?" I said, surprised. "What happened?" I didn't need

to translate for Sister Evangelista.

"Come into the house," said Makan. "We can talk and my daughter will make coffee for us." We followed him into the house, where mats were spread for us to sit.

"It happened several days after you left," began Makan. "He was very violent for about two days. Then he fell into one of his crying spells for an entire day. He wouldn't eat the food my wife prepared for him. Finally, we decided to leave him alone until he was ready to eat. We couldn't coax him to do anything he didn't want to do. It began raining at sunset, and we all went to bed early." He paused and sipped from the steaming glass of coffee his daughter served. "The next morning my wife went to see if he would eat. We heard no sounds from him during the night and assumed he was feeling better. I heard her scream and ran to see what was wrong. The house was empty, but floorboards had been removed. I looked through the open floor, and there he was, floating in the high tide. He must have fallen through the floor. He was face down, tangled in his ropes."

Makan's wife wept throughout the story. I expressed my sorrow to the family again and quietly translated the episode to Sister Evangelista.

"How horrible," sighed Sister. "The poor child. Tell the family that my heart weeps for them."

I translated for the family, and Makan said, "Tell your friend that we greatly appreciate her coming here. It was not meant that she see our son."

"Ask him if he would mind my asking questions about the boy. Tell him it might allow me to help others like him."

I translated for Makan, and he said he would tell Sister anything she wanted to know. For the next half hour, I acted as interpreter for Sister Evangelista.

According to Makan, the boy began having violent temper tantrums when he was about two. He fell into convulsive fits, screamed, frothed at the mouth, broke anything he could reach, attacked people and animals, and beat and scratched his own body. During the first year, the tantrums occurred only about once every three or four months. Their only way to control him was to bind him in ropes until the fits passed, after which he usually fell into a comatose sleep. They called in dozens of shamans, believing he was possessed by *saitan*, but none was able to help him.

As the boy grew older, his violence increased. When he attempted to speak, he stuttered terribly. Eventually, what little speech he knew was totally blocked by his impediment, and his communication consisted of guttural noises and gestures. His violence increased. One day he attacked his sister and almost choked her to death before he could be pulled from her. Two days before, he had hacked a dog to death with a *bolo*. It was then the family decided he should be restrained because his violence was so unpredictable. His isolation, of course, increased when he was tied in the house. He allowed no one to touch him. They couldn't cut his hair or bathe him. About three years ago, the long crying spells began. Even during those periods, however, they could not approach him, since his crying often turned to violence if someone appeared.

Sister Evangelista asked details about his attacks, their frequencies, his history of physical illnesses, his diet. Finally, we ended the discussion, having exhausted what was to be learned about the boy. I asked Sister if she could diagnose the boy's disorder.

"I don't pretend to be a specialist on such matters," she responded. "I'm a surgeon. It appears that severe psychological problems developed as his physical illness increased. Probably there was nothing else the family could do." She sighed. "The tragedies one finds tucked away in these lovely islands break one's heart."

The conversation resumed with Makan and his wife, but was shifted to happier topics. Soon, Sister announced we should leave since she was expected at the clinic that afternoon. I relayed the message to Makan and we rose to depart. Makan and his wife, along with an entourage of relatives and neighbors, walked us to our boat.

As we stood at the end of the wharf, Makan said to Sister, "We greatly appreciate your coming. Perhaps, though, it is better the boy is dead. He is at peace. It is Allah's will."

"God has his own ways," said Sister Evangelista.

I said nothing.

9

The Songs of Salanda

It was one of those quiet evenings on the sea when it seemed the entire earth was holding its breath. Not a sound and not a ripple stirred the watery world around us. We had sailed all day from Bongao to the tiny islands of Lioboran, which are unregistered on most maps of the southern Philippines. The wind was good, but as the islands came into view it ceased, and a hush fell upon us. Masa and I each took paddles and dipped them into the glasslike waters to provide the only sound and motion in our world. We did not speak, both of us tired and sunburnt from our long journey and eager to reach the moorage so we could prepare a meal to subdue our ravenous appetites.

The moorage was the most remote and traditional of all the Bajau moorages in Sulu. The population still lived entirely in houseboats and their contacts with outsiders were minimal. The flat islands protruded slightly above the sea, creating ephemeral interruptions in the waters that stretched in all directions. Momentarily I was struck with the insane notion that if I sailed any farther I would drop off the edge of the earth.

The sun was still bright and golden, but it burnt less harshly on our bare backs as we paddled away from it. The golds began to flow into ambers, and by the time we reached the moorage, the world was crimson. As we paddled among

the moored houseboats, a few shouts of greeting acknowledged us, but for the most part we were ignored. After an-
choring our boat, we erected a *nipa* roof to protect us from
the mists of the night. We began rummaging for food. Masa
cleaned the fish we had caught that afternoon, and I made
the fire that would cook them and the cassava stowed under
the deck. We still didn't speak, being too tired and hungry for
words. Masa sat back to smoke a cigarette as we waited for the
food to cook. I kept the fire going. Finally, our food was ready
and we ate greedily from the cooking pots until we were full.
Masa lit another cigarette from the ashes of the cooking fire,
and we watched the activities of the evening as the sea gently
rocked us.

"It's a very peaceful place," I said, breaking our silence.

"Yes," agreed Masa. "My favorite of all the moorages. When
I was a child, my parents often moored here. This is like home
for me."

"Has it changed much since you were a child?"

"Very little. Some of the people are different. But it is much
the same."

We fell back into silence, entertaining our personal
thoughts. Mine were of the idyllic peace of the little moorage
lost from the world in these remote waters of Southeast Asia. A
half-dozen small islands, a few feet above sea water, enclosed
the moorage to provide a lagoonlike protection. Surrounding
us were about twenty-five houseboats, the nearest one more
than twenty feet away. Cooking fires illuminated the faces of
families as they gathered for the evening meal. Some cleaned
fish while others, especially children, bathed in the clean
waters of the high tide. The moorage sounds, the only noises
in the young night, were comforting rather than obtrusive.

I rearranged myself on the hard deck and lay back to watch
the stars emerge from the darkness left by the sunset. The lul-
labies of mothers tending fussy babies began to fill the night

air. Children's songs interspersed them, as did the romantic ballads of teenagers. I listened to them, only half hearing, and remembered that the songs of the Bajau had become one of the focuses of my research. Another voice, uniquely different, joined the singing. A woman's voice, it grew louder and clearer than the others until it dominated the evening. Other singing halted as the entire moorage stopped to listen to the song. The quality and range of the voice were distinctive. The lyrics were bittersweet with melancholy images. Finally the singing stopped, and the moorage was silenced as by a last lovely note that brings an opera house to an awed hush before the great outburst of applause.

"What a beautiful voice," I finally said.

"Yes," agreed Masa. "Salanda's songs are always beautiful."

"Do you know her?"

"Everyone knows Salanda and her songs. She was once the most famous singer in all of Sulu."

"Why do you say once?" I asked.

"She doesn't sing much anymore. She's too old. She's a mother now."

The following morning, I decided to wander among the houseboats to make myself familiar to the residents before I started the household census and survey that would begin my research in the community. The tide was out and the water was shallow enough for me to wade from boat to boat. Most of the men were away fishing, but the moorage was abuzz with the morning activities of the women. Children collected on a nearby exposed reef to play their version of hopscotch.

I stopped to chat with people I knew, asking them of their travels and of relatives in other moorages. As I was talking to a woman, I heard again the singer who had impressed me the night before. She was singing a lullaby in a nearby boat. I eased out of my conversation and wandered over to the boat.

I smiled at an old woman who was peeling cassava tubers on the front deck. She returned a toothless grin and spat a blob of red betel juice into the water.

"A nice singer," I said.

The old woman laughed. "That's my daughter-in-law Salanda. She's always singing."

The singing stopped and a young woman crawled from under the roof onto the deck, apparently attracted by our voices.

"This is the Melikan," said the old woman. "He likes your singing."

Salanda gave me a wide smile but said nothing. She was a lovely young woman. She wore only a sarong around her waist, and her long, loose hair hung softly about her face and shoulders. Her full breasts were still firm and had not yet become the pendants that characterize most Bajau women after the birth of a couple of children. Her white teeth indicated she was not yet addicted to betel nut. As do many Bajau, she looked more Eurasian than Malay.

"You have a beautiful voice," I said.

"Salanda was the most famous singer in Sulu," volunteered the old woman. "She used to travel to all the islands to sing at weddings and other celebrations. Even the land people paid her to sing. No one could sing like Salanda."

Salanda laughed, tossed her head to get her hair away from her face, and said, "But I am too old now. My voice is no good anymore."

She was no more than twenty-five-years old.

"I heard you singing last night," I said. "I think your voice is still very good."

She laughed again, somewhat embarrassed, but obviously pleased by the compliment.

"You should have heard her before," said the old woman. "No one could sing like Salanda."

"I have a machine that will record your voice. Would you like to hear your voice?"

"I know about recorders," she said, somewhat worldly. "Why do you want to record my singing?"

"Because I think you have a beautiful voice. I'd like to record it so people where I live can hear it too."

"I'm too busy to sing today. I have to go to the island to get firewood."

"It doesn't have to be today. I'll be here for several weeks."

"I'll ask my husband. I'll let you know what he says."

Our conversation drifted to other topics. I discovered that Salanda was distantly related to Masa, not surprisingly, since practically all Bajau are related if their kinship ties can be unraveled. After about fifteen minutes, I moved on to another houseboat. Before the day was over, I had visited every houseboat in the moorage and was ready to begin my census.

That evening, after Masa and I finished our meal and were sitting on the deck watching the evening activities, I asked him about Salanda. She was indeed, he said, a very famous singer. Before she married she had traveled throughout southern Sulu with her brother, singing at weddings and other ceremonies. Her love affairs were equally famous during those years, and she had left a string of lovers throughout the islands she visited.

Her current husband was her third, the one who had fathered her two children. Her other marriages were brief alliances. The first, to an older man, had been totally arranged by her family. Salanda had left him after a few weeks and again took up her singing, this time traveling with a non-Bajau man from one of the neighboring islands, a rather unusual arrangement since most of the land-dwellers consider the Bajau unfit for any kind of social intercourse. After several months with the man, she returned home and within a short time was married to a man much closer to her in age than her first husband. That marriage was no more lasting than the first, however, and before long Salanda was again singing with her brother up and down the archipelago.

Her third and present marriage seemed more successful. She had been married four years. According to Masa, she had had several affairs during this period, but her husband learned of only one, which resulted in a brief separation. Masa seemed to think Salanda had finally graduated from the wildness of her youth and had taken on the responsibilities of adulthood.

As Masa finished his brief biography, the splash of paddles drew our attention to a dugout headed toward our boat.

"It's Salanda's husband," said Masa, as he called out. "Where are you going, Tamba?"

"To see you," was the response as the small boat glided next to us.

Tamba was a rather ordinary young man, probably in his late twenties. He wore only a loin cloth. Huddled next to him in the boat was a little boy, wearing nothing but a necklace. I greeted Tamba and told him I had met his wife and mother earlier in the day.

"They told me you were at the boat," he said. "They said you want my wife to sing into your recorder. Can you come tonight?"

"I'd be happy to," I said, somewhat surprised. Salanda had revealed no particular eagerness to sing for me and I was prepared to spend some time convincing her to do so. "I'll come to your boat as soon as I get my equipment ready."

"We'll wait for you there," said Tamba. He paddled into the dusk.

"That's a surprise," I said to Masa. "I didn't think she'd be ready to sing so soon."

"They're interested in your recorder. You remember how amazed I was when I first heard it."

I crawled under the nipa roof, unpacked my recorder, found some new batteries and tapes, and returned to the deck. We paddled our boat through the waters and moored next to Salanda's houseboat. Tamba was sitting on the deck and invited us to his boat.

We climbed to the deck, and entered the living space under the nipa roof. As on all Bajau houseboats, the living area was very limited. Salanda and her mother-in-law were inside and two small children lay sleeping on mats at the far end. Coals smoldered in the small cooking hearth at the stern. While Masa talked with the family, I untied the several layers of plastic that protected the recorder.

"Do you want me to play the gabbang while I sing?" asked Salanda.

"If you prefer," I said.

She lifted several boards from the floor and, with the assistance of her husband, pulled the instrument from under the deck. Deck boards were replaced and she began assembling the gabbang, an instrument like a xylophone, consisting of a wooden boat-shaped box with an open top. Over the top were bamboo slats that were struck with two rubber-tipped mallets to provide the resonant wooden sounds that often accompany Bajau songs. Salanda played a few tentative notes while I got the recorder ready. Tamba adjusted the small kerosene lamp so its meager flame could better illuminate the space.

"My voice is no longer good, and my songs will be bad," said Salanda, as she continued to tap out melodies. Her demurrer was etiquette and not meant to be convincing.

She hummed as she continued to play the gabbang. Then she moved into words and began singing a ballad about two young lovers, separated because of the enmity of their families, a Sulu Romeo and Juliet. Music and lyrics came easily for her as she sang of their fate. Since Bajau songs are not memorized, she created the lyrics as she went along. Salanda's fertile, sensitive imagination as well as her beautiful voice made her the popular singer she was. Her volume and range dramatized the tragic events of her song.

Before long, people from neighboring boats joined our group to listen. Small children, women with nursing babies, sunburnt fishermen, and decrepit old people pressed their way into the houseboat. As more people arrived, Salanda sang more fervently. She moved on to other stories and other events as she performed musical acrobatics with her voice and the *gabbang*. The boat became so crowded her husband had to refuse admission to newcomers. Those who could not get in anchored their boats nearby to hear the songs of Salanda.

Most of her songs were sad—the sorrow-filled lives of people with no control over their fates. Small children sat enraptured, men sniffled, and women wept unashamedly. After a full hour of singing, Salanda stopped, put down the mallets, and said, "My voice is bad. You do not want to hear any more."

"Sing more," urged someone from the audience.

"Sing about the wreck of the *Zamboanga Star*," said another.

She obviously had no intention of stopping. She needed a brief rest but was eager still to perform for her audience. I took the opportunity to put on a new tape and to compliment her again on the beauty of her voice. She was in her element and she glowed with satisfaction. Her husband looked proud and smug as he sat beside her. The old mother-in-law repaired fish nets by the weak kerosene flame through moist eyes. After another drink of water, Salanda began to play again.

This time she sang of a shipwreck that had occurred several years prior to my arrival in Sulu. Like most of the ballads of Sulu, Salanda's songs were based on actual events which she wove into interesting narratives for her audience. The individuals and places she mentioned were familiar to them, as were the broad outlines of the story. But it was all made suddenly new—the nuances and the innuendoes were hers alone, and her exciting voice enthralled her listeners.

She sang for another half hour before people became restless and began to leave. She finally brought her song to an end,
put down the mallets, and announced that she was finished
for the evening. I told her I would return the next day to play
back her songs if she wanted to hear them. She said she would
be free in the afternoon. Masa and I returned to our boat and
settled in for sleep.

I spent the following morning collecting census material.
It was a particularly hot day and I was happy to have a respite from my work at noon when I fixed a brief lunch. After a
short nap, I went to Salanda's houseboat to play the tapes I had
recorded the previous evening. When I arrived, she and her
mother-in-law were sitting in the boat waiting for me. Today
Salanda's sarong was tied up under her arms. Her mother-in-
law was bare-breasted, chewing her eternal cud of betel. We
exchanged greetings as I crawled into the boat and began setting up the recorder. They responded with amusement when
the music began, but soon Salanda was listening intently to
her voice, first excitedly and then critically. She commented
to herself about the weaknesses of her performance as well
as its fine points. Before long, people from other boats began
to gather to hear the recording. Within a half hour the boat
was filled, and people were standing in the low tide outside.
Salanda was obviously enjoying the attention her songs were
receiving, but she soon became impatient with listening.

"Would you like me to sing again?" she asked, when I
stopped to change the tape.

"Sure," I said, glad to have more recordings of her songs.
"I'll put on a new tape."

As I prepared the tape, she put together her *gabbang* and
began the prelude to her song. After a few tentative beginnings, she moved into a ballad about a young woman who had
many love affairs before she settled down with a handsome,
rich man.

Her audience was mostly women and children, but half-way through her song two young men crowded into the boat and sat opposite Salanda. The ballad evolved into a comic song with many sexual suggestions as the young men began to respond musically to Salanda. The song continued along these lines and everyone turned jubilant as an open musical flirtation bloomed between Salanda and one of the young men. The audience laughed and exclaimed at the racier parts of the ballad. Salanda basked in their admiration as she flirted happily with her handsome singing partner.

It was a delightful song. The events of the story were not unusual, but the repartee between the two singers was drawing upon their musical creativity with marvelous results. Both had become oblivious to the audience as they dwelt upon their sensual story. I checked the tape and noted that it had about ten more minutes to go when I looked up and saw Salanda's husband peer into the back of the boat as he hung a string of fish at the side. His initial expression of delight moved to one of concern as he listened to the lyrics and saw the flirtations of the two singers. He edged his way into the crowd and eventually found a place next to Salanda. When she saw him, her flirtations ceased and her lyrics became innocuous. Her partner stopped singing.

When she brought the song to a rather rapid conclusion, her husband announced, "That's all the songs for today. It's time for us to eat." He glared with obvious dislike at the young man who had accompanied Salanda.

Salanda said nothing and began dismantling her *gabbang* as the crowd dispersed. I put away the recorder and thanked Salanda. She smiled, but still said nothing. I said words of departure to her husband, who responded with a grunt. I waded through the rising tide to my houseboat.

That evening as Masa and I ate a delicious fish we'd baked on our little hearth, I told him of the afternoon's events—

especially the arrival of Tamba and his unhappiness with the situation.

"Who was the man singing with Salanda? Describe him for me," he responded.

I described the young man.

"It was probably Lawani," said Masa. "He's the one Salanda had the affair with last year. Tamba is very jealous of him."

The days at the moorage passed rapidly as I became involved in my research. I finished the household census and was now trying to do an accounting of the fishing done by the families. Each morning I detailed who left the moorage for fishing, and then I interviewed them to record their catches when they returned in the evening. It was tedious but necessary to my research. I was busy in the mornings and evenings but had lots of free time during the days and nights. I spent the days trying to unravel the kinship ties among the moorage residents, and the evenings in conversations with Masa and others.

One evening when Masa and I were finishing our dinner, Salanda's husband paddled up to our boat. A week had passed since Salanda last sang for me, and I assumed her husband's unhappiness had put an end to our recording sessions.

We greeted him and Masa asked him about his fishing that day. They chatted of piscatory matters while I cleaned the utensils of our evening meal. As I joined Masa to talk with Tamba, he said to me, "Salanda would like to sing tonight. Will you come?"

I said I would, and within minutes Masa and I were paddling behind him to the other side of the moorage. The moorage had increased sizeably by the arrival of many houseboats over the past few days. The full moon was approaching, and families were gathering for a wedding that was to take place during the full moon. When we entered Tamba's boat, the *gab-*

bang was already assembled. Brightly colored mats were spread for us, and I prepared the tape recorder for another recording session. Our small group was the only audience as Salanda began singing, but as the sounds of her voice drifted over the moorage waters, others were attracted to the boat. It filled to the point that I feared one more person might capsize it— a fear which Tamba apparently shared since he refused to let any more people aboard. This didn't stop Salanda's admirers, however, as they paddled their boats as close as possible to hear her.

She loved the audience, and as it increased, her singing became more powerful. Again her songs were of love and tragedy. She manipulated the emotions of her audience like the true professional she was. Tears wet their faces as she described a mother helplessly watching her child drown during a shipwreck; their eyes and mouths opened in anticipation when she sang of the dramatic chase that finally resulted in the capture of a notorious pirate; and they sighed with happy relief when, after a tempestuous and lengthy separation, two lovers were finally reunited to live happily ever after. The more she sang, the better she sang. Her lyrics became more exciting, and her voice chased itself through musical labyrinths.

Tamba sat next to her, enjoying some of the reflected limelight. He obviously was very proud of his wife and happy to share in her performance. Salanda stopped briefly for a drink of water, and I took the opportunity to change the tape. When she resumed, she began singing a comic, risqué song about a lovesick young man who tried all sorts of ways to attract a flirtatious young woman who was only playfully interested in him. The song was filled with the sexual innuendoes that the Bajau love in their comic songs. Salanda was having great fun. She paused momentarily to plan her next lyrics as she continued to play the *gabbang*. During the pause, a young man from the crowd joined in to respond musically to Salanda. I didn't know the man and assumed he was one of the new arrivals for the wedding. Salanda responded, and their song soon became one of sexual banterings. The audience laughed and squealed at their various innuendoes, and the singers openly flirted with one another to add to the mood of their song.

As the song grew increasingly sexual, Tamba became increasingly ill at ease. He no longer smiled at his singing wife, but looked at her suspiciously and then at her singing companion. He didn't like the turn of events. After listening unhappily for about five minutes, he reached out and grabbed Salanda's hands, so she could no longer play the *gabbang*.

"That's enough for tonight," he said. Both Salanda and her singing companion stopped. "It's time to go to bed."

"But it's still early," said Salanda, not pleased at being stopped.

"That's all for tonight," Tamba said emphatically.

Salanda said something to him under her breath which I could not hear. She threw the mallets on the *gabbang*, and moved through the crowd to the back of the boat. The tension quickly dispersed the audience, and I put away the recorder. Masa and I said goodbye, but only the mother-in-law responded. Tamba and Salanda stared stonily at one another.

Two mornings after the incident in Salanda's boat, Masa announced that a small flotilla was going to a nearby island to get drinking water. The islands of Lioboran have no drinking water, and the Bajau who moor there must travel to a spring on nearby Tawi-Tawi Island for water. The party of eight boats planned to leave in the late afternoon to take advantage of tidal currents. Masa suggested we go with his brother-in-law to replenish our dwindling supplies. I had never been to the spring and was looking forward to the interruption in my routine.

As our boats assembled at the edge of the moorage, I noticed Salanda and her husband in the group. They seemed to be on amiable terms again. I helped Masa dismantle the roof, and with his brother-in-law we erected the mast and sail.

Other boats were doing the same, and soon our little flotilla was skimming the slightly rippled waters. I found a comfortable spot at the prow of the boat and sat back to enjoy the late afternoon warmth of the declining sun. We sailed for an hour into the setting sun. As we moved within the shadows of the Tawi-Tawi mountains, the breeze diminished and our sail hung limply on its mast. We dismantled it and paddled the heavy boat to the shoals of the island. Once within the shoals, Masa mounted the prow and poled the boat to the shore.

We were the first to reach the beach. As our keel rubbed the sandy bottom, Masa jammed the mooring pole into the shallow waters and we tied our boat to it. I slipped over the side into the warm waters and waded to the beach, which glowed with the golds of the sunset.

A path led inland to a rocky cliff that jutted abruptly upward to a small plateau. Flowing out of the rock, about eight feet above ground, was a spring. Beneath, a pool collected the clear waters before it overflowed into a small stream that ran to the beach and emptied into the sea. We refreshed ourselves at the spring, drinking deeply of its cool waters. We then returned to the boat and got the large ceramic water jugs to fill at the spring. Other members of our party were mooring boats and carrying water jugs to the beach. Children splashed in the water and tumbled on the beach as they explored the new playground. We were the first to arrive at the spring and put our jugs in place for filling. The flow was constant but not great, and consequently it took some time to fill a single jug. While others awaited their turns, they bathed in the freshwater pool and some women took advantage of the abundant supply of water to wash clothing.

For several weeks, my bathing had consisted of a swim in the sea followed by a sparse rinse with a small can of fresh water. I wallowed luxuriously in the fresh water as I repeatedly scrubbed my body with the bar of soap I brought for the purpose. I shared the soap with others who also enjoyed their first bath in many weeks. By the time I finished, a bright moon had replaced the setting sun. Women returned to the boats to cook the evening meals and small groups wandered back to eat. Salanda passed me on the path. Having already eaten, she was returning to fill another jug that she carried on her shoulder. She smiled and made a small comment about the fun of bathing. I responded and went to the boat to join my household.

After eating, Masa and I returned to the spring to see how many more jugs were to be filled. Salanda's husband was filling his final jug as we approached. We sat with him until it was filled, and then walked back to the beach, helping him carry the heavy water. As we hoisted it into his boat, Salanda waded up.

"I'm returning to the moorage with my sister," she said to Tamba. "I haven't seen her for many weeks and she's leaving tomorrow."

Tamba told her to go ahead. Salanda asked her mother-in-law if the children were sleeping. After hearing yes, she waded back to the beach toward a nearby houseboat.

Men mounted the prows to pole the heavy boats through the shallows of the island to the deep waters beyond the reef. It was a beautiful night, the moon turning the sea world into a ghost of the day. One of the men began singing a wind song. Another responded to him, as did another. Soon the night was punctuated by the melancholy songs of the men as they called upon the wind to assist them on the voyage home.

Their pleas to the wind, however, were not answered. When we reached the deeper channel, the poles were replaced by paddles and all took turns paddling across the wide channel that would ultimately take us to Lioboran. It was a long journey home as we paddled, rested, paddled, rested. At three o'clock we finally arrived at the moorage. The sleeping houseboats bobbed on soft waves as we moored our boats to join their slumber.

Tamba poled his boat to the houseboat moored next to us.

He called, "Salanda, come so we can moor the boat and sleep."

The man mooring the boat said, "Salanda is not here. Isn't she with you?"

"She said she was returning with you," said Tamba.

A woman's sleepy voice came from the houseboat. "She told me she was going to your boat when I saw her at the spring." She stepped onto the deck and I recognized her as Salanda's sister.

A chorus of voices quickly confirmed that Salanda was in none of the returning boats.

"She must still be on the island," said Tamba. "I must go back to get her."

No one said anything. It was clear to everyone, including her husband, that Salanda had chosen to stay behind.

Tamba and his brother returned to the island that night in search of Salanda, but they came back the following afternoon alone. We eventually learned that Salanda had left on one of the inter-island launches with Lawani, the young man with whom she had had an affair before my arrival.

I stayed in Lioboran only a few days beyond Salanda's departure, having finished the work I had intended to do there, and I returned to the Bongao area for another leg of my field work. Some weeks later, I went on an extended fishing trip with Masa and his brother-in-law. We were away from Bongao for about two weeks as we fished the waters and visited islands I'd never seen before. One afternoon we sailed into one of the larger villages in that part of Tawi-Tawi and had an early dinner. As we sat back to digest our meal, we heard the sounds of drums and gongs, instruments used to celebrate the various ceremonies of Sulu. After some coaxing on my part, I talked my companions into accompanying me to the village to see what was happening. We paddled our boat to a mooring dock and walked down the path leading to the village. We followed our ears as well as the villagers to the house hosting the celebration. My presence caused the usual stir, but most people were more interested in the celebration, which turned out to be the last night of a circumcision ceremony. We edged our way onto the deck of the house and, with a bit more squeezing, we made it inside. It was a large house hung with brilliant mats and buntings. The object of the ceremony was seated in an ornately decorated corner of the room, dressed in fine new clothes and looking a bit embarrassed by all the attention he was receiving. Sitting not far from the young man were two musicians, a man and a woman. The man sang a song about the occasion while the woman played the *gabbang*. As I was noting the similarity of some of the bunting patterns to the art forms of the Middle East, a familiar voice rose above the mumblings of the crowd. I looked toward the singers. The woman singing was Salanda.

She wore a brilliant blouse and sarong of cerise patterns. Costume jewelry adorned her fingers and wrists. Her dark, luxuriant hair fell about her shoulders as she sang a song of young love. As usual, the crowd's attention focused on her as she started to sing. Eventually all were anxiously awaiting her next word. As her song continued and the audience's appreciation heightened, people stepped forward to leave peso bills at her side to show their appreciation of her songs. She totally ignored them, fully involved in her music. Salanda looked lovely, and she was having the usual effect upon the young men in the audience who were obviously intoxicated by her music and her beauty.

After holding the audience for about thirty minutes, Salanda finished her song and announced she needed a rest. As she rose to leave the room, she noticed us. Rather than being embarrassed at meeting us, as I thought she might be, she smiled and made her way through the crowd toward us.

"Your song was very beautiful," I said after initial greetings.

"Yes," she acknowledged. "My voice has become much better. Are you still at Lioboran?"

We told her we were not.

"I'm here for this circumcision celebration," she said. "I travel all over to sing. We're making lots of money, and I'm seeing places I've never seen before. We might even go to Zamboanga." She smiled happily. "This is the best kind of life for me."

Indeed, she seemed happy and she radiated excitement as she spoke of her new life. We spoke of mundane things as people crowded around to hear her speak. Most of the admirers were young men. She did not ask about her husband, children, or family, and we offered no information. She finally announced it was time for her to sing again. We stayed to hear a few stanzas of her new song and then returned to our boat. My companions wanted to reach a new fishing ground by morning, so we sailed into the night without seeing Salanda again.

About two months later I visited Siasi, a port town in central Sulu. I was there primarily as a break from my work in Bongao, but also to see a priest who was interested in my research. After a leisurely evening meal in his *convento*, heightened by the good cognac he opened for the occasion, he suggested we stroll down to the waterfront to enjoy the moonlit night. As usual on such nights in Sulu, many people were out enjoying the cool brightness. We heard music coming from a house hosting some sort of celebration and decided to see what was happening. We stepped off the main road and walked to the dwelling.

We climbed onto the deck, and the host immediately came forward to welcome us. We were given choice places to sit and were served Coca-Cola, the champagne of Sulu celebrations in those days. As my friend chatted with the host in a dialect I could not understand, I looked around the room. The celebration was apparently the second night of a three-night event honoring the marriage of the host's son. As I idly watched the crowd, an older man with obvious authority cleared space in a central portion of the room and spread bright mats on the floor. As he placed a *gabbang* in the center of the mat, Salanda and Lawani entered the room. Salanda was dressed in a sarong and blouse of brilliant blues. Her hair was in tight curls, the current fashion of some of the land-dwellers, and she wore heavy makeup. Even more jewelry adorned her arms, fingers, and ears than when I had last seen her. She walked regally, knowing everyone in the room was watching her, and sat at the *gabbang*. As the crowd quieted, she struck some tentative chords on the instrument and began to sing. First, in low, rather monotonous tones, she gave the background of the story she intended to weave. Her volume and rate increased as she burst into the dramatic events of a song that told of a woman who lost her children and spent her life looking for them, only to find them dead.

As usual, the crowd reacted emotionally. Tears welled in virtually every eye. When the traditional and expected happy ending did not come, the crowd became restless. As if to satisfy them, Lawani picked up the mallets and beat the *gabbang* as he sang a humorous song of flirtation and sex. Salanda sat beside him, trying to count inconspicuously the peso bills the audience had given her. When she finished, she tucked them into her blouse and looked over the audience for the first time. She saw me, gave a slight start of surprise, and then looked away. We stayed for a half hour longer, but she did not look at me again.

I left Siasi the next day without talking to her.

It was time for a break from Sulu. The winter rains were unusually heavy that year and the succession of grey days was beginning to get to me. I had reached a stalemate in my research and needed a respite. I decided to accept an invitation to present a paper at an anthropological conference in Manila. I took a launch to Jolo, the capital city of Sulu, where I could catch a plane to Manila.

The Jolo of those days was straight out of Joseph Conrad. The harbor hosted not only sailing boats and ships from all over the Philippines but also tramp freighters from Japan, Hong Kong, Greece, Australia, Singapore, and the United States. Its crooked little streets were thronged with pedicabs and brightly painted jeepneys, pedestrians and peddlers. Muslims from the interior, dressed in intense colors, cautiously sought their ways through the crowd. In the marketplace, one could buy colorful parrots in rattan cages, brilliant hand-woven textiles, Chinese medicines from Shanghai, succulent mangosteens, the foul-smelling durian, pressurized kerosene lamps from Japan, and pearls from the Sulu Sea. I loved to wander the crowded streets and get caught up in the excitement of the always-changing activities. Taking such a stroll to kill time until my early afternoon flight to Manila, I walked to the waterfront and sat on a pier to watch the loading of an Italian freighter. The warm sunshine added to my lazy mood. I was almost dozing when I heard, "Melikan! Do you remember me?"

I turned and momentarily did not recognize the woman standing next to me. It was Salanda. She was dressed in the same blue sarong and blouse she wore at Siasi, but the costume was very dirty and torn in several places. She wore a few pieces of cheap jewelry. Her hair was tied back from her face, and she wore a dirty shawl. She was obviously pregnant.

"Salanda," I said in surprise. "What are you doing here?"

"Lawani left me here," she said. "Two weeks ago I woke up and he was gone. He took our money and left. Maybe he went to Zamboanga."

"Are you still singing?" I asked.

"I can't sing by myself. I don't know how to find places to sing." She sat on the box next to me. "Besides, I'm too sad to sing. I have no friends here. You know how these people hate us because we live in boats and don't pray in the mosque. I'm miserable and have no money. I haven't eaten in two days."

"Wait," I said, standing up. "I'll get you some food. Then we can talk."

I approached a street vendor and purchased packets of the rice, fish, and vegetables he was selling. I bought a small bunch of bananas from a fruit stall and returned to where Salanda was waiting. I handed her the food. She accepted it reluctantly, nibbled at it tentatively, and then ate greedily. I watched the stevedores unload the ship as she ate.

"Is that enough?" I asked when she finished.

"Yes. My stomach is satisfied."

"What are you going to do now?" I asked.

"I don't know," she said. "It's hard to do anything with the baby inside me."

"Is it Lawani's baby?" I asked.

"I don't know. Maybe it is. But maybe it's Tamba's."

"Why don't you go home?"

"I'm afraid. Tamba won't want me back."

"But your family will take you back," I said, knowing the ties of Bajau kinship. "And probably Tamba will get over his anger."

She started crying into her scarf. "I would like to go back, but I don't know how to go. I have no money for fare. I don't even know what ships to hide on. These people and this place frighten me." She looked terribly vulnerable.

"I'll give you money to go home," I said. "You must go back. Your family misses you, and they're worried about you. Do you really want to go home?"

"Oh, yes," she said eagerly.

"Come," I said. "Let's find a boat to Bongao. Once you get to Bongao, you'll see some of your people and they'll take you home."

We walked down the wharf and I asked about launches to Bongao. When I found one, I talked to the young captain and told him Salanda would be among his passengers. I paid her fare and bought some food for her to eat on the two-day trip. I went on board with her, helped her find a cot, and gave her some money. In typical Bajau fashion, she did not express thanks, but I knew from her eyes and manner that she was grateful. The captain announced that the launch was leaving, so after a few words of farewell I left. The little launch pulled away from the wharf and I watched it chug into the sea until it disappeared behind an island. An hour later, I was on a plane to Manila.

Some months passed before I returned to Lioboran. The wedding of a friend's son was being held there, so I decided to accompany the family to the moorage. I'd heard news of Salanda since I saw her in Jolo. She had returned to her family and within a week was back with her husband. Her child was born about two months later. Rumors claimed she gave the child to her sister. Some said Tamba wanted nothing to do with the baby since he said it was not his. Others said Salanda gave it away because her sister was childless and she already had two children. Either rumor might have been true.

I didn't see Salanda during the first two days I was at the moorage, and I didn't seek her out. I figured if she wanted to see me, she would come to the boat where I was staying. Late one afternoon I was sitting on a fallen log at the beach, seeking privacy from the hectic activities preparatory to the wedding. I noticed an old Bajau woman walking down the beach, bent under a heavy load of firewood on her back. As she approached, she greeted me, and with a start I recognized the voice of Salanda.

"I didn't recognize you," I said. "I heard you were here in Lioboran."

"Yes, I am here." She looked very old. Her hair was knotted upon her neck in the traditional fashion of Bajau women. Her once firm breasts sagged. Her weak smile revealed betel-stained teeth and lips. She spat a blob of red betel juice at our feet.

We looked at one another silently, having nothing to say. Finally, she shifted the weight on her back, continued walking down the beach, and waded through the shallow waters to the moored houseboats.

I went to Lioboran many times after that visit, but I never again heard Salanda sing. Not even a lullaby.

10

Mike in Manila

It was the Manila of the mid-1960s. The Ermita district was filled with American GIs on R-and-R from the battlefields of Vietnam. Day and night they haunted the streets, looking for ways to pack pleasure into their few hours of respite from a war they would soon rejoin. Most were young kids just out of high school or college, fighting a war they knew nothing about and not understanding why they were objects of hate. And so, not knowing, they hated back. They were scared, but most of them no longer realized it, having lived with fear for so many months. It was a frantic city, with a frantic group of GIs and a frantic group of Filipinos—all seemingly racing to an unperceived Apocalypse.

I was in Manila to present a paper to an anthropological conference at the University of the Philippines. I entered the city from another world, one untouched by the mainstreams of recent history, where life moved in the same patterns it had moved for many centuries. I had frequently to remind myself that a twentieth-century war raged across the South China Sea.

My first evening in the city was at the home of Filipino friends who had invited others interested in my research to join us. It was a pleasant evening of good food, good wine, and good conversation. The party broke up at midnight, and some of my fellow guests dropped me off at my hotel in Ermita. I smiled my way through an assortment of pimps, hustlers, and hookers who offered me a variety of propositions. I decided to have a nightcap before bed and went into the bar off the lobby.

The bar was busy. Most of the customers were Filipinos. In one corner was a cluster of Japanese businessmen who even then were becoming ubiquitous in Southeast Asia. The only other Westerner was an American-looking young man sitting at the bar alone. I went to the unoccupied end of the bar to rethink some of the ideas we had tossed around during the evening. The bartender brought me an un-iced and un-watered bourbon, and I sipped the mellow liquor as I thought about the paper I planned to read the next day. In the mirror behind the bar, I could see the other customers sitting behind me. I noticed the young American watching me. When he caught my eye, he raised his glass and smiled. I raised my glass and smiled back. He extended an open hand to ask if he could join me. I wasn't interested in talking to anyone, but couldn't think of a polite way to say no, so shook my head otherwise. He picked up his drink, and came to the stool next to me. I was prepared for a hustle or a proposition.

"I'm Mike — ." He said his last name, but I didn't catch it. He extended his hand. I shook it and told him my name.

"Are you in the military?" he asked.

"No," I answered and told him I was doing research in the south. I asked him the same question.

"Army," he replied. "On R-and-R from Nam."

"A good place to be away from. Are you in the action?"

"About as thick as you can get." He slurred his words, and for the first time I realized he was a bit drunk. "We spend most of our time dodging bullets."

"What do you do over there?" I asked.

"I'm with the medics. We pick up what's left of them after the shooting."

"Sounds pretty awful," I said, sipping my bourbon.

He looked at me for some time, and then said, "Yeah,

pretty awful." He drained his glass and carefully set it on the coaster in front of him.

"Another one?" I asked.

He shrugged his shoulders. "Why not? Nothing else to do until tomorrow noon."

"And then what?" I signaled to the bartender to bring another drink.

"Back to Nam to join the killing." His voice broke as he ended the sentence, and he swallowed hard to hold back a sob.

"I'm sorry," I said. It seemed inane, but I could think of nothing else to say.

"Yeah," he said, regaining his voice. "So am I."

Someone played the juke box and we listened in silence to a Beatles song.

"I'm scared to go back. I feel sick just thinking about it." He looked at me. "Not exactly brave, eh?"

"You're honest," I said. "I'm sure that everyone over there is scared."

"You don't know how scared," he said softly. "Nam's filled with crazies. Sometimes I can't believe it's actually me over there. It seems like something I'm watching on TV. Everyone is killing or getting killed. And it's only a matter of time before I get killed." He took a long drink from his glass, set it back on the counter, and stared at it. "I wish I wasn't scared. I don't want to be scared when I die."

I could think of nothing to say. I wished I could tell him he was exaggerating the dangers of Vietnam, but I knew he wasn't.

We drank in silence for several minutes.

"How old are you?" I asked him.

"Nineteen. Too young to die, isn't it?"

"Too young to be killed," I said. "Maybe not too young to die. I suppose it depends upon how much you've lived."

"Maybe," he said. "Sometimes I think that even if I survived Nam, I wouldn't want to live. I've seen what people are really like. Strip them of their luxuries and make them grub for survival, and they become savages. Once you know that about people, it's not easy to want to live around them."

"I've long felt that we're the cruelest of all the animals, but I've always managed to find a few in the mob who were otherwise."

"Don't test them," he said. "Scratch them and you'll find the same cruelty." He looked at the clock. It was almost two o'clock. "Ten more hours." He emptied his glass. He turned and looked at me. "I don't have a place to sleep tonight, and I don't have any money for a room. Can I sleep in your room? If you don't want me, just say so, and I'll find a place in the park across the street."

I thought for a moment. "My room has two beds," I said. "You're welcome to one of them."

"Thanks."

The bartender turned up the lights to clear out the bar. I signed for the bill, and we took the elevator to the eighth floor. I unlocked the door to my room and we entered. He walked to the window and looked at the lights on Manila Bay.

"Nice view," he said.

"Yeah. You should see the sunsets." I pulled back the spread from one of the beds and said, "You can take this one."

"It's good of you to let me sleep here," he said, taking off his shirt.

"No problem."

We undressed and got into our respective beds. We lay in silence for several minutes, and then he spoke.

"Do you feel like talking?" he asked.

"Sure," I said. "What do you want to talk about?"

"Anything. I don't like silence. I never have. Even when I was a little kid, I always had my radio on. I got one for my birthday when I was five. I've had one all my life."

"Where's your home?" I asked.

"Upstate New York. A little town you've never heard of. My family's always lived there." He talked about his family. His father was a plumber, his mother a housewife. He had a married sister and a younger brother. He had a dog, too, which he seemed to miss more than the others. They all lived in the little town in upstate New York. He had dropped out of a college that bored him and, shortly after, was grabbed by the draft. He'd lived a sheltered life until he joined the army, and judging from his comments, he'd been in a state of shock since his induction. He was sickened and frightened by the killing and cruelty he'd seen in Vietnam. He talked about some of the atrocities he'd witnessed.

"You have no idea what it's like," he said. "People aren't human over there. You wouldn't believe what they do. They aren't content to just kill. They mutilate the corpses. One guy I know made a necklace of little fingers from the left hands of Viet Cong he killed. And I've seen what the Viet Cong do to us—cut off heads, ears, pricks. The only ones who sometimes seem human are the village people, but even they do some godawful things." He stopped for a minute, and then asked, "Why are people like that?"

"I don't know. The more I see of the world and the longer I live, the more I'm convinced all people have that potential."

We lapsed into silence, thinking our individual thoughts. As I was about to doze off, I heard the muffled sounds of crying coming from his bed.

"Are you all right?" I asked.

"Yeah," he said, sniffing. "I'm sorry, but I can't help it. I'm so scared tonight. Maybe I drank too much."

I raised up on my elbow and looked at him. "You have every reason to be afraid."

"I know I'm going to be killed when I go back," he sobbed. "And I'm scared to die."

I could think of nothing to say and silently cursed the insanity that resulted in wars that killed such young men.

He cried for several minutes and became silent. Then he said, "Can I sleep with you? I need to be near someone."

"Of course," I said.

He crawled into my bed and curled against me. Under other circumstances, he might have been a sexual turn-on, but now he was like a frightened child seeking comfort. He clung to me, and his body shook with deep sobs as he cried out his fears. He cried for about a half hour, occasionally stopping to tell of some horrible battlefield experience. He lapsed into periods of disturbed sleep, occasionally awakening with a start. Finally, he fell into a deep slumber.

I held him all night. Towards dawn I finally drifted to sleep. I awakened a couple hours later to the quiet sounds of his sleep. His head was still on my shoulder. From where I could see his face, he seemed no more than a child. His cheeks were smooth and his color still had the freshness of youth. A slight smile pulled at the corners of his mouth. I watched him for about half an hour and noticed it was nine-thirty when he slowly awakened.

He rolled over to see the clock.

"Man, it's late!" he said. "I've got to catch a plane at twelve." He jumped out of bed. "Got an extra towel?"

I told him there was one in the bathroom. He went in the bathroom and I heard him taking a shower. A few minutes later he came out drying himself.

"That was awfully good of you to put up with me last night." He seemed somewhat embarrassed. "You know, I'm not scared anymore," he continued as he began to dress. "I'm not afraid to go back to Nam, even though I know I'm going to get killed. I'm sure of that. I can handle it now, and I don't care. The world sucks and I want no part of it."

He finished dressing, walked over to the window, and looked out at the bay. I got out of bed and joined him.

"You've been great to me," he said. He gave me a big bear hug and walked out the door.

A month later I was back in Sulu immersed in my research. I thought of Mike occasionally, but like most things beyond Sulu, he seemed miles and millennia away. Then, in the middle of a still night, I was shattered awake from a sound sleep by a terrible explosion in my mind. I suddenly realized Mike had been killed. I gave up sleep for the rest of the night and watched the stars become lost in the dawn as I thought of Mike and all the other dead young men in Vietnam.

11

Interlude in Zamboanga

I was not yet ready to return to Sulu. I had been in Manila for two weeks and made it back as far as Zamboanga. I was saturated by Manila's pleasures. Having wallowed in passions deprived me during my months in Sulu, I'd had enough salads, steaks, clean sheets, warm bodies, bright lights, and anthropological conversations to last many months. But I was not quite ready for Sulu—the monotonous diet, the loneliness of an alien culture, the empty nights, and the sometimes boredom of day upon day of endless sunshine. Thus I was in Zamboanga to spend a few days at the Bayot Hotel until I was better prepared to face Sulu.

The Bayot was my favorite resting place when I went in and out of Sulu. It seemed I always arrived at the Bayot exhausted—either weary of the months on the sea with the Bajau, or drained by the urban conundrums of Manila. But from whichever direction I came, the Bayot was always the same—restful, and sedately old-world in a style reminiscent of Maugham stories of the South Pacific, or Sydney Greenstreet movies of tropical adventure, or Conradian settings of Celebes. Its better days were long gone, and a new, luxury hotel nearby had taken most of its clientele. Frequently, I shared the hotel with no more than a half-dozen other guests.

The Bayot faces the Sulu Sea. A bit to the right and more seaward is the port of Zamboanga with its colorful array of Sulu sails, foreign ships, noises, and smells. In front of the hotel, some twenty miles across the sea, rise the verdant peaks and slopes of the Basilan Islands. Almost every day, the sea between is dotted with colorful sails looking like a flock of brightly colored butterflies skimming the sea's surface, about to rise into the air at any moment. No beach fronts the Bayot. At the lowest tides a bar of sand is exposed, but normally the sea splashes against the concrete wall that inhibits its further invasion into the grounds of the hotel. Usually a few Bajau houseboats bob in the water, the northernmost extension of their numbers. A spacious but not extensive lawn stretches from the sea wall to the screened-in dining room, where empty tables with white tablecloths sit under still ceiling fans—like ghosts waiting for something to happen.

I was eating breakfast at one of the small tables scattered along the sea wall, feeling somewhat colonial as I watched the laboring stevedores at the distant wharf. The meal's remains were cleared by a young waiter, and I sat with a final cup of coffee as I reviewed the projects awaiting my return to Sulu. I became aware that someone had spoken to me.

"I beg your pardon," I said to a Filipino man, about forty, who had taken the table next to me.

"I'm afraid I'm interrupting your thoughts," he replied politely, "but I asked if you were a tourist to Zamboanga."

"Yes and no," I said. "I'm doing research in southern Sulu. I've been in and out of Zamboanga many times."

He asked about my research, and I responded briefly. I was in no mood to talk about the Bajau.

"You mean you live with those people in their boats?"

"Yes," I replied.

"How much longer will your research last?"

"About another year."

"You must have a very free life in Sulu," he said with a note of envy in his voice.

I considered my days of sailing, the occasional visits to uninhabited islands, the unscheduled way in which I did my research, and agreed that I had a fairly carefree existence by standards of the workaday world.

The man, obviously in a mood to talk, continued. "I work all year long and look forward to occasional business trips—like this one—to take me away from Manila." He took a drink and I noticed that he was drinking scotch at this rather early hour. He asked if I wanted one. I begged off.

"I'm on my way to a party," he said. "Would you like to join me?"

"What kind of a party?" I asked.

"A big party," he said. "A friend of mine—one of my most important customers down here—is giving a party. All kinds of people will be there. There'll be plenty of food and drinks."

The drinks didn't particularly interest me, and I wasn't hungry, but the idea of having people to talk to was appealing. I was becoming a bit tired of my lethargy at the hotel.

"Are you sure your friend won't mind?" I asked, certain that he wouldn't if he were a Filipino, who are among the most hospitable people in the world.

"Of course not," replied the man. "It's a big party and everyone will be bringing guests. Come along. You'll have a good time."

"You talked me into it," I said. "When do we leave?"

"As soon as I finish some bookwork," he said, standing up and draining his glass. "I'll meet you in the lobby in about an hour." He started to walk away and then turned around. "I haven't introduced myself," he said, returning with an out-stretched hand.

We exchanged names.

"See you in an hour," he said, and disappeared into the hotel.

About an hour later we arrived at the house hosting the party. It was an attractive Spanish-style home in a fashionable residential neighborhood of Zamboanga. We showed identification to armed guards who called to verify us before we were allowed into the walled residential compound. The homes all had vast lawns, beautifully landscaped albeit somewhat manicured. A young Filipino man, neatly dressed in white jacket and black trousers, opened the door and invited us inside.

Upon entering the lobby, we were assaulted by loud rock music, thick cigarette smoke, and too much air conditioning. We were ushered into a large living room crowded mostly with men drinking from glasses filled with variously colored liquids. I glanced at the furnishings and noted most were rattan and very attractive. In one corner of the room, a bar was manned by three young Filipino men, who were kept busy filling glasses for the thirsty crowd. I reminded myself that it was very early afternoon.

An overweight, balding Filipino man approached us and shouted to my companion, "Mannie! Where have you been? The party started hours ago!"

"Business first," said my companion, shaking the man's hand. "I brought along a friend."

He introduced us, but I didn't hear the man's name above the sounds of the room. He shouted to me, "The more the merrier! Glad you could come. Make yourself comfortable. Drinks are over in the corner. And you'll find other pleasures if you look a little closer." He gave me a rather vulgar wink, and returned to the group he had left to greet us. My companion sighted an acquaintance across the room and left me to my own devices.

I looked at the crowd a little closer. Ethnically it was a rather mixed group, although most were Filipinos. I spotted a few Chinese, several Europeans, some Japanese, and even an Arab. Most were middle aged and affluent, with the accompanying overweight and unhealthiness that combination seems to bring throughout the world. Three young Americans, perhaps Peace Corps volunteers, clustered in one corner. Moving among the men were a dozen or so Filipinas, obviously hired for the occasion. Makeup, clothes, and mannerisms combined to make their vocation obvious.

I excused my way toward the bar and, after many words, finally convinced a bartender that I really wanted a 7-Up with nothing added. I stepped back from the bar traffic and leaned against a wall to sip my drink as I watched the crowd. One of the young Americans came to the bar for a drink. He nodded to me in a way that didn't encourage conversation. He returned to his fellows, spoke to them, and they all tried to look at me inconspicuously. I smiled at them, and they all quickly turned the other way.

"Quite a party, eh?" I turned to see a red-faced, paunchy American man next to me.

"Indeed," I said. "Quite a party."

"What kind of work do you do? Peace Corps?"

"No. I'm an anthropologist. I'm doing research in Sulu."

"Are you now? That's interesting," he said, obviously not sure what an anthropologist was and even less convinced it was anything of interest. "Been here long?"

"A little over a year," I said. "How about you? What do you do?"

"I'm with Royal Canning Corporation. Head of the Philippine branch. Love it here. No desire to go home. Do you like it?"

"Most of the time. I'll probably be ready to go home when the time comes, though. But I like the Philippines. I have some good friends here."

"I know what you mean," he winked and poked me in the ribs. "My wife was here the first year and hated the place. Refused to stay and went back home." He took a long drink from a tumbler that appeared to be full of scotch. "Gets lonely here all alone, you know. So I found myself a lovely little thing. She can't do enough for me. I've got another one in Manila. That's one of the nice things about this country. No one gets upset about it. But I guess you know what I mean." He winked again. "Young, good-lookin' stud like you must have all kinds of women after your dick."

I shrugged my shoulders.

"You should see my house. Makes this place look like a shack in the barrio. I've got eight servants. Can't live like that in America, can ya?"

I concurred that most people in America couldn't live like that.

"My son's coming over to visit next month. He's only fifteen. Guess I'm going to have to send my little girl off to visit her family for a while. If he were a little older, I'd fix him up." He looked around the room. "Have you met any of these girls yet? They're here for the taking, you know. If you see one you're interested in, just let her know. There're rooms in the back you can have for as long as you need them. I'm going to get acquainted with that little number over there." He nodded to a woman across the room, went to the bar for a refill, and made his way toward her.

I sighed with relief when he left, and looked around the room for a more kindred spirit.

I didn't have long to wait, although he turned out to be less than kindred. A tall Filipino man approached me. He was beyond middle age despite his too-black hair. He stood next to me. I nodded to him, and he responded by taking a long draw from his cigarette, letting the smoke drift toward me. He was smoking pot.

"I see you don't like alcohol," he said, looking at my 7-Up. "See the man in the blue shirt?" I turned to see the man across the room. As we watched him, he was approached by a Chinese man who asked him something. He pulled a packet from the bookcase behind him, and handed it to the man.

"He can give you anything you need to enjoy the party," said the man next to me. "And I don't mean just pot." He turned and walked away.

As the minutes and then hours ticked away, I began to wonder if I'd made the right decision in coming to the party. Usually not much of a drinker, I've never learned to interact with people who drink a lot—and everyone there was drinking a lot. Consequently, as the crowd became increasingly drunk, I became increasingly uncomfortable. I was thinking of slipping out when the young American who had nodded earlier approached me. He was quite tipsy, perhaps the reason for his change of attitude toward me.

"We haven't been introduced," he said, holding out his hand. We exchanged names.

"You're not with the Peace Corps," he said rather than asked.

"No," I agreed. "I'm not with the Peace Corps."

"I am. What do you do?"

I told him in as few words as possible.

"Then you're right out there living with the people."

I admitted to being right out there living with the people.

"I usually avoid Americans," he said. "Most of them are so damned crass and arrogant. Sometimes I hate being identified as an American."

I didn't tell him I had similar feelings about being identified as a Peace Corps volunteer.

"You smoke weed." Another of his question-statements as he held out a hand-rolled cigarette.

I declined, and asked him what part of the Philippines he was stationed in.

"Central Mindanao. One of the toughest posts in the country. Really primitive. Those people have just dropped down from the trees. It'd be a good place for you to do a study."

After he took a break to get a drink at the bar, I asked him what he did there.

"Teach English. That's what I'm supposed to be doing. I've almost given up. No one ever comes to school. It's probably just as well. Learning English out there is about as useful as having two asses. To tell the truth, I spend most of my time here in Zamboanga. I figure I'm doing more to help the Philippines by interacting with these kind of Filipinos than those boobies out in the barrio. At least we talk the same language. All they think about out there is fucking and planting rice. You must be in an isolated area, too. How do you stand it?"

He didn't wait for an answer, which was just as well. I wasn't interested in giving one.

"Have you checked out these girls?" he asked as one passed and gave us a professional smile. "Not bad, eh? And free. Mario really knows how to throw a party. I'm going to check that one out." He staggered away.

I looked around the room. The crowd had grown considerably since I first arrived. I saw the man from the hotel a couple of times. We exchanged waves and smiles across the room, but I never spoke to him again. The smoke was thicker, the music louder, and the air conditioner less effective. A new supply of women seemed to have arrived.

I noticed an American woman just as she noticed me. She eased through the crowd toward me. As she stopped beside me, I could tell she was very high on something. I had no idea what it was—the possibilities were so great in that room.

"I like you," she said, as she slipped her hand inside my shirt and pulled at the hair on my chest. It hurt. "Let's find a room."

Her hand was as grey and cold as her face. Her hair was limp, her dress wrinkled, and her feet dirty in tired sandals.

"Sorry, a friend is waiting for me," I said, and eased through the crowd to the other side of the room. By the time I reached the lobby, I had been propositioned by one of the prostitutes, offered a joint, an upper, and cocaine, groped by a serious-looking Japanese man, and invited to another party that night. When I reached the door, I knew I had made the right decision.

"You are leaving, sir?" asked the same young Filipino who had greeted me when I arrived.

"Yes," I replied. "I must return to my hotel. Would you thank the host for me? I can't seem to find him."

"Of course," he said. "But do you have a way back to the hotel?"

"I can get a taxi."

"That would be difficult in this neighborhood. Our driver will take you back."

I started to protest, but he insisted. Minutes later I stepped from a Mercedes-Benz in front of the Bayot Hotel.

I walked through the lobby and nodded to the same clerk who was at the desk when I left. The same bartender was at the bar outside, and the same waiter sat at a table waiting for a customer to break the boredom of his hours. I sat at one of the seaside tables, and almost before I was on my chair the waiter was at my side to take my order.

After some thought, I said, "Gin and tonic." It always seemed appropriate at the Bayot.

I thought of the party I had just left. I had attended variations of such parties throughout my adult life. The settings were different, the faces different, but the ennui, the desperation, and the escapes were the same. It was as if a single, traveling cocktail party moved around the world. People stepped in and out of it, but nothing ever changed. It was universal and cross-cultural—the people, the conversations, the drinks. If I returned to the party next month, or next year, or twenty years from now, the same people would be talking about the same things and drinking the same drinks or taking the same drugs.

I sipped the gin and tonic and looked to the west. The sky

and sea were flowing in reds. Two lonely sails moved across the molten waters toward Basilan Island. A single freighter cast a dark silhouette at the distant wharf. In front of me, a half-dozen Bajau houseboats bobbed soothingly in the gentle waters as families prepared fires for their evening meals.

I was ready to return to Sulu.

12

The Remarkable Mrs. Dickens

She was very pink and a bit plump and was surrounded by important-looking people when I saw her at the airport in Jolo. I was returning to Sulu from Zamboanga, and the plane had stopped at Jolo for passengers. It was one of those rare times when flights flew to Bongao, and I was marveling at the speed of it compared with the incredibly slow ships and launches I usually relied upon to get in and out of Sulu. After much handshaking and well-wishing, she got on the plane. As she passed me, I got a strong whiff of perfume. She smiled sweetly and murmured apologies as she squeezed past a man to ease into a window seat several spaces ahead of me. She settled into her seat and all I could see was her short, wavy white hair. Once we were airborne I forgot her as I tried to identify the dozens of islands we passed over on our brief flight to Tawi-Tawi.

The grass airstrip came into view, and within minutes we swept down and came to a standstill while curious islanders wandered to the field to see what the plane had brought this time. I alighted with the other passengers and waited with them for my luggage to be unloaded by the pilot and co-pilot, the extent of the crew. As I waited for my bag to be tossed out, the woman dressed in pink approached me.

"Excuse me," she said, softly, "but perhaps you can help me."

"I'd be happy to," I said. "What can I do?"

"I'm new to this part of the world," she began. "I'm trying to get to Bongao. Is this it?" She spread her arms to the airfield.

"Not yet," I replied. "Bongao is a neighboring island. I'm going there myself and will be glad to help you."

"How kind of you." She smiled sweetly and her bright blue eyes twinkled. "I have only one bag. I try to travel lightly. There it is."

I turned to see both pilots struggling with a huge pink suitcase. With deep sighs, they heaved it onto the small cart that would transport the luggage to the awaiting launch. After seeing my own bag safely tossed onto the cart, I turned to the woman.

"I haven't introduced myself yet," I said. I told her my name.

"And I am Mrs. Dickens. I'm with the American Embassy in Manila."

She did not seem at all like the American Embassy types I had met before, but I refrained from saying so. "Are you vacationing in Sulu?" I asked. Very few outsiders came to Sulu in those days, and those who did were usually the more adventuresome sightseers.

"Not entirely," she smiled. "Certainly I'm enjoying the beautiful sights of the area, but I'm also trying to take care of some business."

She didn't elaborate and I didn't pursue. "We have to walk to the launch," I said. "There aren't any vehicles on the island. It's about a mile walk. Are you up to it?"

"Oh, yes," she chuckled. "I keep myself in very good physical shape—for just such occasions. Lead the way."

We followed the other passengers along the path that edged the beach to the other side of the island. It was early afternoon and very hot, but fortunately most of the path was

shaded by palm trees. We walked through a small seaside village, and virtually everyone came out to watch us pass. They
were especially intrigued by Mrs. Dickens. Her white hair,
blue eyes, fair skin, and pink dress stood out from the crowd.

"What lovely children," she said, smiling sweetly at a group
of them who gathered to stare at us. She then sighed, "So sad
they have to live in such poverty."

I looked at the children again. They were dressed in shorts
and T-shirts, and to my eyes didn't look particularly poverty-
stricken. I had never considered this village poor.

"Their lives really aren't so bad," I said. "They have enough
to eat, homes, and families. That's more than a lot of kids back
home have."

She smiled up at me as if my naiveté would be forgiven.
"One of my reasons for coming here is to improve their lives.
Our country has so much. We must begin to share more of
our wealth and know-how with the rest of the world."

"Are you with some kind of assistance program?" I asked.

"Yes," she said, as our path left the village and cut through
a small finger of forest. "It's a newly formed program. My job
is to find places where the funds can be used most advanta-
geously. That's why I've come to Sulu—it's one of the most
backward parts of the Philippines."

As usual the reference to Sulu as backward made me
bristle. Not like the rest of the Philippines, yes. But backward,
no. I usually heard it from Christian Filipinos who considered the Muslims of Sulu to be pagans, or from ethnocentric
Westerners who were in culture shock because Sulu was so
non-Western. I bit my tongue and said, "Why do you consider
Sulu backward?"

"Such poor health and education," she said. "It needs more
doctors, hospitals, and schools."

"That's true," I agreed, "but don't you think that before
those programs can help much, the economy needs some assistance?"

"Indeed, yes," she said. "We have plans for that too."

We passed the last clump of trees in the forest and emerged once again onto the beach. "Oh, what a lovely view!" exclaimed Mrs. Dickens. Across the channel was Bongao Island with its somber green mountain towering above villages nestled at the sea shore. "Is that where we're going?"

"Yes. There's the launch we'll take." I pointed to a small launch tied to a rickety wharf. As we found seats in the launch, I asked her, "Who is your contact in Bongao?"

"I really don't have one," she said, as she adjusted her skirt. "I understand a Catholic priest has a school there and some nuns have a hospital. I thought I would work through them. Do you know them?"

"Very well," I said. "I'd be happy to introduce you to them. I'm sure they'll be interested in your program. They're always short of money."

"Those are exactly the kinds of people we want to reach," said Mrs. Dickens, wagging her finger for emphasis. "Programs that are already successfully established which can be enlarged to reach more people."

"Seems reasonable," I said. "But doesn't it matter that these are church-sponsored programs? Usually the government doesn't give money to religious groups."

"But I told you this one is different. The funds come from someone concerned about helping the people, and if this can be done through church programs, it will be done so. Remember this is private money which is simply administered through the Embassy. The ambassador is really doing us a great favor. If you know any worthwhile projects in the area that need money, I'd appreciate your letting me know."

"I'll think about it," I said.

Mrs. Dickens changed the subject to Bongao, and began asking questions about the town. Soon we were docking at the Bongao wharf.

"Have you made any arrangements for lodging?" I asked as I struggled with the heavy pink suitcase.

"I'm afraid I haven't," she sighed. "My decision to come to Sulu was rather sudden, and I didn't have time to wire ahead."

"Just as well," I smiled. "The 'wires' are usually not operating. There's a Chinese hotel in town. You probably can stay there. It's nearby." Thank god, I thought to myself, as I again lifted the heavy suitcase.

We arrived at the small hotel, and the clerk gave lodging to Mrs. Dickens. I saw her to her room and arranged to return in a couple of hours to join her for dinner, following which I would take her to meet Sister Evangelista and the other nuns at the clinic. I then left her and headed toward the convento to see if Father Raquet had a spare bed for a couple of nights.

Mrs. Dickens and I had an unremarkable dinner and then walked to the clinic. I had earlier asked the sisters if we could visit them after dinner. As usual they were delighted to have guests, and they were particularly interested in the program Mrs. Dickens represented. Mrs. Dickens had changed clothes and was flowing in pinks. Her white hair was tied up in a soft pink scarf. A loose pink and white floral dress draped her short, plumpish body, and bright pink slippers shod her feet.

"I hope your accommodations are better than the dinner we had," I said. "Usually the food is quite good. It must have been an off night."

"Everything is quite all right," she assured me. "I travel a great deal, and I have encountered much worse. I am accustomed to roughing it." We were at the edge of town. She paused to look back, and said, "This is quite a lovely little town, isn't it? But it does need a lot of improvements. The houses could really use some paint. I hope our program can help."

I had never considered paint as one of Bongao's pressing needs. Perhaps it was simply a passing thought of Mrs. Dickens.

We arrived at the clinic and were greeted warmly by the three sisters. They invited us into their living room and insisted we have coffee and dessert with them. I needed no coaxing to try the sisters' desserts, which were always delicious.

"What a lovely room," said Mrs. Dickens, surveying the spartan quarters of the sisters.

The room consisted of basics and was not lovely. Sister Evangelista looked at the room as if she had missed something in her past appraisals, and then said, "I had never really thought of it as lovely. I'm afraid we have little time for decorating."

"My program has funds for things of that sort. Just because you are working in the wilderness doesn't mean you should do without the comforts of civilization," said Mrs. Dickens, sweetly.

"That's very thoughtful of you," replied Sister Evangelista, "but there are other aspects of civilization we are much more interested in—such as certain medical equipment. Could you tell us more about your program?"

"This cake is absolutely exquisite," exclaimed Mrs. Dickens, closing her big blue eyes in ecstasy. "You must give me your recipe. Who made it?"

"I'll be happy to give you the recipe," said Sister Evangelista, somewhat hastily. "Now, about your program . . ."

"Oh, yes. The program," said Mrs. Dickens, holding out her coffee cup. "Just a bit more coffee, please. Is this native coffee?"

One of the sisters nodded affirmatively.

"So much better than what we get in Manila," assured Mrs. Dickens. Her cup was refilled and she settled back. "My program is sponsored by private funds designated to develop humanitarian projects in the Philippines. The American Embassy has offered to act as a clearinghouse and to provide certain administrative services."

"May I ask where the money comes from?" said Sister Evangelista.

"The funds are from a private family that wishes to remain anonymous. They have a long-standing affection for the Philippines. I assure you it is all aboveboard. They simply don't want the publicity associated with the projects."

"Do they grant money to church groups?" asked Sister Evangelista.

"Oh yes," assured Mrs. Dickens, taking another sip of her coffee. I noticed for the first time that her fingernails were painted pink. "They've always been very supportive of the many humanitarian projects of the Catholic church in this country."

"What is your organization called?" asked Sister Evangelista.

"The Philippines Development Association," replied Mrs. Dickens. "Could I have some more of that delicious coffee?" She held out her cup which Sister Helena refilled. "Thank you so much." She settled back into her chair. "I am a field representative, and my job is to travel throughout the country to locate worthwhile projects for the Association. After I have investigated such projects and find them worthy of our programs, I ask local personnel to write up proposals for financial aid and send them to our office in Manila. A committee examines the proposals and selects those which seem most in keeping with our goals. I might add that I'm on that committee, and my evaluation of the project is a very important factor in whether or not funding is granted. Would you be interested in the program?"

"We are always interested in getting money to help our work," said Sister Evangelista. "But we would, of course, have to study your program more. Our work is strictly humanitarian and we are totally removed from politics of any sort."

"You need not worry on that account," replied Mrs. Dickens. "We are strictly nonpolitical. Our aim is to help people who need help—whatever their political or religious affiliation may be." Mrs. Dickens shifted her position and crossed her ankles. I glanced at her feet and saw toenails painted the same shade of pink as her fingernails.

"If the program interests you, what sort of requests would you have?" asked Mrs. Dickens.

"A long list," laughed Sister Evangelista. "Our clinic has become too small and really should be enlarged into a hospital. We need more qualified staff to assist us. We need all kinds of equipment, and in order to operate it, we need a larger and more reliable electric generator. Our water system is very inadequate, and the only way we can heat it is over a wood fire." She paused. "I'm afraid I'm sounding terribly greedy."

"Not at all," said Mrs. Dickens. "Those are very real needs. I've heard of the good work you're doing down here. Think of how much more you'll be able to do when you have the proper facilities. How about an airplane or a helicopter? Would that be of assistance to you in reaching the remote islands?"

"Indeed it would," said Sister Evangelista. "It isn't a high priority, but I've often thought of it."

Mrs. Dickens pulled open her pink purse and brought out some pink papers. "I have some literature on our program. If you're interested in applying for funds, the instructions for doing so are on the last page. Yours is exactly the sort of program we're interested in assisting. I hope we may do so."

"You're an answer to my prayers," said Sister Evangelista, sincerely. "You've no idea how frustrating it is for us. We've been trained in the finest medical schools and are aware of the marvelous technology that is available for our work. But each day we see people die who could be saved if only we had the proper equipment or if they could've been reached earlier."

Mrs. Dickens reached over and patted Sister Evangelista on the hand as she dabbed at her moist eyes with a tiny pink handkerchief. "There is no reason why that should ever happen again," she said. "If you apply for our funds, I shall make certain you receive them."

"God bless you," said Sister Evangelista.

Mrs. Dickens smiled sweetly.

The conversation drifted away from the Philippines Development Association and on to more personal matters. Mrs. Dickens asked where we were from, and I returned the question. She said she was born in Ohio. She didn't mention a date, but it must have been at least sixty-five years earlier, perhaps more. She attended college and then taught high school English for two years before marrying a young doctor in the farming community where she taught. They had three children, all of whom were outstanding as children and adults. One was now a physician, another a lawyer, and a third a college professor. Her husband died some ten years previously and she moved to Chicago to be closer to her children. One of her children, the professor, came to the Philippines three years ago as a visiting professor at the University of the Philippines. She came to visit him and subsequently fell in love with the Philippines. She had been here, off and on, ever since, and had become involved in the Philippines Development Association about a year ago. The family sponsoring the program were close friends, and she acted as personal advisor to them regarding the projects of the program.

The hour was growing late, and when Mrs. Dickens stifled a small yawn into her pink handkerchief, I suggested we leave. She agreed it was time to go. "I shall be here for three days," she told the sisters. "Please read the literature I gave you, and if you're interested in applying for funds, prepare a list of your needs. I shall be happy to talk to you further and help expedite the application."

The sisters thanked her profusely and said, given no unforeseen problems, they would be interested in the program. We left the clinic, using a flashlight loaned by the sisters. Mrs. Dickens asked me about Father Raquet and his work in Bongao. I volunteered to introduce her to him the following morning. After agreeing to meet her at nine, I left her at her quarters.

The next morning, after a leisurely breakfast at the *convento* with Father Raquet, I went to pick up Mrs. Dickens. She was resplendent in pink slacks and a matching jacket. She wore a white blouse patterned with tiny pink flowers. Atop her white hair was a broad-brimmed pink hat with a long white ribbon that flowed down her back.

"So kind of you to meet me," she said as we left the hotel. "Is it far to the *convento*?"

"Only a short walk," I said. "If you'd like, we can cut through the marketplace. It's always humming with activity this time of day."

"I'd love it," said Mrs. Dickens.

We turned and crossed one of the bridges that led to the marketplace built on piles over a reef. The market was filled with shoppers and vendors. We walked through the produce section and then went to the fish market, where Mrs. Dickens was properly impressed by the many brilliant colors still fresh from the previous night's catch. Her fancy was caught by a large pink fish, and as she stopped to examine it more closely, a crowd congregated. Few white women made it to Bongao in those days, and none so flamboyantly dressed as Mrs. Dickens. She enjoyed the attention she was getting. We wandered through other sections of the market and were soon back on the main street. When we arrived at the *convento*, Father Raquet greeted us as we entered. I made introductions.

"I've heard so much of your good work down here," said Mrs. Dickens. "I met some of your order in Jolo and they spoke so highly of you."

"That's kind of you to say so," said Father Raquet. "Please sit down. Would you like coffee?"

"I'd love it," said Mrs. Dickens. "I have fallen in love with your native coffee."

"I'm afraid the only coffee I have to offer is instant."

"That will be fine," assured Mrs. Dickens.

Father Raquet opened a thermos jug of hot water and began preparing coffee for all of us. "Is this your first visit to Sulu?" he asked

"Yes. And I love the place. One of the nice things about my position is that it allows me to travel to parts of this beautiful country I would otherwise not see. Like Sulu. I've heard about Sulu ever since I came to the Philippines, but it's so remote from Manila, where I live, that I would never have come here were it not for my job. Has our friend told you of my organization?" she asked Father Raquet as she smiled at me.

"Only briefly," he said as he handed coffee cups to us. "Sugar or cream?" he asked Mrs. Dickens.

"No, thank you."

"Perhaps you could tell me about your program."

"Of course. That is why I'm here," she smiled sweetly. I noticed that her pink lipstick matched her nails. She outlined the nature of the Philippines Development Association and concluded by saying, "And at the moment I am particularly interested in knowing how we may assist you."

"How generous of you," said Father Raquet.

"It is our mission," smiled Mrs. Dickens. "The coffee is lovely."

The coffee was very instant and not lovely.

"What do you consider some of the more pressing needs for your work here and for the town in general?"

Father Raquet laughed. "Do you have the morning free? It will take all morning to tell you."

"I have as much time as is necessary," said Mrs. Dickens.

Father Raquet began reeling off a list of projects he would like to implement to improve the educational and economic life of Bongao. After about five minutes, he stopped and said, "But these are very costly projects . . ."

"Not at all," said Mrs. Dickens. "Our organization has a

great deal of money, and the projects you've mentioned are exactly the sorts of things we're interested in. Please go on."

I sat back in my rocking chair and listened to Father Raquet spill out his dreams for Tawi-Tawi. I'd heard them before, but this time as he told them, there was an extra gleam in his eye with the realization they might actually come true.

"Don't you think more branch schools in the outer islands would be a good idea?" asked Mrs. Dickens. "That way students wouldn't have to come to Bongao and could better afford to go to school."

"Of course," said Father Raquet. "We have long-range plans for such schools."

They talked on, and as they talked, Sulu was transformed from a remote backwater with its myriad of social and economic problems to a shining, contemporary Shangri La.

Mrs. Dickens pulled a sheaf of papers from her purse and handed several to Father. "This will explain in greater detail the nature of our organization. Also, there are instructions for applying for funds. I think it's all self-explanatory. I suggest you write down all the projects we have discussed with an estimate of the costs. Don't be too concerned about the figures— if we feel the project is worthwhile, we'll not hold you to your estimates. Then send them to our office in Manila. I'll be here for two more days and will be happy to answer any questions you may have."

"How long does it take to implement your programs?" I asked, entering the conversation for the first time and with the thought in the back of my mind that if such changes were introduced to Bongao, it would present a great opportunity to do an anthropological study of social change.

"As soon as we can," replied Mrs. Dickens, "although that is often longer than we wish. After proposals have been submitted to us, a field committee from the Association visits the site to further explore its feasibility. Some of our projects have been implemented within three months—others have taken up to a year. Given the nature of the projects you have suggested for Bongao, I would guess that some of them will receive immediate attention."

"You must have a very efficient organization," I said.

"We like to think so," smiled Mrs. Dickens. "We're small, and the people who control the money are directly involved in the decision-making. Consequently, things happen fast for us. Could I have another cup of coffee?"

She handed her cup to Father Raquet who refilled it. She continued. "There's one other person I would like to see here. The mayor. Could I impose upon one of you to introduce me to him?"

"I can introduce you," I volunteered.

"That's very sweet of you," she said. "But I feel I have taken so much of your time already."

"No problem," I assured her.

We left Father Raquet after Mrs. Dickens promised to join him and Sister Evangelista at the convento that evening for dinner. I was invited also, but I had a previous commitment. We walked down Bongao's only street, unpaved and pocked with pot holes, toward the mayor's office near the wharf. I knew the mayor casually. He was not one of my favorite people, a rather simple man who had bought his way into office and was associated with a good deal of corruption.

We paused at the door to the municipal building, a dilapidated affair, to ask a guard if the mayor was in. He replied affirmatively, somewhat overwhelmed by the pinkness of Mrs. Dickens. We entered the building and found our way to the mayor's office. The mayor was seated behind a littered desk, feet propped against a filing cabinet as he read a comic book and smoked a cigar. Upon seeing us, he immediately sat upright and put the comic book away.

"Good morning, Mayor," I said. "I'd like you to meet a visitor to Bongao."

I made the introductions, and then Mrs. Dickens took over. She explained her magnanimous foundation. The mayor hardly spoke throughout her presentation, but stared at her in disbelief—whether in response to her program or her appearance, I'm not sure.

When she finished, Mrs. Dickens said, "So, if you think you could benefit from our funds, I suggest you make a list of your needs and submit it with estimated costs to our office in Manila." She reached into her purse and pulled out a pink packet. "Here is a brochure that explains our program. It has the necessary application forms. Are you interested?"

"Oh yes," said the mayor. He nearly fell off his chair in his eagerness.

"What do you see as some primary needs of Bongao?" asked Mrs. Dickens.

"A new city hall," said the mayor. "And the mayor really should have a better house. I was in Zamboanga recently and saw television for the first time. That would help Bongao, too. Also, we need to pave the street. And the mayor really should have an official car."

I wondered where the mayor would drive his official car since Bongao's one street that could accommodate a vehicle was only about a half-mile long, but Mrs. Dickens smiled kindly and said, "Yes, those all seem like legitimate needs. I think our foundation can find money for them. I noticed," she continued, "that many of these islands near Bongao are quite close. Don't you think it would be a good idea if they were connected by bridges? Wouldn't that ease some of the transportation problems?"

"That's a very good idea," said the mayor, eyes glowing with visions of the new Bongao that was emerging from the pinkness of Mrs. Dickens. "And an airport. It's a nuisance to have the airport on another island." The fact that there wasn't enough flat land on Bongao to land a plane didn't seem important.

"And how about a housing project?" suggested Mrs. Dickens. "Bongao is a quaint little town, but you must admit that the buildings are a little shabby. Some new houses, brightly painted, would totally change the appearance of the town." The color of the paint was not mentioned. "And a sewage system will be needed, too."

"Of course," said the mayor, leaning forward on his desk toward Mrs. Dickens. "And an electric plant. The one we have hasn't worked in five years. Do you suppose we could also have a movie house? The people here would like movies. But maybe if we have television, we won't need movies."

"Yes, one would seem sufficient," agreed Mrs. Dickens.

"The mayor's office could use a speedboat," continued the mayor. "I often have to go on official business to neighboring islands. It would be more convenient if I had my own boat."

"Of course," said Mrs. Dickens. "Your position deserves that."

And so the discussion continued. Before we left, the mayor had requested new uniforms for his staff, new furniture for his new office, a telephone system, a guest house for entertaining official visitors (in which his son would live as host), an official plane complete with pilot for the mayor's use, and numerous other items that would assist him in the execution of his office. I listened first with disbelief, and then with quiet hilarity. It was like a Gilbert and Sullivan operetta. Finally, we stood to leave.

"You will have to make a formal request for these items we have discussed," said Mrs. Dickens, "and submit it to our office in Manila." I noticed for the first time that her eye shadow was pink.

"Yes, yes," said the mayor, almost salivating with greed. "I'll do that and get the letter off immediately. How long do you think it'll take?"

"Probably only a few months for the smaller projects, but the larger ones will take longer. Thank you for your time."

The mayor followed us to the front door, suggesting other worthwhile projects for Bongao.

"Write them all down," smiled Mrs. Dickens.

We walked back to Mrs. Dickens's hotel.

"How many people are on the committee that selects projects for funding?" I asked.

"Only three," she replied.

Surely greater sanity reigned on the committee than seemed to be coming from Mrs. Dickens. I wondered how she could possibly have achieved her position. Her naiveté was incredible. Perhaps she was useful in finding target areas for assistance.

"Have you completed any programs yet?" I asked.

"Oh, many," she said. "Most of them are on Luzon, however. That's why I'm down here. We want to expand our territory."

As we approached the hotel, she gave a profusion of thanks for my assistance. I made appropriate murmurs and went on about the business I hoped to accomplish that day.

I didn't see Mrs. Dickens again until late the following afternoon when she left Bongao. She had planned to stay longer, but a ship was in port so she decided to leave while the means was available rather than await the uncertain next ship or plane. I went to the wharf to see her off along with Father Raquet, Sister Evangelista, the mayor, and a few other officials who had heard of her largesse. She was dressed in pink-and-white stripes, rather resembling a stubby candy cane. On her finger was a glittering pink tourmaline in a simple gold setting.

"I cannot thank you enough for your marvelous hospitality," she told us through her slightly moist eyes. "Being able to meet people like you makes my job so pleasant."

"We're the ones who owe you thanks," said Sister Evangelista. "Your foundation will transform Bongao."

"Be sure and get your applications off as quickly as possible," said Mrs. Dickens. "Bongao has become my personal project, and I assure you quick action." She rummaged through her purse and pulled out a pink pen and matching pad. "Let me get your names so I can send you notes when I get home."

She wrote each of our names in her address book. The weary stevedores hoisted the last of the cargo onto the rusting ship, and a wheezing horn blasted the signal for departure. Mrs. Dickens pecked each of us on the cheek, leaving slight pink traces, and was the last to go up the plank before it was raised. She waved a pink lace handkerchief as the ship groaned away from the wharf. We watched her until the ship turned and she was no longer visible.

"Do you think anything will come of all that?" asked Sister Evangelista, as I turned with her and Father Raquet to walk to the *convento*. "It all seems too good to be true. Are you going to send in your requests?"

"There seems nothing to lose," replied Father Raquet. "Any little assistance we can get will help. How about you?"

"I agree," said Sister Evangelista, kicking a rock from the street. "What's there to lose?"

I left Bongao the following morning for an extended stay in one of the remote Bajau moorages. It was about a month before I returned. I picked up my mail at the post office, found a quiet place down by the wharf with a cold bottle of beer, and settled back to see what was transpiring among my friends back home. After finishing the mail and beer, I sat for an additional half hour before calling on Father Raquet to reclaim the cot in his spare room.

As I approached the *convento*, I heard loud laughter coming from the sitting room. It was unmistakably Sister Evangelista and Father Raquet. I entered the room. Upon seeing me, they laughed even louder.

"What's happening?" I asked, breaking into laughter despite my ignorance of what was going on.

"Read this," gasped Sister Evangelista, wiping tears from under her glasses. "It just came." She handed me a typewritten letter.

I took the letter and read it as they continued to laugh. The letter was written on stationery from the United States Embassy in Manila and signed by someone who seemed to be second in command to the ambassador. The letter acknowledged the receipt of Sister Evangelista's application to the assistance program of the Philippine Development Association, but regretted that there was no such program. It went on to explain that Mrs. Dickens did not represent any agency but rather was the relative of someone at the embassy. It was not stated so directly, but Mrs. Dickens apparently occasionally became unhinged and traveled throughout the Philippines to solve the country's problems as she perceived them. She was known by many aliases (the letter did not mention her real name) including Mrs. Shelley, Mrs. Shakespeare, Mrs. Keats, and several other English literary names. Her heart was in the right place, the letter implied, but her head was not. It was hoped no harm had been done, and the greatest apologies were offered.

"Back to the drawing board," said Father Raquet, as he caught his breath. "Bongao is not going to be catapulted into the industrial age after all."

"We'd all have to leave if it were," added Sister Evangelista. "It would lose its challenge."

"I don't think the mayor will agree," I laughed. "I doubt if he's taking it so good-humoredly."

"You missed the best part," continued Sister Evangelista. "The man who brought the special delivery letter from the post office—." She broke off and doubled over in laughter. A hoot from Father Raquet joined her.

She caught her breath again. "The man who brought the letter from the post office was wearing—." Again she howled with laughter, "—a pink shirt!"

13

To Each His God

I had been in Sulu about eight months when Sister Evangelista arrived in Bongao on the Jolo J to establish her clinic. It was a bright midmorning and I was picking up supplies for a trip to an outer moorage when I heard the ship arriving. Captain Jack, who had navigated the Jolo J up and down the Sulu archipelago for more years than anyone could remember, always announced his arrival by playing scratchy recordings of Sousa marches at full volume. It was the only signal needed. Upon hearing the music, most of the town headed toward the wharf to see who or what might be arriving from the outside world, for in those days the occasional ships that stopped at Bongao were the major links with the rest of the Philippines.

I paid for my purchases at the small Chinese store where I was shopping and headed down Bongao's only street toward the wharf. Father Raquet had told me that Catholic nuns planned to open a small clinic in Bongao, so consequently I was not surprised to see three Filipinas, immaculate in long, white habits, standing on the deck of the converted World War II mine sweeper as it edged against the decrepit wharf. When the gangplank was lowered, the nuns were among the first to alight and meet the gathering crowd of townspeople. Sister Evangelista spotted my red hair and beard above the others in the crowd and moved in my direction with her two companions.

"You must be the anthropologist," she said, thrusting out her hand. "The fathers told me about your work here. I'm Sister Evangelista. This is Sister Maria and Sister Helena."

I admitted to being the anthropologist and shook hands with each. "I heard you were coming to open a clinic," I said.

"A clinic first," said Sister Evangelista, "and we hope that, before long, it will grow into a hospital." She was not a young woman, but her face still held the prettiness of youth. Her smile was easy and her eyes sparkled. She emanated strength and determination, but these were tempered with a gentleness that was her outstanding characteristic. Her companions were rather nondescript by comparison. Both were pleasant, but rather quiet and reserved. Sister Evangelista was obviously the one in command.

"I thought Father Raquet would be here to meet us," she said, her eyes moving through the crowd. "Of course, he didn't know exactly which ship we would be arriving on. Do you know him?"

"Very well," I said. "I'm sure he'll be here soon. Is there anything I can do to help until he arrives?"

"That's kind of you," smiled Sister Evangelista, "but let's wait a few minutes. If he doesn't show up soon, we'll call upon your offer. I'm afraid we didn't travel lightly this trip. We have quite a number of parcels on board."

"You were here a few months ago, weren't you?" I asked, remembering that Father Raquet had told me of her visit.

"Yes, the other sisters were not with me. I came down to scout out the area, to see if it would be suitable for one of our hospitals. I believe Father Raquet said you were working in the outer islands."

"Yes, I was. I'm sorry I missed you."

"We shall have time to become acquainted. I'm very much interested in your research. The boat people of Sulu have always fascinated me. You must stop by for *merienda* as soon as we are settled."

"I would like that," I said, "but it may be some time. I'm about to leave for Bilatan, where I plan to spend several weeks."

"Probably we'll be up to our ears in work until then, anyway." Her eyes wandered over the crowd again and suddenly lit up. "Ah, here comes Father Raquet now. I knew he wouldn't let us down."

I joined them in greeting Father Raquet and stayed until I was sure he was able to accommodate them and their luggage. I then said farewell and headed for my boat, eager to catch the wind which I hoped would carry me to Bilatan before evening.

My stay in Bilatan extended beyond my expectations. It was five weeks before I returned to Bongao. As usual, after being in the outer islands, my first stop in Bongao was the post office, and from there to my favorite little restaurant in the marketplace for something to eat and a San Miguel beer while I read my letters. After finishing the mail and mulling over its contents, I decided to pay a visit to the sisters to see their new clinic. The keeper of the restaurant told me where it was located. I walked to the edge of town to the former Catholic school, now serving as the clinic. Father Raquet had built the small school some years earlier, only to learn it was too far from the center of town for parents to feel safe in sending their children. Consequently, the school was closed and a larger one was built in the heart of Bongao. Apparently the sisters felt they could build a good enough mousetrap to coax people from the town. It seemed to have worked, for as I approached the small building at the edge of the sea, a dozen or so people were milling in front of it, waiting to consult with the sisters about their ailments.

I entered the door and Sister Helena greeted me with a smile. "So good to see you again," she said. "When did you get back?"

"This morning. It looks like your clinic is a great success." I nodded toward the people in the waiting room.

"Indeed," she responded. "We are giving cholera shots today. How about you? Is yours still good?"

I replied that it was, and she told me how busy they had been during their first few weeks in Bongao.

"Is Sister Evangelista around?" I asked.

"She's on lunch break right now. She's target practicing in the back."

Before I could respond I heard the sharp retort of a gun from the back of the building.

"Go through the back," said Sister Helena, motioning to the room behind her. "She'll be happy to see you."

I walked through the room and opened the back door. Some twenty feet ahead stood Sister Evangelista with her back to me and a rifle to her shoulder which she was carefully aiming at a target posted to a tree some one-hundred feet away. She pulled the trigger and instantly the bull's eye shuddered from the impact of the bullet.

"Bravo," I said, clapping my hands.

She turned quickly. "You startled me. I didn't know I had an audience."

"And I didn't know you were a sharpshooter. Is this a prerequisite of your order?"

"Almost," she laughed. She came to me and shook my hand. The rifle was almost as tall as she. "It's a hobby," she continued, "but it occasionally comes in handy."

"How so?"

"When I was in north India some years back, a tiger came into our compound. Had it not been for my gun, he might have mauled some of the children who were staying with us. Ever since, I decided that knowing how to handle a gun is a good skill to maintain. But you didn't come to hear stories of my wild-game hunting. How was your trip to Bilatan?"

"Good," I said. "I managed to see a couple of weddings, a funeral, and several healing ceremonies."

"Anything happen in the healing ceremonies I should know about?"

"Probably," I said. "Are you interested in the local healing practices?"

"Certainly," she said, opening the gun and cleaning the barrel with a cleaning rod. "Years ago, I learned that the best way to introduce new notions of curing is through traditional means."

"Seems anthropologically sound."

"I call it common sense."

"Don't tell anyone, but that's what most of anthropology is."

She laughed. "Will you join the sisters and me for dinner? We'd like to know you better, and also pick your brain about local beliefs on illness and curing."

"I'd love to," I said. "I'll be in town for about a week and have lots of free time."

She thought for a moment. "Tonight is out. We are offering special prayers for some of our sisters in Nepal." She smiled at me mischievously and added, "And you, being a godless anthropologist, I'm sure would not be interested in participating in that."

"Probably not," I said, returning her smile. "It's not that we anthropologists are godless, but rather we're confronted with so many gods that we have trouble choosing only one."

"I've come to believe they are all one," she said. Then she laughed. "Perhaps I stayed in India too long. But back to the business at hand. We must have you over to dinner. Today is Monday. How about Wednesday evening?"

"Sounds good. Can I bring anything?"

"Only yourself," she said, clicking the rifle together, having finished cleaning it. "I would like to chat longer, but duty calls."

We went inside. She placed the rifle in a small closet in the back room and walked with me to the waiting room. We said goodbye and I wandered back to the marketplace.

Wednesday evening found me in the sisters' living quarters above their clinic. It was a beautiful evening, and from my chair I could see the full moon through the opened window casting a tremulous reflection on the slightly restless sea. The dinner—baked tuna, a rice pilaf, and a curry of local vegetables—was delicious.

"If your order always eats this well, I can see one of the incentives for joining it," I said, finishing the last of the food on my plate.

Sister Evangelista laughed. "I'm afraid we don't always eat quite this well, although we certainly always eat properly. It is necessary to keep up our strength for the work we do."

"And unfortunately Sister Evangelista seldom has time to cook," said Sister Helena. "She is a marvelous cook. This is her dinner, a special treat."

"After your weeks in the boondocks, I thought you might need a good meal," said Sister Evangelista, refilling my glass with a chardonnay she'd brought from Manila.

"This is by far the best meal I've had in Sulu," I said. "When did you learn to cook like this?"

"Sister Evangelista has more talents than all the rest of us put together," said Sister Maria.

"I'm a compulsive busybody," said Sister Evangelista. "Whenever I have a few moments I must be doing something. Cooking is one way I like to fill the hours. I find it very relaxing. Unfortunately, it seems I seldom have time to do it any more. I'm afraid I'm a bit rusty."

"Shall we move to the sitting room?" suggested Sister Maria. "The chairs are more comfortable there. Bring your wine."

We went into the adjoining room, which was furnished

plainly but comfortably with rattan. Local mats covered the floor. As we sipped the wine, I asked the sisters about their backgrounds. Sister Maria and Sister Helena were both from Manila, where they had received their degrees as registered nurses. Sister Evangelista was from the central Philippines but had received her M.D. from Johns Hopkins. All three sisters joined the order after becoming disillusioned with professional medicine. Sister Evangelista was a very successful neurosurgeon at Johns Hopkins when she decided the order was in greater need of her talents. They had all recently spent time in hospitals in the United States, catching up on the latest developments in medicine, and were obviously happy to be back in a mission.

"But enough of us," said Sister Evangelista. "Tell us about yourself and your research."

I did as requested, dwelling mostly on my research. Sister Evangelista had a strong grasp of anthropology, and her questions about my research were most astute. They were interested in reaching the Bajau, and she asked if I would be willing to introduce them to some of the moorages, so they might encourage the Bajau to come to their clinic.

"Let us assure you we are not after Bajau souls. Our order is not a missionizing order. We are concerned with saving lives and curing illnesses. Whether or not the people we help are Catholic is of no concern to us. We serve God by helping all our fellow humans."

"I'll be happy to introduce you to the Bajau," I said with sincerity. "I have several friends among them who could use your clinic. When you're ready for the outing, let me know."

"We appreciate your interest," said Sister Evangelista. She then added, "My delicious cooking, as you called it, did not agree with me. My stomach is upset. Will you please excuse me?"

"I'm sorry," I said. "It's time for me to go, anyway. I've kept you long enough."

"Not at all," said Sister Evangelista, standing up. "Please stay and talk further with the sisters. I shall be all right once I lie down."

Sister Maria stood up also. "Let me come with you, Sister. Tell me what you need and I'll get it from the clinic."

Sister Maria and Sister Helena were obviously more concerned with Sister Evangelista's illness than they were with continuing conversation with me. As quickly as possible I took my leave, expressing concern about Sister Evangelista's health. She assured me it was only a touch of indigestion and thanked me for coming.

Several days after my dinner with the sisters, I accompanied a Bajau family to their burial island some twenty miles to the east of Bongao. An infant of the family had died and I was invited to join the funeral party. It was not a particularly sad death. The child had been ill since birth, so no one was surprised when it died. Infant mortality is so high among the Bajau that it generally causes little grief. Consequently, the funeral trip turned into a fishing expedition after the tiny body was deposited in one of the communal graves. After four days out, I developed a touch of dysentery which, within hours, evolved into a severe case. I could keep nothing in my stomach and weakened rapidly. Laka tried traditional curing methods on me to no avail. My last conscious memory of the trip was asking them to take me to the sisters' clinic in Bongao. I passed out shortly thereafter.

When I regained consciousness I was in the clinic. The first face I saw was that of Sister Evangelista. She looked tired and very anxious.

I smiled at her and said, "So I made it."

"Indeed you did." An expression of relief spread over her face. "At times we wondered if you would, though."

"You gave us quite a scare," Sister Helena added. I turned

and saw her standing at the bedside. I also noticed a bottle of dextrose on a pole by the bed draining through a plastic tube into a needle in my arm.

"You've had three bottles of that," said Sister Evangelista, following my glance. "I've never seen anyone as dehydrated as you were. What did you eat or drink that might have brought on the attack?"

"I can't think of anything out of the ordinary."

"Do you boil your water?" she asked.

"No," I admitted sheepishly.

"That's very foolish," she scolded. "Had you reached us a few hours later, you might not be alive now. You must be more careful in the future."

"How long have I been here?"

"Two days," said Sister Helena. "And Sister Evangelista has been at your side most of that time." She turned to her saying, "Our prayers and medicine worked, Sister."

"Especially our medicine," said Sister Evangelista.

I tried to express my gratitude, but Sister Evangelista hushed me and told me to get some more rest as they left the room.

When I next awakened, it was morning and I felt considerably better. Dextrose was still draining into my arm. I lay quietly, enjoying the morning sounds from the sea outside my window. As I was trying to sort through the events of the past few days, Sister Helena entered the room. "Good morning," she said brightly. "You look much better today. You're beginning to get some color back."

"I feel much better," I said. "Thanks to you and the sisters."

She looked at the bottle of dextrose. "I think we can get rid of this and try some solid food." She turned off the flow of dextrose and gently, painlessly removed the needle from my arm, placing a small bandage over the puncture.

"Would you like some breakfast?"

"I'd love it," I said, noticing hunger pangs in my stomach for the first time in several days.

"It won't be much at first," she said. "We'll ease you back into your regular diet."

"You're the nurse."

She left the room and within fifteen minutes returned with a tray of mostly liquid food. "Eat only as much as you want," she said. "Don't overeat. I'll check back later. I must help in the clinic. If you need anything, ring that little bell by your bed."

I thanked her and she left. After sitting up to eat, my strength began to wane and soon I fell back into slumber. When I awakened it was midafternoon and Sister Helena was standing by my bed.

"Hello, again," she said. "You are certainly catching up on your sleep."

"I certainly am."

"Sleep and food are best for you at this point."

"How long do you think I'll be in bed?"

"A few more days," she said. "Don't be concerned about getting up until you have your strength back."

"Is Sister Evangelista in the clinic?" I asked. I was hoping she would stop by.

"She is ill again. The problem with her stomach has returned. Sister Maria and I insisted she go to bed."

"I'm sorry. I hope the hours she spent with me didn't bring it on."

"I don't think so," replied Sister Helena. "Her stomach gives her trouble periodically, and there is nothing she can do but go to bed and take care of it—although she does try to ignore it. She is one of the most dedicated members of our order, an inspiration to so many of the sisters."

After propping me up so I could better see out the window, Sister Helena left. It was late afternoon now, and I could see boats returning from fishing. I watched their billowed sails for about an hour until my thoughts were interupted by a young woman who brought my dinner.

After dinner, I became restless. I was no longer sleepy, and enough of my energy was revived to make me want to do something other than lie in bed. Just as I was beginning to think about getting out of bed, I was surprised by the appearance of Sister Evangelista.

"So you're feeling better," she said, sitting on the side of the bed and holding her palm to my forehead.

"I am, thank you. And how about you? Sister Helena told me you are ill."

"I'm better for the present," she said, smiling wanly. She did not look well. "It's terribly frustrating to be sick. It seems such a waste of my talents, and a drain on the other sisters' time to care for me. I haven't received a satisfactory answer from my God yet as to why it has to be this way." She smiled at me. "Do you suppose one of your gods might have an answer?"

"Is there an answer to everything?"

"I like to think so. I have to find answers, provide meanings to life. Otherwise there is no reason for living, is there?"

"Life itself is reason for me to live," I said.

"But there's a reason for it all," she said. "And my God knows the reason. And eventually I always learn the reason, too."

"How long have you had your illness?" I asked.

"Who knows? Probably for years. These things sometimes develop over many years. I have cancer, you know. Terminal cancer."

I was startled. I had no idea her illness was so serious, thinking perhaps a stomach ulcer caused her periodic discomforts.

"I'm very sorry," I said, not knowing what else to say.

She smiled at me. "Death itself does not disturb me. My

life has been full; I have experienced many things. I am actually looking forward to the experience of death. I have always sought new experiences, and I regard death as another experience in the chain of events."

"Have you known about your illness very long?" I asked.

"I suspected it about a year ago. It was confirmed during my recent stay in the States."

"Do the other sisters know?"

"Yes, but they choose to pretend it is not really terminal. Most people are so reluctant to face the fact that someone is dying. At least they are afraid to face the dying person with the fact. That is perhaps the greatest frustration of dying. There is no one to talk to about it; except God, of course."

"How long . . . before you are bedridden?" I asked, also not wanting to talk about death but realizing she did.

"You mean before I die? It's difficult to say. I had thought I might have another year or so before I am totally incapacitated. But the attacks seem to be coming more frequently now. What I dislike most is the waste of it all. I have these skills for curing and helping sick people, but when I am ill I am unable to use them. And when I reach the point where I cannot get out of bed, I shall have to lie there and let the sisters wait on me—taking their time from people who can be cured and go on living. And who knows how long I shall waste away before I finally die? My God doesn't approve of such waste." She smiled at me. "How about yours?"

"Which one? Some of them do; some of them don't."

She laughed. "One of my goals before I die is to save you from your heathen ways." She stood up to leave. "But I suspect if we looked closely enough at one another's gods, we would find more similarities than differences. I must take advantage of my recovery and get some work done. And I want you to get better, too. Remember, you promised to take me to some of the Bajau moorages. One thing I'd like to do before I die is to see this clinic firmly established. Maybe even a hospital,

God willing." She reached over and patted my hand. "Go back to sleep. I'll stop by later."

About two weeks later, when Sister Evangelista and I had both recovered, I arranged to take her to one of the moorages. I met her at eight o'clock and we walked to the small boat-house where I kept my boat. We had several miles to cover in a limited amount of time, so I decided against the sail and attached my outboard motor. Within minutes we were skimming across a glasslike sea. The sun was pleasantly warm, not yet hot as it would be before noon. Our boat provided the only sound to the soundless day and left a wake of ripples shimmering behind us.

Within fifteen minutes we arrived at the Bajau moorage. It was a sizeable community, a flotilla of some fifty house-boats moored in shallow reef waters. It was Masa's moorage and I was greeted with shouts of recognition as I stopped the motor to paddle my boat among the houseboats. A few cooking fires still burned on some of the boats, while on others, families were preparing for a day of fishing or collecting from the nearby beaches and reefs. Naked children splashed in and out of the clean water of the morning high tide. I paddled to the houseboat of Masa. He and his family were in the boat and flashed smiles of welcome.

"Where are you going?" he asked, in the traditional greeting of the Bajau.

"To see you," I said. "I've brought Sister Evangelista to meet some of the people here. She's a doctor and has heard that some people are ill here."

"We've heard of her," he said.

"Remember when I got sick at Bilatan?" I asked. "Sister's medicine cured me."

The Bajau are always suspicious of outsiders, having suffered a good deal of abuse from them in the past. Consequently, I knew I had to oversell Sister Evangelista in order to convince them she could be trusted. I explained to Masa and his friends that the nuns wanted to help the Bajau with their illnesses. Apparently word had already spread of the sisters' charitable work, so much of my public relations work was already done. Before long, a few adventuresome individuals approached Sister Evangelista with their ailments. I acted as interpreter. Within half an hour Sister had bandaged a severe burn, treated a variety of skin ulcers, provided medication for three cases of malaria—and found herself surrounded by a dozen more people with various pains.

We stayed at the moorage for about two hours. Sister Evangelista did all she could for the patients who approached her. Several of them promised to visit her in the clinic, where she could better deal with their problems. At eleven o'clock we left the moorage. Sister Evangelista was pleased with the inroads she had made into the Bajau community.

"That is why God gave me these talents," she said as I paddled to the edge of the moorage, "to help people who really need help."

"I think you've won some converts to modern medicine," I said. "You'll probably have more Bajau at your clinic than you can handle."

"We can handle them all," she said. "It may take time, but we can handle them all." Her eyes wandered to a little island about a mile from the moorage. "Have you ever been on that little island?"

"Many times," I said. "When I feel a need to be by myself, I often go there. Once I spent a week there. It's a good escape."

"It looks so peaceful. If you have time, I'd like to stop there for a few minutes."

"I have time if you do." I headed the boat toward the island.

I had discovered the island shortly after I arrived in Sulu. It was minuscule, no more than a hundred yards in diameter, but it was a microcosm of the islands of Sulu. On one side was a lovely little bay fringed with white sand and lined with eight palm trees. A little knoll sloped up from the beach and dropped off abruptly to become a miniature rocky coast line. Nestled among the palms on the beach was a small house of nipa thatch, built by passing fishermen. I paddled into the shallow waters of the beach and then jumped out to push the boat into the sand, so Sister Evangelista could alight.

"How lovely," she sighed, surveying the island. "Everyone should have an island like this."

I sat on a fallen tree trunk. She wandered down the beach, examining the flotsam at her feet and occasionally looking up to the loud squawks of brightly colored birds in the palms. She disappeared into the vegetation to climb the little knoll. Sensing that she wanted to be alone, I remained on the log, enjoying the solace the island always provided. No one ever came to the island, since its meager resources were of little value. Occasionally, passing fishermen spent the night, but for the most part the lovely spot was ignored.

Twenty minutes passed before Sister Evangelista returned. Without speaking, she sat on the log next to me. We sat for several minutes in silence.

"I prayed up there," she said. "I was so overcome by the beauty of God's world that I wanted to share my joy with him."

"I know what you mean," I said. "I haven't prayed to your god about it, but I've been overwhelmed by Sulu's beauty. It's a strange feeling, isn't it?"

"A beautiful experience," she said. "You've communicated with God without knowing it."

"I've known it," I said. "I knew I was communicating with something, another realm. You call it 'God.' I don't."

"But it's the same."

"Yes, I suspect it is the same, the stuff that gave birth to all religion."

She looked at me and smiled. "Sometimes I think you're more religious than I."

"You mean there might still be hope for my heathen soul?"

"Perhaps," she laughed. "It's time to get back to work." She stood up, looked out to sea. "Increasingly I feel I must use each of my well moments. They are numbered and precious. When they are gone, I don't know what I will do. I cannot spend my final days uselessly draining time from the sisters which they should be spending on people who can recover. Shall we go?"

We returned to the boat and sped back to Bongao.

It was now the season of the winter monsoons, and one of those days when it seemed the islands of Sulu would not survive the onslaught of the rains. I tried unsuccessfully to occupy my morning, but each attempt was drowned by the incessant clamor of rain beating against the metal roof. Finally, when I could stand the sound no longer, I donned my rain gear and splashed down Bongao's empty quagmire of a street. I didn't know where I was going when I left my room, but I soon discovered it was no day for walking. I decided to go to the clinic to have a cup of coffee with the sisters. When I arrived, they were just sitting down to their morning merienda, and of course they invited me to join them. It was a quiet morning at the clinic, and Sister Evangelista had used her spare time to bake a coffee cake, which she now placed on the table with steaming cups of coffee. She had her usual glass of milk.

"You must have smelled my cake through the rain," she laughed, as she sliced it into generous portions. "I was hoping you would get some before we ate it all."

"That must be what drove me from the house," I said, settling into a chair. "I knew there was some reason I had to leave, but I wasn't sure why. Now I know."

We gossiped about local events as we enjoyed the merienda. It was pleasant to have a leisurely chat with the sisters. Usually when I stopped to see them, they had time for only a quick cup of coffee before hurrying back to waiting patients. But today the rain had kept the ill at home, and the clinic had a holiday air.

After half an hour, Sister Helena and Sister Maria left to do some shopping. Sister Evangelista and I turned to discussing plays. She was telling me about a production of *Richard II* she had seen during her last visit to London when we heard the door to the clinic open and bang shut. Before Sister could get up to see who it was, the door to the small lounge where we were sitting was thrown open, and before us stood an old Muslim man.

We both started at his appearance. In his hand he tightly clutched a beautiful kris. He stood in the doorway, glaring at Sister Evangelista.

"Good morning," she said pleasantly. "We were just having *merienda*. Would you like to join us? Or have you come about an illness?"

The man said in Sama, "I am Mahmud. You have told the people from my village that my medicine is not good."

"Can you understand him?" Sister asked me.

I translated the message.

"There must be some mistake," she said. "I would never do a thing like that. What village is he from? And who told him that?"

I relayed the words to the man, and eyed a chair I might use to ward off his kris should the need arise.

"I am the most powerful shaman on Tabauan. Sitilaini came to you and you cured her illness. And you told her my medicine was no good." He clutched his kris more tightly and looked around the room as if unsure of his next move.

"There must be some misunderstanding," said Sister Evangelista. "Please sit down and have some coffee and cake, and let us discuss the matter."

I translated Sister's invitation to the old shaman, but he didn't move.

"I have great respect for your medicine," she continued. "After all, you were taking care of these people's illnesses long before I came here."

I continued to act as interpreter. These were obviously not the words the man expected, and he looked somewhat puzzled.

"You and I use different kinds of medicine, which are good for different kinds of diseases," continued Sister Evangelista. "You are a shaman. You know that some shamans are good at curing certain illnesses whereas other shamans can cure other illnesses. I'm like a shaman, too. Some of my ways are better than yours, but some of your ways are better than mine. We should work together, since we both want to help people."

I relayed the message. The old man looked even more puzzled.

"I would like very much to work with you," said Sister Evangelista. "I've heard about you. I think we can best cure some patients by working individually, but for other patients I think it would be better if we worked together. Won't you please sit down so we can talk some more?"

She looked at his kris. "You have a very beautiful kris. It must be very ancient."

Again I translated. He looked at his kris, and then back at Sister.

"I made a lovely cake this morning. I'm sure you'll enjoy it." She placed a piece on a plate and put it near an empty chair. "Do you like coffee?"

Much to my surprise, the old man sat at the table across from Sister Evangelista, still holding the kris to his side.

"Do you know my friend?" she asked, nodding to me.

I introduced myself, but he just looked at me.

Sister Evangelista continued as she handed the old shaman a cup of coffee, "I have a patient here that I wanted to talk to you about. Her name is Putini. Do you know her? She is from your island."

The man acknowledged that he knew the woman.

"I have done all I can with my medicine. And now I need your help. Certain *saitan* are still bothering her. They are Sulu *saitan* and I know you are much more knowledgeable about them than I am. Will you try to help her?"

The old man looked at me as I translated the message, and then looked at Sister Evangelista. He nodded his head.

"Thank goodness," she said. "I have tried everything I can think of for her. She needs your help. Let's go see her now."

Sister led the man out of the room, and I followed them. We entered the main ward of the clinic. Only four beds were occupied, and clustered around each was the usual small group of relatives who insisted on staying with their kin. Sister led us to the bed of a woman who was about twenty. Seated on the floor next to the low bed were two middle-aged women, her mother and aunt. They looked alarmed when they saw the old shaman. Sister Evangelista greeted them in the few words of Sama she knew. Then, with me acting as interpreter, she gave him the young woman's medical history. She had apparently come to the clinic with a bad case of malaria and a severe infection resulting from a cut on her foot. Sister successfully cleared up the malaria and the infection, but in the meantime the woman began experiencing seizures caused by what she described as *saitan*. Sister had tried various remedies, but none worked. She now wanted the old shaman to rid the woman of the *saitan* that were haunting her.

The old shaman listened closely to Sister Evangelista. When she finished, he looked at the patient for several moments. He said he thought he could probably help her.

"Good," said Sister Evangelista enthusiastically. "Could you start now?"

"Of course," he said. "I need incense."

"We can get some," replied Sister. She called one of the young women who helped in the clinic and sent her to the store for the incense.

For the first time the old man put down his *kris*. I sighed inwardly with relief. With his gnarled hands, he massaged the young woman's body and asked her questions about her seizures. He also queried her mother and aunt about the illness.

Very shortly the girl returned with the incense and gave it to the shaman. He lighted it in a small dish on the bedside table. He then asked for one of the mats rolled under the bed which the older women used for sleeping. He spread it on the floor next to the bed and assisted the young woman out of bed and onto the mat. He sat cross-legged next to her and placed the incense between them. With his hands held on his crossed legs, palms upward, he closed his eyes and chanted in a language I couldn't understand. He chanted for about five minutes. A babble of sounds in a strange voice replaced the chant, and he fell upon the mat in a trance as the rush of sounds continued. After several minutes he became quiet, his body relaxed, and he fell into a deep slumber. Within five minutes he awakened and sat up.

"She will soon be all right," he announced. "I have talked to the *saitan*."

I gave the message to Sister Evangelista. "I'm so relieved," she said. "I knew you could help her." I translated to the shaman. He smiled for the first time, as did the relatives of the patient.

"Ask him if he would be willing to help me in the future when I need his assistance," she said to me. "Tell him I will help him if he has patients who might be cured by my medicines." I conveyed the words to the shaman.

"I would like to help the woman with her patients," he said. "She's new to the area and needs to learn about the *saitan*. Maybe she can also teach me about her medicine."

I translated for Sister Evangelista. Her face beamed. "That is marvelous. Thank you so much. We'll make a great team. Now would you like to go back and have that cup of coffee?"

"Thank you," he replied to my translation, "but I must go home."

"Don't forget to let me know if I can ever help, and I will be sure to call you to help me."

The old shaman smiled at her, gave the traditional bow of respect, picked up his kris and left the clinic smiling.

Sister Evangelista saw that the patient was comfortably settled back in her bed and then returned with me to the lounge. I closed the door and gave a deep sigh of relief.

"Do you know what that man came here to do?" I asked.

"Most likely to run his kris through me," she said, as she poured fresh coffee for me.

"You're probably right," I said.

"That's always a problem with our work," she said. "We are seen as a threat by the traditional healers."

"You handled this one beautifully. Were you serious about working with him?"

"Of course. That young woman is suffering from delusions triggered by something I know nothing about. All of my medicines cannot cure her. On the other hand, that old man has probably dealt successfully with dozens of such cases. Shamans are among the best psychiatrists in the world. I'll be very surprised if she doesn't have a rapid recovery."

"Weren't you frightened when he came in? You were amazingly calm."

"I was scared out of my wits," she laughed. "In fact, as soon as you leave, I'm going to bed to rest my shattered nerves."

During the next few weeks, I instructed the sisters in the use of my outboard motor. Although the boat was essential to aspects of my research, weeks sometimes passed when I didn't need it. This was a great waste, since at times the sisters hired boats to visit neighboring islands. As anticipated, they learned to handle the boat quickly. Before long they were quite comfortable taking trips by themselves. Sister Evangelista, of course, turned out to be the master sailor. She maneuvered the

boat expertly—better than I, in fact—and delighted in skimming the waters of Tawi-Tawi. Before long the nuns became a
familiar sight on the seascape, speeding across the blue waters
with their white habits flowing in the breeze as they took their
healing services to cure the various ills of the area. Their kind-
ness and concern for the sick won the trust and hearts of the
local population within a matter of weeks. Sister Evangelista
organized a series of seminars with local shamans where she
learned more about their approaches to illness as she taught
them some of her ways. The Bongao clinic was enormously
successful, and within six months the sisters began construct-
ing their small hospital.

It was about this time that I decided to take a vacation to
Manila. I was growing a little restless in Sulu and beginning to
tire of my research. My interpretations of Bajau culture were
becoming too pat and simplistic. I needed a break from my
work to visit friends in Manila and perhaps come back with
some new perspectives on my data. Besides, I was beginning
to hanker for a few of the comforts of home, like clean sheets,
green salads, cold milk, steak—not to mention a nice warm
body to share my bed. So, one cloudy morning I boarded a
little launch headed for Zamboanga—it was one of those periods when planes weren't flying to Bongao. For three days
we chugged through the Sulu Islands, bounced sometimes by
rough seas and now and then stopping at islands to deposit
and receive goods and passengers. Finally, we made it to Zamboanga. I spent a day recovering at the Bayot Hotel and then
caught a flight to Manila.

Manila was as frantic and frenzied as ever. But it was
exactly what I needed after six months in Sulu. For two weeks I
stuffed myself on salads and steaks, enjoyed the luxury of clean
sheets on real mattresses with compatible bodies, and generally gave vent to my various deprived passions. To rationalize
the trip to my work ethic, I gave seminars at two universities,

presented a paper to an anthropological association, and met with colleagues whose research interests were relevant to my own. It was a good break, and one that I needed, but at its end, I was ready to return to Sulu. I again flew to Zamboanga, where I found a launch headed for Bongao. It bobbed for three days as it meandered its way through reefs and islands until I finally reached home.

In Manila, I picked up some periodicals for the sisters. When I took them over to the clinic, I learned that Sister Evangelista had been bedridden almost the entire time I was in Manila. Sister Maria and Sister Helena were busy in the clinic. They suggested I go upstairs to see Sister Evangelista.

Sister Evangelista was propped on pillows in bed and was gazing through the open window to the sea. She smiled a greeting as I entered the room. She looked very ill. She seemed even smaller, and her face revealed the truth of her sixty-some years. I had never seen her look so tired.

"So you have returned from your bacchanalian sojourn," she said, holding out her hand.

I took it in both of mine and pressed it to my lips. "Indeed," I said. "I committed enough sins to fill your prayers for months."

"I got a headstart on you," she smiled. "I prayed for you while you were gone. I knew what you would be up to. But seriously, it is good to have you back. I have missed our little chats."

"And I. The sisters tell me you've been ill since I left. I'm sorry."

She smiled wanly and pressed my hand. "So am I. I am weakening faster than I anticipated. I thought it might be another year before I reached this state. We have asked the Order to send down another physician. I shall never be able to work full-time again."

She spoke matter-of-factly, without sorrow or regret.

"Will you stay here?" I asked.

"Yes, I will stay here. I would like to die here, at the site of my last hospital."

I choked with emotion. I couldn't accept her impending death as calmly as she.

"Please," she said, seeing my sadness. "I am happy. I've talked with my God. He understands. I am not distressed anymore. He'll take me when I am no longer useful here." She squeezed my hand. "What a marvelous life I have had! God blessed me with talents and skills that have allowed me to ease the suffering and pain of so many people. I've seen the wonders and enjoyed the beauties of God's world. I'm not sad. Please don't be sad for me."

Her peace and strength were infectious and the pain within me subsided.

"I've been waiting for you to come back," she said brightly, picking up a book from the bedside table. "I've been reading this book by a French anthropologist named Levi-Strauss. Granted my French is a bit rusty, but he has a very peculiar writing style—not to mention some strange ideas. Do you know the man?"

We spent the next hour discussing the erudite anthropology of Claude Levi-Strauss.

Sister Evangelista's illness worsened over the next few months and she spent more time in bed than working in the hospital. Her replacement was a coldly efficient nun whose razor-blade lips were always slashed into an upside-down smile. She seemed more concerned with curing illnesses than with the people who suffered them. I saw little of her, but I visited Sister Evangelista whenever I was in Bongao. During her good days she worked feverishly at the clinic, cramming as much work as possible into her well moments. When she was ill, she lay in bed staring at the vista of sea, sky, and islands beyond her window. If she was well enough, we talked of matters that intrigued her always curious mind. During her bad days, my visits were spent sitting by her bed, holding her hand and trying to comfort her suffering.

After several months of such bouts and rebounds, she made a remarkable recovery. I went to the clinic one morning to find her as fresh and pert as I had seen her in many months. She was in high spirits and up to her eyebrows in victims of a severe malaria outbreak. She took time out for a quick glass of milk with me and then hurried back to the crowded clinic. It was good to see the woman I'd known during her early months in Bongao, and I left the clinic for the first time in many weeks without thinking about her impending death.

The next morning I slept in. I had been up very late reading a book I wanted to finish, and it was ten o'clock before I decided it was time to face the day. As I pulled on my shorts, one of the maids from the clinic knocked on the door.

"A letter from Sister Evangelista, sir," she said, handing me a white envelope with my name on the front.

I thanked the woman, closed the door and turned to read the letter. "I have borrowed your boat to visit your lovely little island. Please come at noon—not before. I have talked with my God, and He has decided it is time. Perhaps you should bring Father Raquet with you." It was signed by Sister Evangelista.

I finished and was tempted to go to the island immediately, but I respected Sister's instructions. Shortly after eleven, I walked down to see Father Raquet. I told him of the letter and asked if he would accompany me. By noon we were speeding toward the little island.

As we approached the island, I could see my boat moored at the miniature beach. We anchored next to it and walked to the little clump of coconut palms. Propped against the base of the largest tree was Sister Evangelista. Her habit was perfectly arranged, her eyes were closed, and on her lips was a gentle smile. Without examining her, we knew she was dead. Father Raquet fell on his knees to offer prayers.

I turned and walked to the top of the little hill. I sat on a large rock and gazed at the hazy summits of Borneo until the beatitude of Sister Evangelista eased my pain.

14

A Death in Sunshine

Iheard about the old American man who lived on Tandubas Island shortly after I arrived in Sulu. Local lore claimed he had been there since the days of American rule in the Philippines and was married to a Muslim woman. I didn't put much stock in the story and stored it away with some of the others I'd heard, such as the one about the little people on Tawi-Tawi Island who disappeared each time they saw someone watching them, or the tale of the great snake atop Mount Bongao which demanded bananas before it allowed visitors to go up the mountain slope to see the sacred graves on the peak. Sulu was filled with these stories. They were interesting from an anthropological point of view, but I never took them too seriously.

But even if the old American man existed, I wasn't too interested in meeting him. Most such American and European expatriates I had encountered in Asia were dull, as dull in Asia as they would have been back home. Consequently, I had no intention of looking for the old man who reputedly gave up America for life on one of the remote islands in the southern Philippines. Events, however, turned out otherwise.

I'd been in Sulu over a year when Masa and Biti, their two young sons, and I were on a fishing trip in the eastern waters of Tawi-Tawi. The islands were new to me, some of the most remote of Sulu, and I was enjoying my adventure into new territory. Biti's houseboat served as fishing boat and living quarters. We enjoyed beautiful weather on the trip and our fishing efforts paid off. Each day we sought reefs known to Masa and Biti, tossed out our nets, and harvested hundreds of brightly colored fish. In the late afternoons, after we butchered our catch, we sprinkled the fish with salt and placed them on every available surface of the boat to dry. It was a good trip. We worked hard, ate well, and slept soundly. The days were hot but invigorating, and the nights were cool and restful.

On the morning of our fifth day out, Masa looked at a sunrise that was having trouble breaking through a very grey sky. He announced we were in for some bad weather. Biti crawled out of the house with sleep still in his eyes and seconded Masa's prediction. At noon the weather worsened, and it was agreed we should head for shelter on the coast of one of the nearby islands. Within sight was a small village nestled in a little bay that seemed to offer the protection we were seeking.

As I dropped the heavy stone that served as our anchor into the boat, the wind came up—first as a light breeze that ruptured the glassy surface of the sea, and then as a gale that lifted the nipa roof from the boat and tossed it into the water. Swells playfully tossed our boat, and then began breaking and drenching us with sea water. We strained at the paddles to get the boat out of the angry waters, occasionally shouting warnings and exclamations at one another. After about a half hour, we reached the little bay. We dropped anchor, reassembled the roof, and fell under its protection to recuperate from our stormy trip. We were soaked, and since the few items of clothing we had were soaked also, we had no choice but to sit in the gloomy boat in our wet clothes. Masa made a quick survey of the fish in the hold and announced that we had lost very few, although most would have to be redried.

"How long do you think the rain will last?" I asked, having come to rely upon the Bajau for weather forecasts.

"Probably it will end tonight," said Masa, as he rummaged through a can, looking for cigarettes. "Maybe tomorrow morning."

I didn't relish the idea of spending the remainder of the day and the night in wet clothes in the wet boat.

"Do you know anyone in this village?" I asked.

"No," said Biti. "These are not our people."

"Maybe if we go ashore they'll let us sleep overnight," I suggested.

"We couldn't sleep with these people," said Masa. "This is Tandubas. These people are sorcerers, the most powerful in Tawi-Tawi. It would be dangerous to go to their houses."

I didn't pursue the subject, thinking the sun might come out before the day was over and dry us out, or the men might change their minds when faced with the prospect of sleeping in the soggy boat. We eventually found pursuits to occupy us. Biti slept with the two small boys curled beside him, while Masa repaired his fishing nets and sang a jaunty song about the weather. I reread the stack of letters from home that I'd picked up in Bongao on the day we left. Most were from friends and were filled with bits and pieces of news to keep me in touch with what was happening in a world so remote that I sometimes almost lost belief in its existence. After reading the letters several times, I finally put them away, found a less wet spot, and fell asleep to Masa's song of the rain.

I don't know how long I slept—perhaps an hour. I was awakened by Masa telling me people from the village were approaching. He and Biti were alarmed.

"They can't be trusted," warned Masa, as we watched a boat with two men approaching us.

"I'm sure they're simply coming out to see who we are," I said, having some time ago become aware that the Bajau are distrustful of anyone who is not a relative or a fellow Bajau.

When they were within a few feet of our boat, I stepped out onto the deck in the heavy drizzle and greeted the men. "Where are you going?" I asked, in the traditional greeting of the Bajau. The men were obviously surprised to see a red-bearded foreigner emerge from a Bajau fishing boat.

"We came to see if you have fish for sale," said the older of the two, recovering from his surprise. "We didn't fish last night, and it looks like we won't be able to fish today. Will you sell us some fish?"

"I'm sure we will," I said. "Let me ask my friends."

I crawled back under the roof and spoke to Masa and Biti. "Let's tell them that we'll give them some fish if they'll find us a dry place to sleep tonight."

"We can't sleep with them," said Biti. "They can't be trusted."

"They won't harm us," I insisted. "I'm an American, and you know the people in Sulu like Americans." That was true in those days. "And you're my friends, so they won't harm you."

"You can sleep with them," said Masa. "We'll stay here."

I was irritated at my friends' stubbornness, but given their history of abuse by outsiders, I could understand their concern. "Shall we sell them some fish?"

"We will give them some," said Biti. "Then maybe they'll leave us alone." He began to put together a string of dried fish as I crawled back onto the deck.

"My friends are getting some fish for you," I said.

"You're an American?" asked the older man.

"That's right," I admitted. "And where is your home?"

"Here," he said, nodding toward the village. "It's unusual for an American to visit this area. Where do you stay?"

"I live with the Bajau."

"That is why you speak Sama," said the man.

"Yes," I said. "My friends have taught me." By then, Biti and

Masa had crawled onto the deck with a generous string of fish. Masa tossed the fish into our visitors' boat.

"How much do I owe you?" asked the older man.

"Nothing," said Masa. "We've had good luck this trip. You can have the fish for your families."

"That's very good of you," said the man. "Would you like to come ashore. Our house is dry."

"We have work to do here," said Masa, including Biti in his lie. "But maybe our friend would like to go."

"I'd like to very much," I said, looking forward not only to leaving the wet boat but also to glimpsing another of the many subcultures of Sulu.

The men poled their boat next to ours and I jumped aboard. I told Masa and Biti I'd be back soon. The older man thanked Masa again for the fish, and the younger man poled the boat toward shore.

"My name is Kanta," said the older man. "This is my son-in-law Abasa."

I told them my name and added I was happy to meet some people from Tandubas.

We reached the village, and the men maneuvered the boat between two pile houses built on the shoreline. After securing the boat with ropes, Kanta motioned for me to follow him as he climbed a rickety ladder to the deck of the larger of the two houses. We crossed the deck and opened a closed door to enter the gloomy interior of the shuttered house.

Sounds of surprise and alarm came from the inhabitants when they saw me.

"He's an American," explained Kanta, "living with the boat people."

About a dozen adults and children were in the house. At my entry, they all approached to examine me more closely. By now I was accustomed to being scrutinized like a visitor from another planet whenever I visited the remote islands of

Sulu, so I smiled amiably as they looked me over. The women went to the back of the house where the kitchen was located. Kanta asked me to sit with him on mats that were spread on the floor for us.

We sat, and as the rest of the household crowded around us, I asked him questions about his family and Tandubas. Before long, the women returned with glasses of steaming coffee and dishes of various Sulu foods.

In traditional Sulu style, the coffee was syrupy sweet. The other dishes were variants of rice and cassava. They tasted good as I remembered I had eaten very little that day.

"We have an American on this island," said Kanta. "Have you heard of him?"

"I heard there was an American here," I said, "but I didn't know if it were true."

"Indeed it's true," said Kanta. "My son-in-law Abasa is his son." He pointed to the young man who accompanied us in the boat.

"Your father is American?" I asked.

"Yes," he replied. "He lives in the next village. I live here with my wife." He nodded toward an attractive young woman holding a baby on her lap.

"I'd like to meet your father," I said.

"If he were well, he'd come to meet you. But he's been sick for several days. Maybe you have some medicine that will help him?"

"I don't have very much medicine. What's wrong with him?"

"I don't know," said the young man. "He is very old. His illnesses are probably the illnesses of old age. Would you like to visit my home village and see him?"

"Yes, I would." I was genuinely curious to meet the old American man now that his existence was confirmed.

"It's too late to go today," said Kanta. "And the weather is bad. If you stay overnight, maybe we can go in the morning."

"I would like that," I said.

"I'm sure he'll be happy to see you," said Abasa.

I wasn't sure about that, since the man had obviously chosen to isolate himself from his countrymen. The conversation drifted to other topics and I began to learn about the island. It was a small agricultural island. The people were primarily subsistence farmers who raised copra as a cash crop and fished the seas for the protein element of their diets. Like most of Sulu's people, they were Muslims. If Kanta's household was typical, the Tandubas people lived in matrilocal extended households. His household consisted of his wife, his mother-in-law, and his three married daughters with their husbands and children. Kanta was the village headman. I learned nothing of the sorcery my Bajau friends feared and chalked it up as another Sulu legend.

The rain continued and the household resumed the various activities my arrival had interrupted. Two of the women wove mats while a man repaired his fish nets. Kanta's mother-in-law worked at sewing, and a young mother cut her son's hair. Others slept as Kanta and I talked away the afternoon.

As dusk approached, Kanta suggested we return to the houseboat to see if Masa and Biti would like to stay overnight in his house. I knew they wouldn't, but I also knew I had to work out logistics with them for my visit to the old American man, so I agreed to Kanta's suggestion. It was still raining. The houseboat was anchored where we left it, and as we poled up to its side, Masa greeted us. The men declined to stay overnight in the house, but agreed to meet me in the same location the following noon. They planned to go fishing in the morning if the rain stopped, and they would return to the village at noon to pick me up. If it was still raining by morning, they would simply remain where they were until I returned.

After a few more words, I returned with Kanta to his house. When we arrived, the evening meal was ready and we ate the generous portions the women served. After dinner, we lounged on mats on the floor around the flame of a small kerosene lamp. Friends and neighbors dropped by, apparently in response to the rumor that an American was in the village. Before the evening was over, I'd learned a great deal about the village and had met a good many of its inhabitants. The rain was still falling when I joined the slumber of the rest of the household.

I awakened shortly after sunrise to greet a clean morning swathed in sparkling sunshine. I stepped onto the deck with Kanta and watched fishermen preparing their boats for a day at sea while farmers left for their fields, *bolos* strung from their belts and baskets strapped to their backs. All greeted me with the smiles that come so easily for the peoples of Southeast Asia. The houseboat of Masa was gone, the two men having gained an early start on the fish. Kanta's wife called us inside, and we sat on the floor with the rest of the family to enjoy an ample breakfast of island produce. Upon finishing, Kanta announced we would leave for the village where Abasa's father lived. Abasa accompanied us.

The path we took led through palm trees along the sandy shoreline. The crystal clear, aqua waters of the reef licked at the white sand. The sky was a soft blue puffed with cotton-candy clouds. A cacophony of animal sounds came from the awakening island's interior. The path was wide enough to accommodate a motor vehicle, although there were, of course, none on the island. We encountered people walking to their farms, mostly children and women whose husbands were among the fishermen whose boats we could see on the shining waters. Brightly colored birds squawked and fluttered through the trees and occasional monkeys surprised us with their antics in the limbs above. I marveled anew at the idyllic beauty of the Sulu Islands and felt good to be alive in such a place. I thought of the old American man and could understand why he chose to stay here.

Kanta and Abasa were veritable guide books to the island. They pointed out features of the natural landscape along the way and related bits and pieces of local lore. At one point we came to a small islet of strangely shaped rocks that somewhat resembled a boat. According to Abasa, many years ago pirates invaded the island while the men were away. They kidnapped the women and children and were about to leave when Allah intervened and turned them and their boat to stone so their captives could escape. At another point we saw turbulent riptides some distance off shore. These were caused, claimed Kanta, by the struggles of two daughters of a sultan who irritated their father so much by their bickering that he tied them together and tossed them into the sea. The riptides were the result of their continual conflict. I made mental notes of the stories, and told myself that someday I'd return to Sulu to research its rich oral literature.

After about thirty minutes we reached our destination. It was a village not greatly different from the one we had left, albeit somewhat smaller. Its houses with nipa-thatched roofs were built on piles and were scattered along the white sand beach that edged a half-moon bay. Tall palm trees stood behind the houses, their graceful fronds serving as umbrellas against the heat of the tropical sun. Beyond the village stretched the sea, with the mountains of Tawi-Tawi Island looming phantomlike in the distance.

Our entry into the village caused a minor commotion. People shouted to Abasa and Kanta, asking who I was. They replied that I was an American and had come to visit "Brook." We walked to the far side of the village and stopped before a walkway that led over the shallow beach waters to a house built on piles and surrounded by a large deck. The deck was covered with various potted plants, most of them bougainvillea with their profuse, brilliant colors adding riot to the unpainted boards and nipa of the house. As we approached the deck, a young woman came out and greeted Abasa and Kanta.

"This is my sister," said Abasa. He turned to the woman. "This American is living with the boat people. He's come to see Father. He might have medicine for him."

The young woman smiled warmly and we entered the house. Unlike most houses of Sulu, the interior was divided into rooms. The room we entered appeared to be the central living area. Attractive mats adorned the walls and fish nets hung from the rafters at one end. Typically, there was no furniture. Three small children, wearing no clothes, were interrupted from their play by our appearance. A teenaged boy and a woman in her midtwenties rose to greet us.

"This is my other sister and my younger brother," said Abasa. We smiled acknowledgments at one another. "How is Father?"

"He seems better today," said the older sister. "He has just finished eating."

"This American would like to see him," said Abasa.

The older sister motioned to a room off the living room. I followed Abasa into the room with the others. It was a small room with two large windows that opened onto the small bay. Colorful mats hung on the walls and covered the floors. Lying on mats and propped up with pillows was the old American.

I had no clear preconceptions of the man, but I did expect him to be somewhat misanthropic and not very happy with a visitor from a country he had abandoned some thirty years before. I was wrong.

"Come in," he said warmly in English. "Please sit down. I'm sorry we have no chairs."

"Father," said Abasa, "this is an American who is living with the boat people. We brought him to see you. He speaks Sama."

"You speak Sama," he said matter-of-factly. "That is good. We can converse in Sama. I'm afraid my English is rather rusty. I speak it so seldom. It's good of you to visit me. My name is William Brook."

He was a handsome man. His hair was thick and snow white. His years in the tropics had left their mark on his brown, leathery skin which accented the blueness of his bright eyes. He appeared to be of medium height, and his body was lean and strong. He wore only a sarong.

"I'm pleased to meet you," I said. I told him my name as I settled myself cross-legged on the floor. "I've heard about you ever since I came to Sulu."

"And what brings you to Sulu?" he asked.

"I'm an anthropologist," I said, and briefly explained the nature of my research. "I've been here over a year, but this is my first visit to these islands."

"They are beautiful, aren't they?" He smiled at me.

"Indeed they are. I never tire of the beauty of Sulu."

"Nor I. Otherwise I suppose I wouldn't have stayed here so long."

"And how long has that been?" I asked.

"I have been on Tandubas since 1938. I first came to Sulu in 1935. I worked in the customs office in Bongao for three years. That was in the days of American rule. Probably you were not born yet," he added with a twinkle in his eye.

"Just barely. What part of the States are you from?"

"Kansas—a small town in Kansas which may have disappeared by now," he said.

"Have you been back to the States since you first came to the Philippines?"

"Never," he said. "I used to think that someday I would go back for a visit. But now I know I never will. I'll die here with my family. There's nothing for me in America. Probably all the people I knew are dead by now. And I am happy here, so there is no reason for me to leave."

"I can see why you would be happy here."

"It is a good place," he said. "But like any place, it has its problems. Sometimes the people quarrel and fight about silly things. I still get impatient with them at times." His eyes wandered to the open window. "Sometimes I can hardly believe I have been here so long."

His daughter adjusted his pillows to make him more comfortable. He smiled at her and continued speaking. "I didn't intend to stay here when I arrived. I visited Tandubas several times when I was working in Bongao and decided that when my job ended in Bongao I would live here for a few months. I always liked the outer islands and thought it would be interesting to live the lives of these people for a while before I returned to the States."

"I've often thought the same," I said.

"I stayed with the family of Kanta when I arrived. I was lonely until I learned the language and made friends. Then I met the mother of these children. She was a lovely woman. We fell in love and were married. Before I knew it, I was the father of a family. And now, all these years later, I'm still on Tandubas. I never dreamed I would spend the rest of my life here." He paused to entertain private thoughts. "My greatest sadness is that my wife died about six months ago."

"I'm sorry to hear that," I said.

He smiled at me. "We had a good, long life together. And we have good children." He looked at them warmly. "So I have no complaints. I am a lucky man."

"You were never homesick for America?"

He thought for a moment. "No, I don't think so. Sometimes I used to wonder what happened to certain people and how things might have changed. But I don't think I was ever homesick. My family wasn't close, and my friends back there weren't important. You don't realize what a fine life I have here. And what beautiful children I have. Otherwise, you would understand."

Already I had begun to understand. I could sense the great love the children had for their father. Their concern for him was evident as they carefully adjusted his pillows and mats to make him more comfortable and as they respectfully listened to his every word.

"The only thing I still miss about the States," he said, "is Hershey's chocolate. I always loved Hershey's when I was young. But I haven't been able to get any here for years. I don't eat much candy anymore, but for some silly reason I'd like to have a Hershey's candy bar before I die. Do they still have Hershey's in America?"

"I think so," I said. "Some American candy bars are for sale in Bongao, but I don't think I've ever seen Hershey's."

"No, none are there," he said with a smile. "I've frequently asked."

"If I find some, I'll send them to you," I said.

"That would be kind of you," he said, "but they'd probably never reach me. Such things have a way of getting lost in transit in Sulu."

"Your son told me you are ill. What is your illness?"

"I'm afraid it's nothing but old age. My rheumatism gives me the most discomfort. Some days I am fine, but other days—like the past few days—I have trouble moving around. So I stay in bed and let my children and grandchildren wait on me. Did you see my grandchildren? They're peeking in the door behind you. They're shy when strangers come. They are my greatest joy. If you weren't here, they'd be in here with me. I can't imagine my life without the children."

I turned to look and caught a glimpse of three pairs of wide, dark eyes that immediately disappeared when they saw me turn. The adults laughed at the children's shyness.

"Do you have any medicine for your rheumatism?" I asked.

"No. We have no medicines here besides the native ones. Some of them are quite effective, but they don't seem to help my rheumatism."

"I have some aspirin," I said. "My grandfather had rheumatism, and aspirin was the only relief he could find. If you wish, I'll leave you the bottle of aspirin I have."

"That's very kind of you, but I don't want to deprive you of your medicine."

"I can get more in Bongao." I rummaged in my shoulder bag, pulled out a bottle of aspirin, and gave it to him. "If aspirin helps, you can order more from Bongao."

"Thank you," he said. "How many do you think I should take?"

I suggested he take two every four hours.

"Take some now, Father," suggested his younger daughter.

"Yes," he said. "I may as well try it." He took two tablets from the bottle and swallowed them with a sip of water from a glass handed to him by his daughter.

Our conversation drifted back to his life. From his wife's family, he acquired a parcel of land which he farmed with his own family. With the small amount of capital he accumulated from his job with the United States Government, he bought more land and invested in a small motor launch, which he and his brother-in-law operated among the eastern Tawi-Tawi Islands. They eventually bought several other launches. The business was now doing well in the hands of his sons and nephews. As he grew older, he became increasingly interested in farming. He told me of his garden located beyond the house and regretted he was not feeling well enough to show me the fruits of his agricultural efforts.

What impressed me most about the man was his happiness and contentment. He had found both on Tandubas without seeking them. Apparently he had never been unhappy in his homeland and had made no conscious decision to leave it and find his Shangri-la in Asia. It had simply worked out that way. And I suspect that had he returned to the little town in Kansas, he would have found equal happiness.

I liked Mr. Brook immensely. He radiated goodness. The warmth and generosity emanating from him were returned by those who received them. I liked him easily because he liked me, and I'm sure most people reacted to him in my way. There were dozens of questions I wanted to ask him, but I refrained from probing into his personal life.

After an hour or so of conversation, it was apparent he was growing tired. Glances from Abasa and Kanta indicated it was time for us to take our leave. I thanked him for his hospitality and told him of my pleasure in meeting him. He responded graciously and said he hoped I would visit him again if ever I were in these waters. I told him we would probably be returning to this area in a few days on our way home, and with his permission I would stop to see him. He said he hoped I would do so, and after a few more formalities we left and were soon retracing our steps down the seaside path.

True to their word, Masa and Biti were waiting for me in the waters fronting Kanta's house. I thanked Kanta and his family for their hospitality, told them goodbye, and helped to put up the sail to catch the breeze that would take us farther east to the fishing grounds we hoped to reach that afternoon. The breeze was a healthy one and we skimmed across the rippled sea. By late afternoon we reached our destination. Since the tides and currents would not be proper for fishing until morning, we anchored our boat off a small islet. While Masa and the boys dismantled the sail and put up the nipa roof under which we would sleep, Biti and I began dinner. I built a fire in the small hearth at the back of the boat while Biti selected some fish and cassava, the staples that had sustained me since arriving in Sulu. We ate to a setting sun that incarnadined our watery world. After dinner we sat on the open deck and watched the stars appear in the darkening sky. Finally, the activities of the long day took their toll and one by one we retired under the nipa roof to find a spot for sleep. I felt the gentle rock of the boat and heard the soft splash of the sea, and then I slept until a golden dawn awakened me.

We fished for three more days. Masa and Biti timed our arrivals at the various reefs expertly, and we began to run out of space for the fish that seemed to throw themselves into our nets. Our hold was full, and we were in high spirits from the success of the trip. At the end of the third day, Masa announced we should begin our trip back to Bongao the following morning. I asked if we would be passing near Tandubas on our way home. Masa replied that we would. I said I would like to stop for a brief visit with Mr. Brook, and the men agreed it could be arranged.

We lifted anchor before the sun was fully up the next morning in order to take advantage of the currents and wind. Under the expert navigation of my companions, we sped over the gentle surface of the sea. The wind continued through most of the morning and by early afternoon we reached the village of Mr. Brook. Masa and Biti deposited me at the beach with a long string of fish and I walked to the Brook house. Mr. Brook's elder daughter met me on the deck.

"I've come to see your father," I said, "And I brought you some fish."

She accepted the fish and said, "Father isn't here. Your medicine is very good. He felt so well today he went to his garden." She thanked me for the fish and dropped them in the shade of the house.

"Is the garden near?" I asked.

"Yes. Would you like to go there?"

I replied that I would. She called into the house, and we were joined by a boy of about twelve.

"This is my son. He'll take you to the garden. My father will be happy to see you."

I thanked her and returned with the boy to the beach. I told Masa and Biti that I was going to the garden and would be back within an hour. They agreed to wait. My young guide led me from the beach into the fields that lay beyond. The sun was hot, but fortunately the walk was short, and within ten minutes we were greeted by Mr. Brook. He was pulling weeds from a patch of cassava, wearing only a sarong and a native sun hat. He looked much better than when I last saw him. Two boys, about eight and ten, were helping him.

"You've come back," he said, as he walked toward me. He took my hand and shook it warmly. "How was your fishing trip?"

"Great," I said. "I left a share of our catch at your house."

"That's very kind of you," he said. "And again I want to thank you for the aspirin. It has done wonders in alleviating the pain of my rheumatism. I feel like a young man again." He laughed and pointed to a tree at the edge of the field. "Let's sit in the shade. The sun is fierce today." We walked to the tree and found places to sit among its roots. The boys joined us, happy for the excuse to quit work in the garden.

"This is where I like to spend part of my day," he said. "If I don't spend some time digging in the soil, the day doesn't seem complete."

"Perhaps it's your Kansas background coming out," I suggested.

"Maybe you're right," he laughed. "Gardening has become one of the chief pleasures of my old age. I grow a little bit of everything here. Would you like to see my crops?"

He obviously wanted to show them to me, so I expressed interest. We walked among the carefully tended plants. The garden probably covered about a half acre, and as Mr. Brook noted, it seemed to have a portion of almost everything that can be grown in Sulu. One end contained a big stand of cassava next to a healthy field of corn. Scattered throughout were tomatoes, squash, beans, peppers, eggplant, banana plants, papaya trees, and several vegetables I couldn't identify. It was meticulously tended. Weeds were virtually absent and the soil was carefully hoed. Weak plants were propped up and tied to stakes. Neat paths connected the various plots. Almost central to the garden, surrounded by bougainvillea, was a pile of white sand enclosed by a low stone wall, forming a rectangle about four by eight feet. Placed on the sand were small bowls containing flowers and bits of food. We stopped in front of it.

"This is the grave of my wife," said Mr. Brook. "When I die I will be buried next to her."

"It is a good place to be buried," I said, looking out over the sea that stretched beyond the village clustered at the base of the low rise we stood upon.

"Yes," agreed Mr. Brook. "My wife and I worked many years in this garden. She, too, loved it. We decided some time ago that we would be buried here."

"Are burials such as this typical in Tandubas?" I asked, knowing that in other parts of Sulu, communal cemeteries were common.

"No," said Mr. Brook. "Most people are buried in the cemetery near the village. My children didn't like the idea of burying their mother out here, but they knew it was her wish. They'll bury me here, too."

He picked some bougainvillea blossoms and placed them on the grave. Then he turned to me saying, "Come and see my tomatoes. I've never had such tomatoes."

He led me down a path past the grave to the edge of the garden, beyond which the forest began. He proudly showed me the robust tomato vines studded with large green tomatoes, some turning to shades of pink. My attention was attracted, however, to what appeared to be another grave behind the tomatoes at the garden's edge. A pile of white sand was covered with small flags made of green, yellow, and white cloth. Small white bowls containing tobacco, food and cigarettes were placed about the area.

"Is that another grave?" I asked.

He smiled. "No. Not in the usual sense. That is for the *saitan*. Do you believe in the *saitan*?"

"I don't disbelieve," I said, anthropologically. "My experiences with them have been rather limited. Do you believe in them?"

"Of course," he replied. "One cannot live very long in Sulu without believing in the *saitan*. They offer the best explanation for unknown things. Each day I leave offerings for the *saitan* in the garden. That's why my garden is always so successful."

"Are you a Muslim, also?" I asked, knowing that the community in which he lived was Muslim.

"No," he said after some thought. "I don't think I am. I go to the mosque with my family. But I have never cared much for Allah and the things he is said to do to people. He's too intolerant for my taste. Allah is from outside anyway. The *saitan* were in Sulu long before Allah came with Islam—although they were probably called something else then. The *saitan* are the true spirits of Sulu. They don't demand much except respect. And that seems to me the nature of life. It shouldn't be complicated with all the laws and regulations of Allah. The *saitan* are like Sulu—if you cooperate with them they are good; if you offend them, they are bad. Such, it seems to me, is the way of the world. Don't you agree?"

"I suppose so. I've never been much attracted to organized religion, either. Its laws always seemed so arbitrary."

"That's what I mean about Allah. It's different with the *saitan*. If you treat them kindly, they will do the same for you. We have so many *saitan* here—in the ground, in the trees, in the mountains, on the beach, in the sea, in the tomatoes, in the corn. It seems to me the longer I live, the more *saitan* I find. But they are essentially the same. Sometimes I think they're all simply one *saitan* that expresses itself in many ways. That's why I have only one altar in my garden. It's for all the *saitan*. I see them as all the same. I've always treated them well, and they've treated me well. The *saitan* only punish people who don't treat them with respect."

"What do they consider disrespect?" I asked.

He thought for a moment. "Three weeks ago some neighbor children were playing games at the edge of the garden. They didn't mean to be destructive, but during their play they trampled down some cassava plants. The next day two of them became ill. The *saitan* were angry at the children for destroying plants that were intended as food, so they made the children ill."

"Did they recover?"

"Oh, yes. The *saitan* were simply teaching them a lesson. I'm sure they'll be more careful where they play in the future."

He spotted a ripe tomato, plucked it from the vine, and handed it to me.

"Eat it," he said. "They're quite delicious."

I bit into the tomato, and as he promised, it was delicious. We wandered through the rest of the garden. The children followed, saying little, but attentive to our every word.

As much as I would have liked to stay longer with Mr. Brook, I finally had to take my leave. I knew that Masa and Biti were eager to continue their journey home, and I did not want to delay them any longer.

"I must go," I said. "My friends are waiting for me."

"So soon? I'd hoped you would be able to stay overnight."

I explained we had a hold full of fish and my friends were anxious to return to Bongao.

"Come," he said. "I want to give you something."

I followed him to the tree where we had rested in the shade. At the base were several baskets filled with garden produce. He selected the largest basket and handed it to me.

"This is for you and your friends. Some produce from my garden."

I thanked him, and after a few more words we shook hands warmly.

"I hope you'll visit me again," he said.

"I'd like to very much," I said, "but it will probably be some time before I'm in this area again."

"Whenever you are, you're welcome to stay at my house."

I thanked him and, with my young guide, returned to the village. I stopped to say goodbye to Mr. Brook's daughter and then rejoined Masa and Biti in their boat. Winds and currents were still in our favor, so we set sail immediately. We sailed into the night, anchored off a small island to sleep, and sailed all the following day. By evening we reached Bongao.

The next few months passed rapidly as I approached the end of my stay in Sulu. Days blended together, becoming indistinguishable from one another until they were weeks, and then months. My research had its ups and downs, but the enchantment of Sulu never left me. Frequently, I had to remind myself that another world existed beyond Sulu, one to which I would soon return. And when I was reminded of that other world, I savored my days in Sulu more. I experienced some of the most carefree days of my life. I had no time tables, no deadlines. I worked when the spirit moved me, but not until. I occasionally traveled in my small boat to some of the remote, uninhabited islands of the area to spend several days in solitude, wandering the lovely, lonely beaches, absorbing the heat of the seductive sun and the cool darkness of the warm nights. I walked reefs at low tide to explore the endless array of brilliantly colored life in the tidal pools. I climbed to the mountaintops of some of the high islands to gaze across the Sulu Sea at the ghostlike summits of Borneo. Some days I thought I would never be able to leave Sulu, and I envied Mr. Brook for the happy life he had found here. But on other days, I realized my enjoyment of Sulu was partly based on the realization that I would soon be leaving. If I knew I would never leave, I would not have devoured its visual delights and sensual offerings as I did.

Finally, my last month in Sulu began. My research was completed, but I had purposefully left one month to tie up various loose ends. Among them was a final visit to Mr. Brook.

I planned to return to Sulu as soon as possible, but I didn't know when that would be. And since Mr. Brook was an old man, it was quite possible he would not be alive when I returned. As I began to think of a suitable gift I might take him, I remembered his desire for Hershey's bars. I asked a friend in Bongao who regularly smuggled goods from Borneo to the Philippines if he would look for some Hershey's bars during his next run. I'd never seen them for sale among the contraband in Bongao, but that didn't necessarily mean they were unavailable in Borneo. Much to my delight, he returned from a run three weeks before I was scheduled to depart with six somewhat crumpled Hershey's bars. They would be the perfect gift for Mr. Brook. Early the following morning, I boarded a motorized launch for the eastern Tawi-Tawi Islands. One of its stops was Tandubas.

It took us two days to reach Tandubas. The little launch stopped at practically every village along the way. The crew consisted of twin brothers who spent most of their time wiring together the ancient engine. The passengers we picked up and deposited were local people en route to visit relatives, usually accompanied by a few chickens, a string of fish, and baskets of produce. We anchored overnight off a small island within sight of Tandubas, and after a simple breakfast of bread, coffee and fruit, we chugged on to Tandubas.

It was about nine when we arrived at the village where Mr. Brook lived. It was a clear day, clean and sparkling after the showers of the night before. I jumped from the launch as it anchored at the little wharf. I planned to stay overnight and then rejoin the launch when it returned the following afternoon on its way back to Bongao. Smiles acknowledged my return to the village. As I approached Mr. Brook's house, I shouted greetings to his two daughters who were pounding rice on the deck. They smiled back at me.

I crossed the walkway to the deck and said, "I've come to see your father. How is he feeling?"

The younger daughter burst into tears and held a scarf to her eyes.

Tears came to the older daughter's eyes as she said, "Our father is dead. He died several hours after you left."

I was stunned and momentarily could say nothing. "I'm so sorry," I finally said. "I didn't know. What happened?"

"He was working in the garden with the children. He fell over. The children came to the house, but by the time we got there he was dead."

"I'm so sorry," I repeated. "Your father was a very good man. I was very fond of him."

"Everyone loved him," said the daughter softly. "We all miss him so much." She, too, began sobbing into a scarf she held to her face.

I felt awkward and tongue-tied in the presence of their grief. Finally the older daughter regained her composure and asked, "Would you like to see his grave?"

I replied that I would. The two sisters walked with me down the same path I had walked to visit Mr. Brook in his garden. We walked in silence among the sounds of the sea and the surrounding fields and forests. They led me through the garden. At the center, next to the grave of Mr. Brook's wife, was a new pile of glistening white sand, enclosed by a low stone wall and covered with small, white bowls containing offerings of food and flowers.

"He wanted to be buried next to our mother," explained the younger daughter. "This was their favorite spot."

"Yes, he told me so," I said. "I'm sure they are happy here."

We stood for several moments in silence. The elder daughter spoke. "If you'd like to stay here, you may. We must return to the house. We're expecting our brother's family this afternoon and must prepare for them. We hope you'll stay with us for a while. Can you find your way back?"

"Yes, I can. Thank you. I'd like to stay for a few minutes."

They walked through the garden and disappeared down

the path. I sat on the low wall of Mr. Brook's grave and thought of the kindly old man I'd known so briefly. Few people have attracted me so immediately and so deeply as did Mr. Brook. Sad as I was at his death, I wasn't grieved by it. He had found his niche in life on this little island miles and millennia from his native land, and I was sure he had found a comparable niche in death.

I sat at the grave for almost an hour, thinking of Mr. Brook as I became absorbed into the expanse of sea and sky that cradled the island. When I stood up to leave, I remembered the Hershey's. I took the package from my shoulder bag, and I placed the candy bars, one by one, atop his grave. I walked back to the village and felt happy to have shared a few brief moments of life with Mr. Brook.

15

Amak

Depending upon whom you asked, Amak was a pirate, a patriot, a smuggler, a philanthropist, a revolutionary, a *hadji*, or a murderer. To me he was a good friend.

I was traveling with a Tausug crew from Ungus Matata to Bongao in a rickety old launch that shook its way through the limpid waters of a hot, sultry morning. We attempted a shortcut through a reef, a risky maneuver since the tide was out. As the boat shuddered through the shallow waters, we suddenly heard the crunch of wood upon coral. Without a word spoken we all knew we were grounded. We manned poles in an attempt to dislodge the keel, but it wouldn't budge. Finally, we gave up, turned off the exhausted motor, and resigned ourselves to waiting until the tide returned some hours later.

I spoke no Tausug and the crew spoke no English so most of my communication with them consisted of gestures. Using such, I indicated that I would like to explore the nearby island, about half a mile across the reef. My companions let it be known that it was out of the question and kept repeating "Amak," a word I didn't know.

I didn't give up the idea of going to the island, a fairly sizeable one with a small village set on piles along its white beach, but until my companions changed their minds, I decided to catch up on my journal. I soon became lost in my writing while the others found comfortable spots on the deck to sleep.

I wasn't aware of the three men approaching the launch until they were upon us. They had walked across the exposed reef from the village, and all wore sarongs and wide smiles when I looked up at them.

"Are you an American?" the oldest of them asked in English.

"Yes, I am," I answered, somewhat surprised. I hadn't spoken English in over a month. It felt strange upon my tongue.

"I'm Lamir. These are my sons."

I told him my name and about our problem with the reef. By now my companions were awake and looking at our visitors with a good deal of suspicion.

"What island is this?" I asked.

Lamir told me about the island. It was named Secubun. The inhabitants were farmers who fished the reef and raised a little copra for cash. He then asked about my research, and after a few other questions about me, he and his sons left. When they were out of hearing, my companions began talking excitedly, with the word "Amak" recurring in their discussion. They tried to convey their excitement, but it was hopeless. All I understood was that someone named Amak lived on the island and he was to be feared. Privately, I thought it strange that Lamir hadn't invited me to the village since Sulu people are usually very hospitable. Perhaps this island was a deviation from that tradition, I thought as I returned to my journal.

Some twenty minutes later, I again saw three figures approaching the launch from the village. As the men neared us, I could see they were the same three who visited us earlier.

"My friend," said Lamir, "I'd like to invite you to our village for dinner. You can eat and relax until the tide returns and then be on your way."

"I appreciate that very much," I said. "Are my companions invited too?"

He spoke to them in Tausug and from their response I could see they were declining his invitation. He spoke more earnestly and still they declined.

"They say they cannot leave their boat."

I thought a moment. There seemed no reason why I shouldn't accept, so I did. As I made movements to leave the boat, the Tausug men expressed concern. They spoke to Lamir and he responded, telling them I was going ashore. They changed their minds and made preparations to leave also.

We walked over the bare reef under the hot sun. Conversation was minimal as we threaded our way around the tidal pools. As we approached the village, we were met by what appeared to be the entire population. They all smiled and shouted "Melikan!" at me. They crowded tightly around me, most of them simply staring, but the more curious reached out to touch my skin, run their fingers over the hair on my arms, or to tug lightly at my beard. I felt uncomfortably like a specimen from outer space, but tried to keep a friendly smile. A child was pulling at the hair on my leg while another was exploring my crotch when a loud voice shouted something that quickly dispersed the curious crowd. I looked up to the house from which the voice had come.

Standing on the deck was a man who was probably not as tall as he looked from my vantage, but even at that, was tall for a Sama. He wore only *sahwal*, the loose trousers common in southern Sulu, of brilliant cerise and a multicolored cloth tied around his head. He was powerfully built with strong arms and a full chest, but his most commanding feature was his face. It was demanding, rather than handsome, with a strength that flowed from his muscular body. He glanced at me briefly with fierce eyes and then went into the house.

"We'll go this way," said Lamir, as he directed me to the house where I'd seen the man.

I followed him up the ladder to the deck, and then into the spacious interior. The floor was covered with brightly colored mats; colorful buntings hung on the walls. Several windows provided ample light and air. Propped on multicolored pillows in the far corner of the room was the man who had briefly appeared on the deck. He was even more striking among the colors of the room. He looked at me angrily through heavy eyebrows.

"This is my brother Amak," said Lamir. "And this is the American."

"Come and sit down," said Amak. "Your companions, too."

I sat on the mat near Amak while the others sat some distance away. Villagers gathered on the deck to peer in the open windows and door.

"Where did you learn English?" I asked as an opener.

"From an American teacher here in Sulu before the war." He said something I could not understand to three women sitting on the other side of the room. They immediately left and Amak became silent.

"Is this your home island?" I asked, thinking of nothing else to say and becoming uncomfortable in the silence.

"Yes. I was born here." He again fell into silence, looking at me intently. Then he said, "Have you heard of me?"

"I'm afraid I haven't," I said. "Should I know you?"

He ignored my question and asked, "Do you like our food?"

"I like what I've tasted, but I haven't eaten much. I've been eating Bajau food."

"If you can eat their food, you'll certainly like ours. My wife is preparing a dinner for you."

By now the room was filled with people of all ages crowding in to look at me, but keeping their distance as if afraid to approach Amak too closely. Some whispered among themselves, but most listened intently to our conversation although I doubt if many of them understood English.

"They're very curious," said Amak, nodding toward the crowd. "There hasn't been an American on this island since the war when your soldiers drove out the Japanese. Most of the young people have never seen an American."

"How long were the Americans here?" I asked.

"Only a few days. The Japanese garrison was small and it didn't take long to destroy it. But the Americans were very generous during their stay and the people remember it."

I thought of the ramifications of all the chocolate bars and cigarettes that GIs passed out around the world. "Where were you during the war?" I asked.

"I was young," he said, "but old enough to fight. I fought with the guerrillas in Mindanao and Jolo. Some of my companions were Americans. I came to respect the men of your country. You are a brave people."

I always feel uncomfortable with most generalizations about a people, whether they be complimentary or derogatory. "Some of them are; some of them aren't," I said. "You were fortunate to meet some of the better ones. Believe me there are plenty of Americans who are neither brave nor respectable."

"Every country has its good and bad people. I'm sure yours is no exception. But I have good memories of the people I knew from your country. And we in Sulu have reason to dislike your people," he continued. "You, too, were once conquerors. But you finally left us alone."

"Mostly because we realized there wasn't the wealth here we thought there was."

"Whatever the reason, you left. But now we must fight again to be free of foreigners."

"What foreigners?" I asked.

"The Christian government that dictates to us from Manila. They're worse than the Americans. At least the Americans didn't move Christians on our land."

"What kind of work do you do?" I asked, attempting to move away from politics.

"I'm a businessman."

"What kind of business?"

"All kinds."

This was getting nowhere. Fortunately at about that time, the food began to arrive. And it continued to arrive until I was surrounded by plates and bowls.

"What a feast," I said. "Surely this is not all for me."

"It's for you to eat as you will. We'll eat what is left. Your friends will join you." He spoke to my companions in Tausug and handed a plate to me.

"Eat," he said to me.

I took small portions from each dish, but before I sampled even half of them, my plate was full. The crowd watched my every move, and eagerly awaited my reaction to my first bite. Fortunately, it was delicious and I could honestly respond with enthusiasm. Not all the food was equally tasty, but I cleaned my plate and sampled the remaining dishes. Finally, I could eat no more and told Amak so. He said something to the women and they collected the dishes and took them outside to the kitchen. Steaming sweet coffee was brought in and we sprawled on the mats and pillows like two potentates as the women served us.

"Please tell your wife and the others who helped prepare the food that it was delicious, and I am very grateful for it," I said to Amak, who conveyed my message to them. They smiled and nodded to me.

I stayed for another hour or so. We talked mostly of local events. He was well informed and expressed curiosity about my research. He obviously had no great interest in what I was doing, but thought it all right. As did most Sulu people, he regarded the Bajau as rather harmless dregs, and if I wanted to live with such people that was my business. He avoided speaking of himself. Whenever I raised personal questions, he dodged them, so I soon ceased to do so. The afternoon passed quickly, and I was surprised when my companions said the tide was high enough for us to continue on our way.

We prepared to leave and I again thanked Amak and his family for the dinner and their hospitality. He sent two young men to accompany us to our launch, which now required boats to reach. When we got to the launch, it was floating, and before long we were once again chugging our way toward Bongao.

Several days later I spotted Father Raquet's white cassock in the Bongao marketplace. He was having a great time bargaining with an old woman who was trying to overcharge him for a bunch of bananas. After he finished the transaction, I walked up to him and said, "I thought you were still in Manila. When did you get back?"

"Hello! I didn't see you. Look at the lovely bunch of bananas I got for only twenty centavos." He held up the bunch for me to see. "I got back yesterday. The conference was awful. A bunch of theoreticians totally out of touch with the reality of the Philippines. Besides Manila was getting to me. You know how I feel about Manila. After a week away from Sulu, I begin to get homesick. So how are you?"

"I'm fine. You look great this morning."

"Ah, who wouldn't on such a morning?" He held his arms up to the blue sky. "Can you believe that some people think Sulu is a hardship mission? My relatives back home still write sympathetic letters to me about my hardships here. Little do they know that I live in one of the loveliest spots on earth. But let's keep it to ourselves," he said, with a twinkle in his eyes. "We don't want the rest of the world down here."

"Scout's honor," I laughed.

"I'm glad I ran into you. I was going to call on you or send a note around. A friend in Manila gave me a bottle of wine that looks very promising. You're the only other person in town who might appreciate it, so if you've nothing better to do, come around for dinner tomorrow night and we'll open it. I'll even do the cooking. I don't want Tia's cooking to ruin the wine."

Tia was the ancient cook who had been with him for years. Her bizarre and sometimes disastrous dishes were a joke between us. After many years together, he hadn't been able to convince her that fried eggs are best served hot off the stove, not after an hour of refrigeration.

"How can I refuse such an invitation? What time?"

"Eight. I must run now. I've got a desk full of paperwork to catch up on. See you then."

"Can I bring anything?" I asked the small, retreating figure.

"Only yourself," he shouted through the crowd.

The following evening, I walked to the *convento*. It was a soft, cool evening. Stars were beginning to brighten the dark sky, but a rising full moon promised to absorb many of them. Father Raquet responded to my knock and invited me into his sparsely furnished living room.

"We're eating in style tonight," he said, as he directed me to the screened-in balcony off the living room. "Tell me this is not class!"

The table on the balcony was set for two. Candles, usually reserved for blackouts when his generator failed, provided light which softened the crude tableware of the *convento*.

"Bongao has never seen the like," I said.

"Let's sit immediately. Things are finishing up sooner than I expected. It's been a long time since I've cooked. First, the wine."

He opened the bottle, a California chardonnay, as he told me of the friend who gave it to him. He poured some in my glass and said, "Tell me how it is."

I tasted the wine, and said honestly, "It's lovely. You have a good friend."

He finished filling my glass and then filled his own. "Ah, yes. It is nice," he said after sampling his.

We enjoyed the wine as the full moon made its appearance in the sea beyond the balcony. He served the dinner and we yielded to our appetites for the next half hour. It was a tasty meal of baked fish, rice pilaf, green beans, and a delicious flan for dessert.

"Tia is probably angry because I took over the kitchen tonight," he said as he finished his flan. "But that's too bad. I've subjected my stomach to enough of her disasters to warrant occasional freedom in the kitchen."

"You should do it more often," I said. "That was delicious."

"Have some more wine." He refilled our glasses.

"How long has Tia been with you?" I asked.

"Since creation," he laughed. "Almost as long as I've been in Sulu."

"And how long is that?"

"Let me think," he said thoughtfully. "The years have gone by so quickly. Especially these last ones. I came in 1934. You figure it out."

"A long time," I mused. "You've seen a lot of people and events come and go."

"Yes, indeed. The characters I've met here would fill a book. Several books."

"Speaking of characters," I said. "I met one the other day you may know." I told him of my encounter with Amak.

"You met Amak?" He said, surprised. "He's one of the most wanted men in Sulu—if not the entire Philippines."

"Who wants him?" I asked.

"The Philippine Constabulary, among others," he replied. "He's a pirate, smuggler, kidnapper, murderer—so they say. But he's also one of the most generous men I've ever known."

"You know him?"

"I've known Amak and his family for years. You've met one of the legends of Sulu. Let me tell you about him."

Father Raquet refilled our wine glasses and settled back in his chair. "I knew Amak as a child before the war. As you know his family is from Secubun, but he used to come to Bongao to a school staffed by the American government. He came to my attention because he was such a good student. His teachers always raved about him. I was imprisoned in Manila during the war, but when I came back after the liberation, I learned that Amak had been with the guerrillas in Mindanao. He apparently gained a liking for the restless life because he soon became involved in smuggling between here and Borneo. Everyone was smuggling in those years so it was no big deal. But when the Philippine government decided to crack down on it, it became a big deal, and Amak was one of the chief offenders. When smuggling became too dangerous, he and his men, mostly relatives, resorted to piracy. The Philippine Constabulary claims he's killed more than two dozen men, and he probably *has* killed some of them. His exploits have become legend. He couldn't possibly do all the things attributed to him, but he makes a good scapegoat when the P.C. can't find their man. They've been trying to catch him for years, but he always manages to elude them."

"You said Amak is a generous man. How so?"

"Amak supported my school for years. I don't think we would have made it through the early years without his help. He's a strong believer in education—he feels that one reason Sulu's been subjected to outside domination is because of the lack of education and sophistication of its people. Some years ago he realized our order is not after souls—pity us if we were! Muslims aren't the converting kind! We're interested in educating people so they can compete in the larger world. He has no respect for the schools the Philippine government has established in Sulu—if you've visited them, you know why—but admires what we're trying to do. In the early years, I never questioned the money he gave me. I knew it was from smuggling, but everyone was smuggling in those years. It was almost legal! However, after the stories began to circulate about his pirate activities and murders, and when the government began to crack down on smuggling, I decided I couldn't accept his money with a clear conscience. It wasn't easy to turn him down, partly because I genuinely do like Amak, despite his infamy, and partly because we really needed the money."

He stopped to look into his wine glass. "He told me he understood my position and respected my feelings. Then I began to receive large donations from his family. I knew the money was coming from Amak, but what could I do? They claimed it was their gift to the school. So I used the money for scholarships for students who could not otherwise afford to attend. The money is going back to the people and it salves my conscience."

"Why has the P.C. never caught him?" I asked.

"Because everyone protects him. He's a great hero among the local people. He's very generous to them. He never bothers Sulu people, but God protect any outside vessel that comes into these waters. The locals see nothing wrong with his smuggling. As you know, many people smuggle in Sulu. They've traded with Borneo and Indonesia for centuries, and aren't about to stop simply because artificial international boundaries have been drawn across their routes. A successful smuggler here is comparable to a successful businessman back home. His battles with the P.C. have made him a hero, too. As you surely know by now, the P.C. are considered oppressors here, rather than protectors—and with some justification."

"He sounds like a real character," I said.

"And to top it off, he's a *hadji*! He made the holy pilgrimage to Mecca. He visited me when he came back and told me he was very disappointed in what he saw. He expected Mecca to be sacrosanct, I think. He's never used the title and never wears the white turban."

"Too bad I didn't know all this when I met him. I wonder why he invited me to his village."

"He genuinely likes Americans. He saw the best side of us during the war. Also, he probably wanted someone to talk to. He's a bright man with a curious mind. Before he became an outlaw, he used to visit me often. At that time, he was interested in theology. I fear, though, he is a godless man. He cannot accept the Muslim or the Christian god."

"I wonder if I'll ever see him again," I mused.

"Very unlikely," said Father Raquet. "He's seldom seen anymore."

Our conversation drifted to other topics as we lingered over the final drops of wine and watched the moon climb higher into the sky.

About two weeks after my dinner with Father Raquet, I began working on a paper I'd promised an anthropological journal. I had thought the paper through and knew exactly what I wanted to say, but I was having trouble finding time to write it. When I write, I need blocks of uninterrupted time, and these were not forthcoming in Bongao. Each time I got into a thought, someone knocked on the door or something outside caught my attention. After several frustrating days, I decided to pack up my boat and go to the uninhabited island I sometimes sought for solitude. I arrived at midmorning and unloaded my typewriter and provisions into the small fisherman's hut that stands on the islet. I arranged a comfortable place for typing and began pounding away. Ideas flowed smoothly onto the paper, and before I knew it, the sun was far into the west. I closed the typewriter, stood up to stretch my tired back, and decided to walk down to the beach. I was pleased with the progress I had made that day and thought of what I would write next as I watched birds find sleeping places in the palms above me.

The far-off sound of a motor caught my ear, and I looked across the darkening sea for its source. Soon a black vessel became visible. A streamlined version of the local launches, it was thrust rapidly through the water by powerful engines. As it reached the reef, the engines were silenced and it drifted toward the shallow waters of the island. Two men with automatic rifles slipped over the side and waded toward me. Immediately, I recognized one of them as Amak. The other one carried a large bundle over his shoulder.

"Hello, American," said Amak. "We meet again."

"Hello," I said. "It's good to see you again," not really sure it was.

"Are you here alone?" he asked.

"Yes," I said. "All by myself."

"The boat people tell me you have medicines?" he stated as well as asked.

"I have some. Nothing too valuable."

"I have a wound that has become infected. Maybe your medicine will help."

"I have some penicillin capsules and ointment. They might help."

"Is anyone coming to stay with you?"

"I'm not expecting anyone," I said, wondering if it were the wise thing to admit.

"I need a place to stay for several days until my arm heals. I'd like to stay here."

Since I was squatting on the island, I was in no position to refuse his request. "Be my guest," I said. "I'm doing some typing, but otherwise I won't disturb you. I came here to have some solitude for writing."

"I won't bother you." He spoke to his companion who then carried the bundle to the little house, left it inside, and returned to Amak. After a few comments to Amak, he waded back to the boat where other men helped him aboard. They started the engines and disappeared into the darkness.

"The food in the bag should be plenty for both of us," said Amak. "Have you eaten yet?"

"No. I was just thinking of doing so before you arrived."

"Maybe we can try your medicine first," he suggested. "My arm is very painful."

"How did you injure it?" I asked.

"Maybe you'd better not know," he replied. "Do you know more about me than when I first saw you?"

"Yes," I admitted. "I talked to Father Raquet."

"A good man, Father Raquet. Then it's best we don't talk about me. It's for your own good. I had an accident."

"Let's go in the house. I have a lantern."

We went inside, and I lit the lantern as Amak placed his gun on the floor. I examined his wound, a severe slash in the bicep that needed much more medical expertise than I could provide. In spite of the clean bandage and the attempts at dressing it, it was badly infected.

"That really needs the attention of a doctor," I said.

"It's too dangerous for me to try to see the doctor in Bongao. Do you have anything that might stop the pain?"

"I only have aspirin."

"Anything," he said. However he may have received the wound, I felt sorry for the man. He was obviously in great pain. I found the aspirin and shook out two tablets for him. He swallowed them before I could get a glass of water.

"The wound probably should be stitched together," I said.

"Can you do it?"

"I wouldn't know where to begin," I said.

"Will you try?" he asked. "What do you need?"

"Needle and thread, I suppose. It will probably be terribly painful."

"A little more pain won't bother me."

"Maybe I can just clean it out and tape it together. If you remain inactive, it will probably heal. The important thing is to get rid of the infection."

I gave him a couple of penicillin tablets, after he assured me he had taken them before with no side effects. Then I heated water and cleaned the wound as best I could. I cleaned it a second time with alcohol which brought grimaces from Amak. I dressed a gauze bandage with penicillin ointment and then secured it firmly in place, closing the gaping wound.

"I can think of nothing else to do," I said, when I put on the last strip of tape. "You shouldn't use your arm at all. I'll make a sling for it. How do you feel?"

"Let me rest a minute." He lay back on the mat, cradling his gun, and closed his eyes. "I'm grateful for what you have done."

"Let's see if it works first," I suggested.

"It doesn't matter. You've done the best you can."

"Does it still hurt?"

"It hurts, but not like before. I feel sleepy."

I put away the medical paraphernalia, and when I glanced at Amak again, he was sleeping soundly. It looked as if he was out for the night, so I found something to eat and then lay down beside him. I woke up once during the night and heard his quiet breathing. When I awakened again it was dawn, and the space beside me was empty. I looked up and saw Amak sitting in the doorway with his gun. He saw me and smiled, the first time I'd seen him smile.

"I missed dinner last night," he said.

"You did. How do you feel?"

"Better. Much rested and in less pain."

"You should have some more penicillin." I found the tablets and handed them to him with a glass of water. "Try some more aspirin." I gave him the tablets.

I rummaged through the supplies he brought and combined some ingredients with the ones I had, and made a palatable breakfast. When we finished, he said, "You have work to do. I won't bother you." He walked down to the beach with his gun and sat on a fallen log and looked out to sea.

I went to my typewriter and after a few bad starts was able to regain the thread of my thoughts from the previous day. While I typed, Amak returned to the house and went to his mat where he soon fell asleep cradling his gun like a child. After about three hours of writing, my reserves were exhausted, and I decided to call it a day. I put my finished papers away and returned the typewriter to its case. The snap of the lock awakened Amak and he sat up abruptly with his gun drawn and a cry of pain as he turned his arm.

"I'm sorry," I said. "I should have been quieter."

He rubbed sleep from his eyes and mumbled something I couldn't understand.

"Are you hungry?" I asked.

"Yes," he said. "Let me prepare the food."

"Sit still," I said. "It's time for more penicillin." I gave him two more tablets which he obediently swallowed. I fixed lunch and we ate the tinned affair in silence. Following the meal, I suggested we sit on the beach where it would be cooler. For the first time since arriving, he set his gun aside in the corner of the room.

"My arm seems less painful," he said, as he settled onto a fallen log on the beach.

"Let's hope it's healing," I said, as I sat against a tree trunk. "How long will you stay here?"

"My launch will be back in three days. I hope I'm not disturbing you too much."

"As long as I have time to write, I enjoy the company," I said. "Where will you go from here?"

"It's best you not know," he said.

"Do you have children?" I asked, trying to change the subject to something harmless.

"I have ten children," he replied with a smile of obvious pride.

"Ten children! Your poor wife!"

"I have three wives. Another reason why the Christians think I'm a savage."

"Do they all live at Secubun?" I asked.

"Only one, my first wife. One lives in Sabah, and another lives at Sulawesi. Those are the places I visit regularly. Four of my children are at Secubun, three at Sabah, and three at Sulawesi."

"Seems a convenient arrangement," I mused.

"If I were a Christian, I would have only one wife whom I couldn't divorce. Then I would have mistresses and illegitimate children to whom I owed no responsibility. As a Muslim, I'm bound to care for all the women I marry and for all my children. But yet the Christians call us savages."

"Not all Christians call you that," I said.

"The ones in the Philippines do."

"Father Raquet wouldn't agree."

"He's not like the Christians."

"Why do you dislike Christians so much?"

"Why should I like them? I'm talking about Filipino Christians who live in Sulu, especially the military. They interfere with our trade; they try to move settlers onto our land; they decide upon laws for us to live by; they think we're pagans; they take the fish from our waters. Why should I like them? The Christians should stay in their islands and leave Sulu to us."

"But don't blame *all* Christian Filipinos," I continued. "Most of them want no more than the Muslims do—a decent life. Don't hold them responsible for their government's decisions. People are often the puppets of their governments."

"True, but sometimes people have to be hurt in order to

destroy the governments they blindly follow. That's what must be done to the Christians in Sulu until we Muslims are allowed to again rule ourselves."

As with most political arguments, this was getting nowhere, so I changed the subject. I asked him about his activities during World War II, and he reminisced about his wartime experiences. We spent the rest of the afternoon in conversation. It became increasingly obvious to me that he had come to the island because he needed a place to hide while his wound healed. I guessed he was being pursued by the P.C., didn't feel safe in his customary hiding places, and wasn't up to the rigors of a trip out of the Philippines and a possible encounter with the P.C. Thus, he'd chosen me, my island, and my medicine. He couldn't have picked a better hideout. The local people knew I occasionally came to the island and they never bothered me. It had no resources to interest anyone and so was bypassed by strangers in the area. I discovered some time ago it was the perfect hideaway, and apparently Amak had come to the same conclusion.

I cooked a big meal that evening and we ate heartily. Amak's appetite had returned and he seemed much better. I continued to administer penicillin and occasional aspirin and he said the pain in his arm was gone. His gun remained in the corner of the house, and he didn't pick it up again until he left the island. After dinner we returned to the beach, which had become our favorite spot, and watched the tide come in with the setting sun as a backdrop. After a bit of conversation, but mostly silence, we decided to retire. I slept soundly and when I awakened at dawn, Amak was preparing breakfast. He handed me a cup of coffee and I drank it silently as the sleep cleared from my head.

"Did you sleep well?" I asked him.

"Yes," he said. "My arm feels much better. Will you change the bandage today?"

"Later this afternoon. It still looks intact."

We ate the breakfast and lingered over coffee.

"I'll leave so you can write," he said, standing up. "Do you have some books I could read?"

I handed him a couple of news magazines, a book of short stories, and a collection of anthropological essays.

"How about the things you write? Do you have any of them?"

"They're not very exciting. I have a couple of reprints of articles I wrote about the Bajau." I rummaged in my bag and found the crumpled articles. I handed them to him and he walked down to the beach.

I set up my typewriter and was soon immersed in the article. It was going well and I would be able to finish the first draft the following day. I planned to stay another day or so for rewriting, and then return to Bongao. It was early afternoon when I decided to quit for the day. I put away my materials and walked to the door. Amak was still sitting at the beach reading the material he'd borrowed from me. I walked down and sat next to him.

"What are you reading?" I asked.

"About the United Nations," he said, holding up a news magazine. "Sometimes I forget that so many things are happening in the rest of the world. I wish I were a better reader so I could understand more of what I read."

"Practice does it," I said. "The more you read the better you read."

"I tried to read your articles about the boat people," he said. "I didn't find them very interesting."

I laughed. "They're written for other anthropologists. Most people would agree with you."

"When I read magazines like this, I think of all the places to see in the world. Some day I'd like to travel to some of those places, but I probably never will."

"Father Raquet told me you traveled to Mecca. Did you enjoy that trip?"

"I enjoyed seeing the places along the way, but I didn't like Mecca."

"Why?"

He thought for a moment and then responded, "Too many hypocrites. Everyone is trying to take advantage of the poor pilgrims who go there. They lie about the things they sell you and try to cheat you everywhere you turn. It's too bad the prophet's sacred birthplace has become a den of thieves. It's as if the *hajj* were invented to provide a good income for the people of Mecca."

"Were you impressed by the ceremonies in the great mosque?"

"No," he said without hesitation. "We were herded through like goats. I became very disappointed in my religion when I went to Mecca. I thought it would be an experience that would make me a better Muslim and make me closer to Allah. But it was the opposite."

"Do you still believe in Allah?" I asked.

He thought for some time. "I suppose I do," he finally said. "Someone must be responsible for the world. But I believe more in the spirits of Sulu, the *saitan*. They're more important to us here in Sulu than is Allah. I think the people of Sulu are much more religious than the people of Mecca even though they tell us our Islam has too many superstitions and we're still pagans. But they don't understand. We must worship the *saitan*. They influence every aspect of our lives. Do you believe in the *saitan*?"

"I believe they're very real to the people of Sulu."

"That means you don't believe in them yourself," he said.

"I have my own spirits to contend with back home. I don't want to become involved with the Sulu spirits."

He laughed. "I can understand that. If your spirits are as tricky as ours then you have plenty to keep you busy. People should be allowed to worship in peace. That's something the Christians haven't learned yet."

"Muslims have done their bit of missionizing, too," I reminded him.

"I know," he said, "but I don't approve of it. Missionaries have come here from the Middle East to reform our religion. I don't think that's right. All people need some kind of religion. And if they have one that helps them through their lives, why try to change it? I don't believe all the things my people do, but their beliefs help them through the troubles of their lives."

"Father Raquet is a missionary," I said.

"But not a religious missionary. Maybe his order is, but he isn't. Did you know he even teaches classes about Islam? Father Raquet is the finest man I know. He doesn't know it, but he's a Muslim, not a Christian."

He laughed at his joke and our conversation drifted to his wound. He was eager to have the bandage changed, so we returned to the house and I boiled water to clean it. I carefully removed the tape to avoid the pain of tearing it from his skin, but more important, to avoid reopening the wound. Finally it was loosened, and I removed the bandage. The redness was almost gone and it was obviously beginning to heal.

"It looks good," I said.

"Yes, it's beginning to heal. You're a fine doctor."

It looked as if the infection was gone. I cleaned the wound with warm water and alcohol, dressed it with more penicillin ointment, and wrapped it with a clean bandage. When I finished, Amak lay back on his mat to rest.

"How can I repay you?" he asked.

"You owe me nothing," I said.

"I do," he insisted. "You don't know how important this is for me. What can I give you?"

"I've received so many favors from the people of Sulu, I couldn't begin to repay them. Doing small things like this is a way I can try. You owe me nothing."

"I understand," he said. "You are a good man."

The next day we again awakened at dawn, and after a leisurely breakfast I worked on my article. By noon I'd finished the first draft and sat back with a sigh of relief.

"You've finished?" asked Amak, looking up from his magazine.

"Almost," I said. "I have some rewriting to do, but the big job is out of the way."

"When will you go back to Bongao?"

"Probably the day after tomorrow."

"My boat will come tonight. I'll leave you in peace again."

"I'll miss you," I said. "I've enjoyed our conversations."

"And I," he said. "It's good to talk to an outsider who doesn't think we're a bunch of savages."

We ate lunch and took naps afterwards. When we awakened, I cleaned and dressed his wound for the final time. It was healing nicely and with proper care would soon be back to normal. I gave him some penicillin tablets and told him the dosage he should take. I also gave him some ointment, gauze, tape, and alcohol, and emphasized the need to keep the wound clean.

That evening we ate an early dinner and then sat quietly on the beach to await the boat. Shortly after sunset, the sail of a fishing boat appeared from the darkness.

"Here is my boat," said Amak.

"I was expecting the launch to return," I said.

"It's too obvious in these waters. This boat will take me to the launch."

When the boat drew nearer, he called to it. Someone responded, and within minutes a man was pulling the prow onto the beach. Amak spoke to him in a dialect I couldn't understand. He didn't bother to introduce him, but took him to the house. They returned momentarily, Amak with his gun and the man with his bag.

Amak turned to me and said, "I'll never forget what you've done for me."

He climbed into the boat and the man pushed it into the

water. I watched them silently disappear into the darkness. I walked back to the house and for the first time felt loneliness on the small island which had always provided solace.

As planned, I returned to Bongao two days after Amak left. The paper was finished. I was pleased with it and mailed it at Bongao's post office. During the next few days, I learned of Amak's latest exploits, and many of my surmises about his visit turned out to be correct.

He and his men had attacked what they thought was a trading launch from the Visayas. The launch, however, had been a decoy with six Philippine Constabulary aboard. During the fight that ensued, two P.C. had been killed, and Amak had received the wound I treated. The encounter raised Amak to even greater hero status in the eyes of the local people since, only two weeks previously, two fishermen were killed by the P.C., who mistook them for smugglers.

It was a good two months before I saw Amak again. I was at Lioboran, the most isolated of the Bajau moorages in Sulu. On navigational maps, the waters are marked "uncharted" and are truly treacherous. The flat-bottomed Bajau boats have no trouble navigating the reefs, but outsiders usually avoid the area.

I had been in the moorage for about a week, attending wedding and healing ceremonies. Many boats were congregated for the events, and I saw people I knew from other moorages. Lioboran was far from any other settlements, and the Bajau were enjoying their sense of isolation from a sometimes hostile world. I waded to one of the little islands I had not yet explored, mostly to get some privacy from the festivities, but partly to see if it held anything of interest. It was a hot day and my enthusiasm for exploration soon evaporated. I sought a shaded beach to watch the Bajau boats across the reef.

My attention was caught by a vessel threading its way

through the reef toward the moorage. It was a motorized launch and its crew seemed to know the reef as it rapidly moved closer. As it neared, I recognized its dark hull—Amak's launch. My first thought was that he was seeking another hiding place. But I soon dismissed this as I realized Amak would not risk being trapped on these reefs, which virtually imprison boats at low tide. I waded back to the moorage to meet his launch and to see what he was up to. The launch stopped at the outer edge of the moorage, as close as it could come to the houseboats.

"Hello, my American brother! How are you?" he shouted.

Amak was standing on the deck dressed in his usual attire of *sahwal* and turban. "Look at my arm. All healed." He bulged his bicep in muscle-man fashion and laughed. "You're a great doctor. I recommend you any time."

"I'm glad you've recovered," I said, wading to the launch. "What brings you here?"

"I came to see you and your friends. Come on up." He helped me onto the deck where we sat as his half-dozen crew members gathered around us. They, too, were dressed in *sahwal* and turbans and greeted me with smiles. Hollywood could not have created a more believable lot of pirates. Various battle scars adorned their bodies, and each had a bladed weapon or a gun at his side.

"You look like you're ready for battle," I said, nodding at the blade at his waist.

"Always prepared," he laughed. "You never know when a P.C. may pop up. I heard you were here. I brought some gifts to repay the help you gave me."

"I told you, you owe me nothing." Since Amak's last escapade I was reconsidering the man. As amiable as he might be on some levels, he was obviously a violent character.

"I knew you'd say that, so I brought gifts for your friends, the boat people. I have rice and sugar and bananas and sardines and Cokes. It's my way of thanking you—and giving these poor people a treat."

And a way of winning them to your cause, I thought to myself. Amak was known for the periodic largesse he heaped upon villages, and it was, of course, one of the reasons for his great popularity among the local people.

"I'm sure they'll be happy to receive the gifts," I said.

He called to a nearby houseboat and told the inhabitants to come over for some free food. One by one, houseboats began to arrive for the food, and then as word got out that it was genuinely free with no strings attached, the launch was surrounded by boats getting their shares of the food Amak and his men were pulling up from the hold. The crew took over the distribution, and Amak came to the bow where I was sitting.

"Where do you go from here?" I asked as a conversation opener.

"I never tell people where I'm going," he said. "It's best for everyone."

"I suppose so," I said.

He looked at me intently, sensing my feelings. "I hope I haven't offended you by giving away this food. Sometimes I do it to get support from people, but that's not the reason this time. The boat people are timid and few in number. Their support is not important to me. I had to do something to repay what you did for me. I knew I couldn't give you a gift, but I had to do something. I hope you understand." He looked at me earnestly.

"I understand," I said. And I did. No Sama liked to feel indebted, and especially a Sama like Amak.

"I still haven't repaid you, but I feel better about it," he said.

"Let's consider the matter closed," I said.

By now Amak's stores were almost exhausted, each boat in the moorage having received some of his food. He shouted a question to his crew and they responded. Following further conversation with them, he turned to me and said, "We must go. The tide is lowering. If we don't go now, we'll be marooned until the next tide."

I stood to leave. "Thanks again, brother," he said. "We'll meet again." He turned to give orders to his crew. I climbed over the side and stood in the receding waters as I watched his launch thread its way through the reef to the deep waters.

Several months later I saw Amak again. I was at Tungbangkao, a Bajau community located about twenty-five miles east of Bongao. It was night and I was staying up late to transcribe notes from an interview with an old shaman. My eyes were beginning to tire from the weak flame of my small kerosene lamp, but I wanted to finish the job before I retired, so I persisted. Apart from the rustle of my paper, the only other sound was the gentle lapping of the sea around the piles of the house where I was staying alone. I heard paddle-splashes outside, and then steps on the deck. Before I could get up, Amak appeared in the doorway. He looked angrier and more fierce than usual as he stood there, momentarily saying nothing.

"You surprised me," I said. "I didn't hear you coming."

"I can't stay long," he said. "You must do something for me."

"If I can, I will."

He handed me a soiled, bulky envelope. "Give this to Father Raquet. Don't tell him I gave it to you. Tell him it's for the school, so more Sama students can go to school."

"What is it?" I asked.

"Money," he said. "Five thousand pesos."

"Why can't your brother give it to him?"

"You haven't heard what happened this afternoon?"

"No," I said. "I've been here all day. What happened?"

"The P.C. attacked my home village. I haven't been there in months, but they somehow found out I was there. They came in an old launch, and no one suspected them. They fired into the house where they thought I was staying. Eight people were killed—three were my children. And my brother. And an old woman, and three men. All were my relatives."

"I'm truly sorry," I said. "Sit down. I'll fix some coffee."

"I don't have time. I can't stay in Sulu. It's not safe for me in my own home. And it isn't safe for other people for me to be around. I must leave until I decide my next move."

"Where will you go?" I asked.

"Probably Sulawesi." He sat on the edge of the only other chair in the little house. "Now can you see why I must continue to fight the P.C.? They'll not stop slaughtering us until we let them do whatever they want, until they've taken all our fish from the waters, until they've taken all our land from us for Christian settlers. I've never killed women or children. I've only killed those who deserved to be killed, who would have killed me." He sobbed and put his head in his hands. "And now they've killed my brother and my sons."

I walked to him and put my hands on his shoulders. "Amak, I wish I could say the things that would make you feel better, but I don't know the words. Maybe there are no words. But my heart aches for you. Our lives play terrible tricks on us at times."

He looked up at me with watery eyes. "You're my only brother now. You're one man I truly trust."

"You can trust me, Amak. You can always trust me."

"And you'll make sure Father Raquet gets the money?"

"I'll see that he gets it."

"I must go. My men are waiting."

"Where is your launch? I heard nothing."

"At the edge of the reef. I paddled in by myself." In spite of his stated eagerness to be on his way, he seemed reluctant to leave. "Maybe I'll not see you again. Maybe you'll be gone when I come back."

"Maybe," I said. "But I'll come back to Sulu someday."

He looked down at the papers on the table. "What are you writing now? Another paper for other anthropologists to read?"

"I'm afraid you're right."

"When you finish writing for those anthropologists, why don't you write for the other people out there? Tell them about Sulu. Tell them what the people such as Amak are really like. Tell them why we have to fight and kill and steal."

"Maybe I'll do that," I said.

He stood up to leave. I stood up also. He stepped forward and gave me a strong hug which I returned.

"I'll miss you, my brother," he said.

"And I you."

He turned and went out the door. Momentarily, I heard the dip of paddles in the sea. I went to the deck to watch him depart, but I saw only blackness in the moonless, starless night.

As usual, my departure was delayed. It was two days after Amak's visit when I finally arrived in Bongao. I was eager to get rid of the bundle of money, so I went directly to Father Raquet's office.

He turned at my entry and we exchanged usual greetings. "A friend of your school gave me money to be used for educating Sama children."

I handed him the envelope and he opened it silently. He counted the money and said, "This is a very good friend. Do I know him?"

"He asked to remain anonymous," I said.

"I see," said Father Raquet. "One shouldn't question such a generous gift for such a worthwhile cause. Tell him I greatly appreciate the gift, and I'm sure the children who benefit from it will be equally appreciative."

"I'll tell him," I said. I expected more resistance from him in accepting the money without knowing its source. He seemed unusually reflective and certainly was not his usual self.

"I suppose you haven't heard about Amak," he said, after a rather long pause.

"Heard what? I just got in a few minutes ago."

"He was killed two nights ago by the P.C. His entire crew was killed. They caught them by surprise near Simunul."

"Oh my god," I whispered. I always assumed that some day Amak would be killed, but I wasn't prepared for his death now.

"He was a friend of yours, wasn't he?"

"Yes," I said. I couldn't hold back my tears.

"He was a friend of mine, also. A great man in his own way. And a great friend to my school." He looked at the bundle of money.

"Will there be a funeral?" I asked.

"The P.C. won't give up his body. He's been decapitated and his body is on the wharf at Batu-Batu where his head is impaled on a pole as a warning to others."

"Good god!" I said. "Who did that?"

"I assume the P.C. commander at Batu-Batu. He's a vicious man. I'm going over to try to convince him that it's a savage act and is simply furthering the anger of the people. Would you like to come with me?"

Within minutes we were speeding toward Batu-Batu in Father Raquet's boat. It was a beautiful morning, but my thoughts were with Amak, the man and his cause. As I had done many times, I wondered what he might have become with different beginnings. But it was useless speculation. He was as he was. And now he was dead.

We arrived at the P.C. compound on the outskirts of the town. Armed guards greeted us defiantly, but upon seeing Father Raquet, they allowed us to pass to see the base commander. We were ushered into a room and told to wait there while the guard went into an inner room.

"It's best I see him alone," said Father Raquet.

"Of course," I said. "I'll stay here."

The guard returned shortly and told Father Raquet he could see the commander. He went in and I sat on the hard wooden bench to wait. Ten minutes later the priest returned with an envelope in his hand.

"He saw my position," he said. "Let's go claim the body."

We left the office, walked out of the compound, and headed toward the wharf. A group of perhaps a hundred local people were gathered, held back by several dozen armed P.C. officers. Father Raquet approached them and asked for a particular officer. A man stepped forward and Father handed him the letter from the base commander. After reading it several times, he allowed us to pass.

"We'll go to the body first," said Father Raquet. "Then I'll talk to the crowd."

The officer consented. Father and I walked to the end of the wharf where Amak's decapitated and badly wounded body lay. Two dogs sniffed at it, and flies buzzed at the wounds. Father chased the dogs away. Impaled on a pole at the end of the wharf was the head of Amak. It was the face I had often spoken to, frozen in a fierce expression of defiance and anger. I turned away and looked to the sea as Father Raquet fell on his knees to offer prayers. Upon finishing, he walked back to address the crowd. When he finished, he returned to Amak's body with the crowd of Sama. Two days of weeping were past and no tears were in their eyes now—only anger, hate, and defiance.

Amak was dead, but his cause was very much alive.

16

Sulu

When I left Sulu, I thought I would soon return. That didn't happen. After completing my doctorate, I accepted a university position and settled into the comfortable routine of academe. I corresponded regularly with Father Raquet and he kept me informed about the Bajau. None of my Bajau friends in Tawi-Tawi were literate, so there was no way I could write to them. When I began to plan a return field trip to Sulu, the conflicts foreshadowed by the circumstances of Amak's death escalated into a major civil war. For almost a decade, Sulu was off-limits to outsiders.

I became involved in research in another part of the world, but I knew that some day I would return to Sulu. I repeatedly asked permission from the Philippine government to visit Sulu, and I was repeatedly denied. Finally, after several years of futile attempts through the Philippine consulate in San Francisco, I decided to go to Manila to see if I could use personal contacts to get into Sulu. If necessary, I was prepared to slip in without permission.

In Manila, I saw several officials before I was finally granted an interview with the general in charge of Sulu affairs. He asked me to write a formal request, stating reasons why I should be allowed to visit Sulu when no others were. Several foreign journalists had written uncomplimentary articles about events in Sulu, and consequently the government was reluctant to let foreigners into the area for fear of what they might write. I wrote an impassioned but nonpolitical statement explaining the reasons I should be allowed to go, emphasizing my desire to visit Masa and other friends. I delivered the letter to the general's second-in-command, who told me his superior could not get to the letter for three weeks, at which time he would give me his decision. I asked if there were any possible way he might be able to read it sooner, a task that would take five minutes at the most. I was assured he could not fit it into his busy schedule, and I was given a date when I could expect an answer.

I left, feeling very frustrated. I didn't want to stay in Manila for three weeks, so I decided to visit other parts of Southeast Asia until the day when I expected to hear the general's decision. When I arrived in Bangkok a couple of weeks later, two days before the general's decision was due, I called the Philippines to see if my request had been approved. I got through immediately and learned that permission had been granted for a one-week visit to Sulu, the beginning of which had started two days previously. I immediately booked a flight to Manila, flew all night, and arrived in the early morning. I went directly to the military post where I picked up papers to get through military bureaucracy in the south. After some pleading on my part, the general decided my one-week visit would start that day. I rushed to the airport, got a flight to Zamboanga, presented my papers to the commander there, and was able to catch a plane to Bongao. Thus, within twenty-four hours after I left Bangkok, I was back in Sulu.

The flight to Bongao was not an easy one emotionally. I'd heard some news of the conflict in Sulu from the occasional letters I received from Father Raquet before he left Sulu for an assignment in Mindanao. Additionally, I'd read the stories that sometimes made the news services in the U. S. After a decade of warfare, the Philippine government had finally subdued the secessionist attempts of the Sulu Muslims, but not before some destructive, bloody battles throughout the islands. I knew the Bongao area had been the scene of some fierce combat and bombing. I knew the Bajau were not involved in the fighting, but I also knew they were innocent victims of it. So when the small plane circled and finally landed on the airstrip at Sanga-Sanga Island in the late afternoon, I thought I was prepared for the worst. Twenty years later, I was back in Sulu.

The runway, once nothing more than a grass strip, was now paved and had a small terminal building with a permanent staff. As I stepped from the plane, my first impression was of military personnel everywhere. Several military vehicles, including a tank, were parked along the airstrip next to the plane. I was met by army officers, who told me they had been informed by wire about my visit. They would look after me while I was there. I soon discovered they meant to follow me everywhere I went, and I later learned they thought I was a CIA agent. I was escorted to a military vehicle and we were soon speeding down the new road that cut through Sanga-Sanga Island. We crossed the channel between Sanga-Sanga and Bongao on a newly constructed bridge, which ended at a paved road that encircled Bongao Island, replacing a former path. We met numerous other vehicles on the road, mostly military, but also an assortment of jeepneys, busses, and motorized cycles.

When we arrived in Bongao, I recognized virtually nothing. Most of the town had been destroyed in a fire—the result of secessionist fighting several years earlier—and the new town bore little resemblance to the old one. A network of roads failed to accommodate the crowded, noisy vehicles vomiting pollution into the air. Bongao had had only one vehicle during my years there—a truck without an engine.

I was told the population of Bongao now numbered about one hundred thousand. It was about five thousand when I lived there. Much of the new population was military personnel and their dependents; the rest were refugees fleeing the outer islands, where the most intense fighting occurred. My escorts pointed out with great pride the urban amenities of the new city, including a new hospital, three movie houses, a roller skating rink, a pool hall, a nightclub complete with go-go dancers, and a variety of bars and sleazy clubs catering to the military. Radios and tape decks blasted from everywhere, and television was available during the evening hours. I later learned of widespread drug use and an epidemic of venereal disease.

My military escorts took me to the convento, where they arranged for me to stay with the resident Filipino priest. The young priest was very nervous in the presence of the soldiers, and before the evening was over, I discovered he was terrified in Sulu. He was considering leaving the order rather than stay in Bongao. He seemed as frightened of the Muslims as he was of the military. Shortly after dinner I went to my room, the events of the long day having exhausted me. The next day I would try to locate some of my Bajau friends, but I was fearful of what I might find.

The next morning I walked around the new Bongao to see if I could find any Bajau or learn of their whereabouts. I was a stranger in a strange city. Nothing was familiar except the natural features of the landscape which were unaltered by the throbbing mass of people. Everything was constricted and I sensed great tension in the air—tension among the military brought on by fears of Muslim attacks, and tension among the Muslims brought on by fears of military attacks. By accident, I found the Wu family. Some years earlier they had left Sitangkai to help rebuild Bongao. They had a large store that sold a little of everything. It was managed by the two younger sons, who supported their older brother and sister, both now middle aged. The father had died many years earlier. I found my way to the hospital founded by Sister Evangelista. It was greatly expanded but had the same atmosphere of caring and concern.

All the sisters were, of course, unfamiliar to me, but they welcomed me with great hospitality, having heard of me and read
my publications on the Bajau. I asked them about the Bajau,
and they gave me directions to a small Bajau community at
the outskirts of town, not far from the hospital. I walked there
after *merienda* with the sisters.

The Bajau community was a collection of perhaps two
dozen houses built on piles over the shallow reef connected
to land by a walkway. Few Bajau lived in houseboats anymore.
I walked to the houses and made inquiries in my rusty Sama
about friends from the past, especially Masa. No one knew his
exact whereabouts. Some thought he'd gone to Borneo, some
said he was in Sulawesi, and others claimed he was in Lioboran. I met several people I knew as children who were now
adults with children of their own. The little community was
rapidly becoming Muslim; many of the young Bajau had married Muslims, and most of the community attended a nearby
mosque on land. After learning all I could about Masa, I wandered back to the crowded marketplace to see if I could find a
place to eat.

After eating, I walked around the waterfront to find a
launch going to Lioboran. Many inquiries later, I found one
that was leaving early the next morning. I made arrangements
to be on it, and then I explored the new Bongao.

It was a city alien to the sleepy little port town I once
knew. It was a conquered land. The military was everywhere,
and when I was able to shake my military escorts and talk
to local people, I heard horror stories of military atrocities
against the local population. All was told in whispers, with
nervous glances to see if anyone was listening. Large sections
of the new city consisted of housing constructed for dependents of the military establishment.

Sulu Province had been divided. What was once southern Sulu was now Tawi-Tawi Province. A new capitol building
had been constructed on the side of Mt. Bongao. It was so

far from town, however, that people were afraid to go there, so government affairs were conducted in a small set of offices in Bongao. The bureaucratic jobs of the new government had brought in many outsiders. Much money had been poured into the province by the corrupt Marcos regime in an attempt to satisfy local Muslim demands and convince sympathetic Muslim nations that the Philippine government was sincerely trying to help its Muslim minorities. But, it was all superficial. A hospital was built, but with no equipment or personnel to staff it; a new university was situated on Sanga-Sanga Island, but it was incomplete and already crumbling; the new power plant was inoperative most of the time; and the new water system provided water for only an hour a day.

The destruction of the environment was appalling. Virtually all the trees on Bongao and neighboring islands suitable for construction had been cut down to build shelter for the exploding population. Beaches and reefs, robbed of sand for concrete construction, were invaded by the sea, totally altering coastlines and destroying coastal vegetation.

My favorite little island hideaway, where Sister Evangelista chose to die, was now a barren rock, raped of its sandy beach and reef for construction in Bongao. The island that housed the ta'u-ta'u images of the saitan was gone, also raped of its sand; only a few ta'u-ta'u clung to the dead tree on the barren rock now swept by the sea.

Litter was everywhere. In the days when I knew Sulu, plastic and glass were rare items which if found, were carefully kept as containers. What were once some of the most spectacular beaches in the Philippines now had no sand and were littered with broken fragments of glass and plastic.

The next morning I boarded the launch for Lioboran. By what was more than coincidence, two army officers were also on the launch. I didn't expect Lioboran to be unchanged, but I was unprepared for what I discovered. When I knew Lioboran, it was a half-dozen small islands surrounded by extensive reefs and inhabited by a couple of dozen Bajau houseboats usually clustered in a small, protected inlet. Now it was a town of several hundred houses, built over the reef, connecting three of the islands.

The reefs were intensively cultivated in *agalagar*, a seaweed that was now the area's most important export. *Agalagar* cultivation had been introduced some fifteen years previously. Unfortunately, it was most successful on the reefs inhabited by the Bajau. People from all over Sulu came to participate in the new boom cash crop, and most of the Bajau were driven out by the aggressive newcomers. Only a few were left, and they, too, had become *agalagar* farmers.

Virtually no one fished anymore, mostly because few fish were to be had. Dynamite was introduced as a way of getting fish some years back, with the result that most marine life on the reefs was destroyed. It had been one of the richest fishing grounds in Sulu. But the population that once ate fresh fish twice a day now ate canned sardines and corned beef.

The only old friend I found was Biti, Masa's brother-in-law, who seemed much older than his fifty years. I asked him about past acquaintances. Some, of course, had died of natural causes. Old Laka had died years ago and was buried in a special grave, as befitted a powerful shaman. But many other Bajau were displaced by the invading *agalagar* farmers or were shot by the military. Three Bajau families were slaughtered by a group of drunken soldiers who, for kicks, opened fire on their houseboats. Salanda was among the victims. Four fishermen were killed because they refused to give two soldiers their catch. Several young Bajau women were murdered after being raped by soldiers. Biti's estimate was that probably two-thirds of the Bajau population had either died or been driven from the area. My observations concurred. I became so depressed by the litany of deaths that I stopped asking about people. Reluctantly, nonetheless, I finally asked about Masa. I wasn't sure I could handle his death.

Biti's face lit up, however, as he told me that Masa had sensed the sickness in Sulu early and had left with his sons, now adults, for Borneo, where life was less violent. Biti hadn't seen him in years, but occasionally he heard about him. Apparently Masa still lived in his boat, although his sons were confirmed house dwellers and Muslims. He owned two launches and operated a successful business with his sons among the small islands of eastern Borneo.

I lay awake very late during my last night in Sulu, trying to digest all I had seen. I kept reminding myself that I had known the Bajau and Sulu for one brief moment in time. Indeed, to old Philippine hands, the Sulu I had known probably seemed as much changed as did the present-day Sulu to me. For change is the nature of culture. Sometimes it is relentless in its demands and there are casualties. Traditional Bajau culture was such a casualty. Although many individual Bajau had died, most lived on. Those who stayed in Sulu were doing what the people of Sulu have done for centuries, adapting to change. They were becoming Muslims, the last of the Sulu people to do so.

As sleep continued to elude me, I considered how a young anthropologist arriving in Sulu today would view the islands. That young anthropologist might very well be a woman, since women now comprise about half the profession. She would probably find today's Sulu as beautiful, exciting, and exotic as the Sulu I found in the early 1960s. It is a different Sulu, but it is still distinctively Sulu. She would find stories and characters to rival the ones I discovered. She would not see the boat-dwelling culture I saw, but as she explored the contemporary cultures of Sulu, she would discover that aspects of Bajau boat culture persist. For although traditional Bajau culture has joined the thousands of other cultures that form the accumulated past of human history, it has left its imprint on Sulu for many years to come.

I left Sulu without seeing Masa, who had been my chief reason for going there. But I'm glad I didn't see him. It would not have been a happy reunion. The Sulu he and I knew together does not exist anymore. The seas we sailed with so little concern are now filled with fear; the fish we fished from those once rich reefs are few; and the faith that life could always be sustained in those enchanting waters is badly shaken.

I realize now that my years in Sulu were a lull in a long, stormy history. The world war was over; the civil war had not yet begun. I know I was very young, the islands were intoxicatingly beautiful, and the passage of time has tended to romanticize my years there. But I cannot help believing that the Sulu of then was a special spot in the world.

I shall never return to Sulu. I cannot. My lovely Sulu is gone.